Order

CeeCee Crow

Smut by Design

Print ISBN: 978-1-971405-13-1

Publisher: Smut by Design

CeeCeeCrow.com

BEFORE WE BEGIN

You came back.

I love you for that.

Now I need you to know something.

I love these characters.

Every single one of them.

Keep that in mind.

— CeeCee

Content Warnings

Thank you for reading *Order*! This is the final book in Nova's trilogy, and it contains themes and content that may be triggering to some readers. Please review the following warnings before proceeding:

Major Content Warnings:

Captivity & Torture

- Kidnapping, imprisonment, and prolonged solitary confinement in darkness

- Interrogation while bound and restrained

- Torture by repeated forced cold-water exposure ("cleansing")

- An untreated dislocated shoulder, including an on-page joint reset

- Starvation, hypothermia, and sensory deprivation

- Being strapped into a chair for forced experimentation

- A secondary character psychologically broken by torture (dissociation, repetitive looping speech)

Trauma & Recovery

- Believing loved ones are dead and grieving them

- Survivor guilt and self-blame

- Food insecurity behaviors (eating in secret, hoarding, fear of food disappearing)

- Physical scars, bruising, and injury recovery

- Identity crisis tied to discovering one's parents were not biological and were assigned

- Learning one's entire life was orchestrated as an experiment

- Grief that remains unresolved (biological origins never answered)

Emotional & Psychological Themes

- Found family and belonging

- Learning to trust and accept care after long-term isolation

- A character processing the reveal that her suffering was deliberate and institutional

* Coming to terms with manufactured vs. chosen love

Harassment, Power Dynamics & Institutional Violence

* Systemic oppression and institutional violence

* Human experimentation; a person's entire life used as a controlled test

* Threats of mass murder used as coercion (referenced)

* Antagonist psychological manipulation and gaslighting

* Siege, ambush, and a town surrounded by hostile forces

* Children placed in danger during the attack

* Forced displacement and the choice to leave home

Physical & Supernatural Violence

* Animal shifter combat and battle sequences

* Painful, involuntary, and forced transformation

* A forced-shift program that traps subjects permanently in animal form

* Distorted "failed experiment" shifters

- On-page death of a character (violent, implied rather than graphic)

- Serious injury and blood, including a near-fatal wound

- Use of sedatives/darts and character incapacitation (extended unconsciousness)

Romance & Intimacy

- Reverse harem romance (one woman, multiple male love interests)

- Multiple explicit sexual scenes, including group and multi-partner encounters

- Explicit oral sex (giving and receiving)

- Bondage/restraint (rope) and power-exchange dynamics, including praise/dominance

- Anal play and voyeurism

- A scene that begins as one partner is waking (consent given and enthusiastic once awake)

- First-time experiences on-page

- Fated bonds and mark changes on-page

- Possessive and protective male characters

Additional Notes

- Strong language throughout

- References to past systemic suppression and genocide of abilities

- Revelation that a parent's death was institutional policy

- A character left to live with the consequences of their actions (no clean redemption)

Series-spanning threads left open (an unresolved biological origin, a system left cracked but not destroyed)

This list is provided to ensure a safe reading experience. If any of these topics are personally distressing, please read with care.

Thank you for your support and for seeing Nova's journey through to the end.

CONTENTS

Chapter 1
NOVA

Dark.

The hum of something moving under me. My wrists behind my back, long past hurting.

I don't know how long I've been here.

It doesn't matter.

They're gone.

And I don't know how I can live with it. I don't know how I can live with myself.

They're gone and it's because of me.

I couldn't think about it when I saw Locke drop — his eyes rolling back, the sound he made when he hit the ground — I couldn't because I had to focus on the threat in front of me, that bastard Silas standing there smiling like it was nothing. And as soon as I said yes, as soon as the word left my mouth, he killed them all anyway.

It took seconds.

Seconds and they were all gone and I was completely and utterly alone again.

I didn't even get to say goodbye.

I don't know how to live with that. I don't know how to make sense of a Locke lying on the ground with the Locke that opened the door that first day like I was someone worth opening doors for. I don't know how to stop thinking about how many times Vaelor made me coffee, adjusting it every single time, never once making it a thing, just quietly trying to get it exactly right.

I don't know how to forget the way Trey tastes or the way Kyron carried me down the street and I couldn't make myself pull away from him no matter how hard I tried. I don't know how to stop thinking about my date with Rane and how I never wanted it to end. And I will never know how to find calm again without looking into Beckett's eyes.

I knew how to live before them. I did. Fifteen years of knowing exactly how to survive, how to stay invisible, how to need nothing and no one. And then the system found me and dragged me in and I was terrified.

But then I met them.

And for the first time in so long I actually felt safe. Safe enough to let my guard down. Safe enough to let them see me. Safe enough to want things. To let them do things for me. To stop flinching every time someone got close.

And then—

Oh.

Oh god.

I love them.

The realization lands in the dark and I have to stop myself from shaking because I know it in my bones.

Everything I am is theirs. It was theirs the moment I walked into that house. I just didn't realize it until now. And now... Now they're gone and I'm here and my heart is back there in the Hollow. In the middle of that road... And that's where it'll always stay.

I don't know how to go on without them.

I don't know how I'll ever stitch myself back together. I'm not sure I'm supposed to try. I just know that the dark is the same no matter how long I sit in it and my face is wet and I can't make it stop.

The vehicle slows.

Stops.

I don't move. I don't care.

Hands haul me out. My legs don't work. Someone grabs me and I pull away anyway — just my body refusing to be handled one more time — twisting, throwing my weight, blind and broken and doing it anyway because it's all I have left—

I freeze.

A mouth at my ear through the fabric.

"Keep that up," Silas says, almost soft. "And I'll go back."

I go still.

I don't know what's left to go back for.

But I can't risk it. Even now. Even like this. I can't.

I stop.

With his hand on my arm, we walk. Inside somewhere because the floor levels out and the temperature drops. One foot and then the other. That's all.

A door opens.

I'm jolted, shoved forward.

The bag comes off as my knees hit hard on the tile.

Light everywhere, all at once, after days of nothing. I can't see. Just white burning into my eyes and I turn away and blink until the shapes bleed through.

White walls. Clean floor. The shape of a man near the far wall.

"Brought her just like you wanted, Father."

He steps forward. Comes into focus slowly and then all at once.

I know exactly who he is.

"Ah," Laith says. "Excellent."

No.

Chapter 2
LOCKE

I open my eyes but I don't know where I am. I'm looking at a ceiling, but it's not our house. The light is wrong. My neck hurts like a bitch and I can't remember why I'm on my back.

I need to move.

"Hey. Take it easy." Lena, with a cold compress on my forehead and her hand on my shoulder pushing me down. "You've been out a while."

"I'm fine." I sit up anyway. The room tilts, then steadies.

The Community Hall. Cal is at the door, Jonah at the far wall, Brent by the kitchen entrance with his arms crossed.

There are mattresses around me with bodies on them. Rane with a dart mark on his neck, still out. Kyron beside him. Trey, Vaelor, Beckett. All here. All breathing. All unconscious.

Great.

I count them. Count again.

"Where's Nova?"

Lena's eyes go wide. She looks at Cal, then at Brent, then at Jonah. Her mouth opens but nothing comes out.

Brent walks over. His face is flat and controlled. Barely.

"She's gone, Locke."

I stare at him.

"What the fuck do you mean she's gone?"

The hall goes quiet. Mara freezes halfway through the room with a tray. People in the doorway stop moving.

"We couldn't get to you," Brent says. "Not without casualties. You were surrounded. When we finally broke through, you were all down. Darts in every one of you."

"And Nova."

"Gone."

"How long?"

"Yesterday morning. You've been out a full day."

A day. She's been gone for a full day.

"There were bears," Cal says from the door. "Memory bears. But not just Memory. Shadow ravens. Reverie wolves."

Three Houses coordinated together. That's not Silas. He doesn't have the pull for cross-House assets. That's Laith. That's Order leadership.

"This was sanctioned," I say.

"At the highest level." Brent's jaw is tight. "Silas was the face, but whoever organized the extraction had resources from three territories. That doesn't happen without the top signing off."

I look at the guys on the mattresses around me. Six men, all taken out with darts before we could do a single goddamn thing.

They knew what we could do. They planned for it. Hit me first because I'd have shifted fastest. Had darts ready for all of us before Silas even opened his mouth.

"Where did they take her?"

Brent looks at Cal. Cal looks back.

"Nightmare Order headquarters is our best guess."

The most heavily secured location in the realm, built on the ruins of the convergence space.

Mara sets her tray down and walks over. She adjusts a blanket over my legs without saying a word and I don't stop her.

People keep coming in to check on us. Darcy appears in the doorway with her kid on her hip. She doesn't say anything, just stands there looking at the mattresses and the space where Nova should be.

The whole town is here. The people she stood up for. The people she promised to fight for.

Of course she did.

I should be on my feet. I should be planning, maybe breaking a few things.

But I can't move.

"We'll figure this out," Brent says. "We'll find a way—"

"No."

He stops and stares at me like I hit him.

"Three Houses coordinated against us. They walked into the Hollow like it was nothing." I look at him. "We'll never get her back."

"Don't say that."

"She's gone. Really gone."

Brent opens his mouth, then closes it. He doesn't argue because there's nothing to argue with.

Lena replaces the compress on my forehead. I let her because it gives her something to do and I get it.

Somewhere behind me a kid asks why the big man is sad. A mother hushes him.

I'm not sad. I failed her. That's different.

She's everywhere in this town. Every room, every face, everything they built because of her. And she's not here.

Beside me, Rane is waking up. He groans as his hand goes to his neck where the dart hit.

His eyes open, unfocused. He looks at me and whatever he sees makes his face go white.

"Locke?"

I can't say it again.

He looks around the room and counts the bodies. Gets to the same number I did.

"No," he says.

I close my eyes.

Chapter 3
RANE

It comes back in pieces.

The crow. The bears. The sound Locke made when he hit the ground. And she...

No.

I sit up too fast and the room spins. My hand goes to my neck automatically — the dart mark, still tender — and I have to breathe through the spin until the Community Hall stops moving and stays put.

Fuckers.

Mattresses on the floor. Bodies on them. All the right people in all the wrong positions.

And the one person that should be here, isn't.

"Hey." Brent pulls up a chair in front of me like he's bracing for something. "Take it easy. You've been out a while."

I look at the space between the mattresses.

"I know."

He opens his mouth and I can see it coming.

"She's gone," I say.

He stops, closes his mouth.

"You were conscious," he says.

I nod. I can't look at Locke right now. I can feel him on the mattress behind me, the particular quality of his silence, I know what it means. And I can't...

"What happened out there?" Brent asks. "Locke was down before — he doesn't know the full—"

And that's it. That's the crack.

"We were walking." I'm on my feet before I know I'm standing. "Normal morning. That's the thing. It was a completely normal morning. Trey was telling Eli about the stag thing and Zoe kept interrupting and I was trying to defend myself, which wasn't going great, but whatever — and Nova was right there. Right next to me. Sun out. Everything fine—"

Brent opens his mouth.

"I'm getting there." I'm already pacing. "And then the crow loses it. This bird has been chill for weeks. Sits on the railing, sits on her shoulder, basically a pet, right. And suddenly it's in her face screaming and we're all trying to shoo it away because we think it's just being weird—"

My hand goes to the dart mark again. I make myself stop.

"And then I look up and they're everywhere. The whole street, full. Bears. I don't know what else. How did we not hear them? How do you not hear that many—" I shake my head. "Locke starts to shift. Because of course he does, he's Locke. And they dart him. One shot. Down before his bones even finish cracking."

I snap my fingers.

The sound lands too hard in the quiet hall.

"Gone. Just like that. And I'm trying to get to him but the shifters are already between us and there's nowhere to go and—"

"Rane." Cal, from the wall. "Laith, was he there?"

"No, but his fucking son was." I exhale. "Silas walks through the bears like they opened for him. Smiling. Talks like he's explaining a scheduling conflict — says the Order doesn't like our cluster. Says we forced their hand by existing." I swallow. "Said Nova shouldn't exist. Exact words."

Brent's jaw tightens.

"He said she manipulated us. Into bonding. Into believing she belonged. Said it was sick." The pacing gets faster, shorter. "Vaelor growled at him and Silas tutted. Like he was a fucking dog that barked at the wrong time. Asshole. And then he—"

I stop.

The next part. I don't want to say it.

"He gave her a choice." It comes out flat. "Come with them voluntarily. Or he kills us. All of us. The town. Everyone here."

I didn't think the hall could get quieter, but it does.

Outside, someone's kid is laughing at something. The sound is from a completely different world.

"And she said yes," I whisper.

Something shatters in my chest when I say it.

I hear Locke make a sound like a wounded animal.

I keep moving because stopping is worse.

"She looked at me first. Right before. Right at me, and I could see she'd already decided, it was already done, and I wanted to say something — I don't even know what — and then they hit all of us. Fast. Couldn't have been more than two seconds after she agreed." I press my palm flat against the mark on my neck. "Pre-planned. They had it staged for the moment she said yes."

I take a breath willing myself not to fall apart.

"They knew she would."

My throat closes.

I push through it.

"And that's the last thing I saw. Her face."

Trey groans from one of the mattresses. His eyes open. He blinks at the ceiling, at the room, at the people in it.

"Fuck," he says, quiet.

I start moving again.

"So the question is what we do. We can't just sit here. Three Houses coordinated — Shadow, Memory, Reverie — which means this isn't just Silas, Silas doesn't have that reach, this is Laith, this is Order leadership at the top, and if that's who signed off then we're dealing with—"

I catch Locke looking at me.

He's turned his head on the mattress. His green eyes with that expression I refuse to deal with right now. Like he's watching me come apart and I can't...

I stop.

Stare at him because he needs to stop.

"Don't look at me like that."

He doesn't look away.

"I'm processing. This is how I process. You break things, I talk. It's the same."

"It's not the same."

"It's exactly the same except mine doesn't leave holes in the wall."

Kyron opens his eyes on the mattress beside Trey. Doesn't speak. Doesn't move. Just stares at the ceiling which probably means he's already five moves ahead and none of them are good.

I keep talking. The formation of the bears. How fast the team moved. The timing, the positioning, whether there were more we didn't see. I'm mid-calculation when Vaelor gets up from his mattress without a word and walks into the kitchen.

A cabinet opens.

He's cooking.

Seriously?

She's gone and he's cooking and I wish I didn't understand as much as I do.

I'm trying to remember the exact position of the shifters when Beckett opens his eyes.

He doesn't sit up. Doesn't move. Just lies there with his arms at his sides, staring at the ceiling like Kyron. His face is blank like everything is switched off. Like he went somewhere else in his head and shut out everything else.

"Beckett?"

Nothing.

"Beck—"

"I know." Flat. Empty. "I heard you. All of it."

He still doesn't move.

I open my mouth. To keep going. To keep the words coming, to stay ahead of the thing I can feel gaining on me—

"Enough."

Quiet. Not sharp. Just done.

I close my mouth.

The hall is silent except for Vaelor in the kitchen and that kid still laughing outside and my own pulse that's pounding in my skull.

She looked at me.

Right before she decided. Right at me.

And I couldn't do anything to stop it.

Chapter 4
BECKETT

I can't look at anything else.

The ceiling. The same water stain in the corner. I've been here since I woke up and I knew the second I opened my eyes — before Rane said a word, before anyone told me anything — I just knew. The same way you know when a room has changed while you were gone. Something missing from the air.

She's not here.

And it keeps circling. The way she looked at Rane right before. The moment I saw it — and I did see it, that's the thing I can't get away from — I saw her face settle into something decided and I had one second where I understood what was happening and then the dart hit and the ground came up and that was it.

One second.

It cost everything.

She'd barely finished saying yes before I was already gone. But I heard it. Even under, somewhere, I heard it. Small and quiet and certain the way she does everything.

I should have been faster. I keep coming back to that and I know it's useless and I keep coming back to it anyway.

She sacrificed herself. Stood there and did the math the same way I do, except hers ended with her walking away with them instead of us lying in the dirt. And the worst part — the part that's been sitting on my chest since I woke up — is that I knew she would. I knew it before it happened. I've known it for months.

I've watched her whole life in miniature, in the small things. The way she ate like the food might disappear. The way she made herself small in doorways, in rooms, in conversations. The way she found the edges of every space and stayed there. I know what that is. Not just surviving — that's too clean a word for it. It's making yourself invisible so completely that eventually you forget there's anything left to see.

I know what that costs.

I've done it too. Different walls, different corners, same architecture. You give up everything that makes you a target and you call it living and after a while you stop noticing what's gone.

She was learning to be exactly who she was meant to be. That's what I can't put down. Reach for things. Stay in the room instead of finding the exit. It was slow and uneven and half the time she didn't even know she was doing it but I noticed.

I always noticed.

And now she's gone and the ceiling has the same water stain it had the day we got here. Rane is talking. Vaelor is in the kitchen. My hands are doing nothing. That one second keeps running on a loop in my mind, but it doesn't change the fact that she's not here.

And I let it happen.

Chapter 5
KYRON

I can't believe she did it.

I've been lying here running it back since before Rane opened his mouth and I keep landing in the same place. We were right there. All of us. She looked at us and she — did she even hesitate? Did she even —

Rane's still talking.

"Would you stop." I don't mean for it to come out that loud.

Rane stops mid-sentence. Looks at me.

"Just — stop. Please."

"Kyron—"

"She left." I sit up. "Okay? She looked at us and she left. Can we just — can we sit with that for five minutes without running the play-by-play."

The hall goes quiet. Not the good kind.

"That's not what happened," Rane says. Careful. Like he's approaching something that might bite.

"I was there too."

"Then you know she didn't—"

"She chose to walk away. I watched her do it." The words taste like something I'll regret, but I don't care because my chest feels like it's caving in. "We all watched her do it."

Brent shifts from the wall. "Son—"

"Don't." I look at him. "Don't do that."

He closes his mouth.

I get up because I can't stay sitting for this. My skin feels wrong. Too tight. The owl is right underneath the surface and has been since I woke up. I've been holding it back through sheer stubbornness because shifting in the middle of the Community Hall seems like the kind of thing that doesn't help anyone.

I stand at the window instead. The Hollow outside. It looks like a normal morning. People moving, doing whatever they're doing like nothing happened.

"She was scared," Rane tries again. "She saw Locke go down and she panicked and—"

"She wasn't scared." I turn around. "That's the thing. She wasn't scared at all. You said it yourself. She looked at you and she'd already decided. That's not panic. That's a choice."

"A choice to save our lives—"

"A choice to leave."

"Kyron." Locke. Low. Warning.

"I'm not wrong."

"You're not right either."

I look at him on the mattress. Still flat on his back. Still staring at the ceiling. The bruise on his neck from the dart has gone purple overnight.

"She had options," I say. "She always has options. She just didn't pick us."

Nobody answers that.

Good. Because I'm tired of people finding ways to make this okay. I'm tired of reframing it into something that makes sense. She was there and then she wasn't and every version of that story ends the same way — she's gone and we're here and she made that happen.

I should have known. I've noticed every single thing about her from the first day — the exits, the bread, the way she went still when someone moved too fast — and I missed the most important one. That she'd always find a way to disappear when it counted.

I should have known better.

"Maybe Silas had a point," I say.

The room goes very still.

Rane's face falls. "Don't."

"I'm just saying—"

"I know what you're saying and don't." He's on his feet now. "Don't do that to her. Don't do that to yourself."

"Why not? We trusted her. We let her in. We—" My voice cracks. I hate it. "We built something and she walked away from it the first time it got hard."

"She walked away to save your life." Rane's voice has gone tight. "To save all of our lives. To save this whole town full of people she'd known for like five minutes. That's not — Kyron, that's not someone who doesn't care. That's someone who cares so much she—"

He pulls at his hair and takes a breath.

"She didn't have a choice," Rane says. Quieter now. Certain. "You know that. She didn't have a choice."

I can't breathe.

Locke, sitting up on the mattress now. "He's right."

Something rips open in my chest.

"She did." My voice comes out strange. Raw and scratching and I can't make it stop. "She had a choice and she made it and she didn't even—"

The shift comes up so fast I can't catch it.

I don't try.

The owl comes out of me hard. Bones cracking, spine bending wrong, the ceiling dropping toward me as I grow into the space. Someone shouts. Something hits the floor. Wings fill the gap between the mattresses and there's not enough room in here, there's not enough room anywhere, and then I'm through the double doors and the cold morning air hits me like a wall.

I climb.

Up. Away. The Hollow dropping below me, small and still and exactly the same as it was yesterday.

I climb until my wings ache. The air is thin and cold and clean and there's nothing up here except sky. Nothing up here that reminds me of her.

I don't know if I'll ever come back down.

Chapter 6
VAELOR

I don't remember deciding to get up.

I just wasn't on the mattress anymore and then I was in here, and the pantry was open. My hands were already moving and I can't seem to stop.

That was an hour ago. Maybe two. I've stopped checking.

There's eggs. Someone stocked this place well before everything fell apart — Lena probably, or Mara, one of the women who's been keeping the Hollow running while we've been falling to pieces. I find a cast iron pan and set it on the burner and stand there watching the heat ripple up from the surface.

Scrambled eggs. Then the rest of the oats. Then something with the potatoes in the back of the pantry that are going to go bad if nobody uses them.

I work through it methodically. One thing at a time. My hands know what to do even when the rest of me doesn't.

From the hall I can hear Rane talking. And Kyron's voice, tight and wrong. It's quiet for a while and then I hear Kyron again. It's not until something falls over and there's a sound I feel in my back teeth — bones cracking, a rustle of wings — that I finally pause. The double doors bang open and the cold comes in for a second before they swing shut again.

I keep my eyes on the pan.

I don't know what to do with any of that. With any of this. What I know is that people need to eat. That's something I can do. That's something that makes sense because nothing else does.

I find flour in the back cabinet.

My hands are already measuring before I realize what I'm making.

Bread.

I stop and look down at the bowl. At the flour on my hands. At the way my body just went there without asking me first.

She reached for it before anything else. Every meal, every table — her hand would go to the bread like she needed to confirm it was real before she let herself believe the rest of it was too. I started making extra. I never said anything about it. I just made sure there was always enough for her.

I don't know when I started doing it. I just did.

My face is wet.

How did...

I shake my head. It doesn't matter.

I stand there with flour on my hands and the bowl in front of me. I can't make myself move. Or make myself dump it out and I can't make myself keep going and I just — stand here like an idiot. The burner is still on. Something's going to burn.

I don't have it in me to care.

The kitchen door opens.

I know it's Cal without looking. He doesn't say anything. Doesn't ask if I'm okay or tell me it's going to be fine. Which is good, because I might punch him if he did. He just looks at the bowl and looks at me and pulls out one of the stools at the counter and sits down.

That's it.

My hands start moving again. Not because it makes sense. Just because I don't know how to stop now that I've started again.

The bread takes a long time to make. Cal stays the whole way through. Neither of us says a word.

When it's done I put it on the counter and look at it for a long moment.

I stand there looking at it. The bread on the counter. The way she'd come in here and steal a piece or three and I'd let her because some habits don't end because your situation changes.

Cal's hand lands on my shoulder. Heavy and steady and he just leaves it there.

I put my hand over my face.

I don't know if I can make the tears stop either.

Chapter 7
TREY

I've been up for a while.

Back against the wall, watching the guys do whatever it is they're doing.

I can't really focus on it because I keep coming back to the same thing.

I never told her.

The night Cal sat with me on the porch and didn't push and somehow that made it easier to say the things I'd been carrying. The way he saw things that maybe I wasn't ready to see before that. *Does she look at you? You know what I mean.* And I did know. I knew exactly what he meant because I'd been paying attention to every one of those moments and telling myself they didn't count, that I was reading into it, that wanting something to be true doesn't make it true.

And Cal just looked at me and said *then you're not stuck. You're just not there yet.*

I believed him. That's the thing. I actually let myself believe it. Stopped waiting for some system confirmation that was never going to come anyway and just — let it be real. Let her be real. Let the idea that she was mine the same way she was theirs be something I could hold onto. Maybe even let myself want.

And then they took her.

Fuck. This isn't helping.

I watch Locke on the mattress.

It's digging at me because this isn't him. He's flat on his back, not moving, not breaking anything. Locke who went into boiling water without thinking twice. Just lying there with something cracked open behind his eyes that he's not letting out and not letting go of either.

The thoughts keep coming even as I watch Locke lose himself.

Because I need to know, does it even matter? The bond, what Cal said, what I never got to say to her — does any of it matter now.

It has to.

She has to matter enough that it matters.

I push off the wall.

"Alright." Just loud enough that I have their attention.

Beckett looks up. Locke doesn't move.

"I get it." I look around the room. "I do. It's killing me too. I never even got to—" I stop, trying to hold it together. "But look at yourselves. Look at what we're doing."

Nobody answers.

"She's out there right now. Alone. With people who told her to her face that she shouldn't exist." My voice stays steady. "And we're in here. Falling apart. Like it's over."

Locke's jaw tightens.

"Kyron's in the sky because he's decided she abandoned us. Beckett's checked out. Rane you haven't stopped talking since you woke up and I get why but talking isn't doing anything." I look at Locke. "And you — you don't do this. You don't lie down."

Something moves across Locke's face. The look of a man who knows he's doing the wrong thing and hates that someone said it out loud.

"She made a choice. A terrible, brave, stupid choice because she thought that's what she had to do. She's somewhere right now not knowing if we're okay. Not knowing if it worked. Thinking she left us in the dirt and it might not have even been enough." My throat tightens. "Imagine how she feels. Imagine what that's like."

"None of you would let her go. I've known you five minutes in the grand scheme of things and I know that much. So stop acting like this is the end. She's waiting. She doesn't know it yet but she is. And she deserves better than us falling apart in here while she's alone with them."

This isn't about us, not anymore. The moment she walked into my life, that was it. And we're just going to sit here and do nothing?

I can't live with that.

The door creaks open.

"You're right."

Chapter 8
NOVA

I've been looking at his face for five hours.

I didn't want to. I didn't have a choice. When you're on your knees with your hands tied behind your back and nowhere else to be, you end up memorizing things you'd rather not. Like the pause before each question. The way his mouth moves when he's deciding how much to reveal. The smile that means nothing at all.

My knees stopped hurting a while ago.

He's asking about my parents again. He keeps circling back to my parents like eventually I'll crack open and hand him something. What I remember. What they told me. Whether they mentioned — and here the pause — certain things. Certain places.

I don't fill the pause.

Why would I tell him anything. They've taken everything. I have nothing left to trade and nothing left to protect and no reason on earth to give this man a single word.

And some of it I genuinely don't know. I was eleven. I have fragments. A smell. A light in a room I can't fully picture anymore. I don't know what's real and what I built to survive it.

I'm not going to explain that to him.

He asks another question. I hear him talking but I'm not even trying to make out the words.

I think about them.

The way I was drawn to them from that first moment. Standing in that doorway looking at Locke for the first time and forgetting how breathing worked. Not because of what he looked like, but there was that too. But because something in me knew before my brain had any say in it at all.

Rane talking too much at dinner and somehow it was the most comfortable sound I'd ever been inside.

Vaelor's hands. How careful they always were. How he never once made it feel like charity.

Beckett in the hallway, not asking for anything. Or when I took that single step toward him before I decided to. And that quiet — I didn't know you could feel quiet inside your own head. I didn't know it was something a person could give you.

Kyron's arms carrying me down a street and never wanting him to put me down.

Trey's mouth. The weeks I spent not thinking about it and then the moment I stopped pretending and thought about nothing else.

All of it. The pull toward all of them, from the very first day, before I had any idea what it was. Before I understood what I was walking into.

I understand now.

"Answer me."

His voice, sharp. Close.

I jerk.

He's leaned forward. Right in my face, and I didn't hear him move. His composure has a crack in it. Small, but it's the first one I've seen.

I look at him. Look back at the wall.

He sits back. Smooths his jacket. I'm pretty sure I can see the wheels turning inside his head at this point.

"The marks," he says. The words sound calm but there's impatience underneath. "The men in your cluster — their House marks don't change. That is not something that happens. That has never happened in four centuries of documented bonds." His jaw tightens. "You're doing something to them. Consciously or not. And I need you to tell me what."

I think about Rane's wrist. My mark there, no longer dream.

"The phoenix." He tries a different angle. Leaning back. Casual, almost like he's not coming apart on the inside. "I know what you are. I have a very detailed account. I'm not asking you to tell me something I don't know — I'm asking you to confirm it. That's all. Just confirm it."

I breathe through my nose.

"Your parents." And again with the parents... "They came to someone when you were a baby. Looking for answers. They were frightened and they loved you and they made choices trying to protect you." He pauses. "I wonder if you know what those choices cost."

Nothing and screw him for thinking he can hold them over my head like that.

"How did you find the Hollow." He's procedural now. The questions coming faster. "Who told you it existed. How did you get there. What are they building. Who helped you." Each question tight against the last.

"What do you know about the marks. What do you know about what you are. Why did your cluster form the way it did. Who has been helping you."

I blink. Once. Each time his face gets too close.

He stands up abruptly.

Walks to the far wall. Stands there for a moment with his back to me.

When he turns around the composure is mostly back. Sort of.

"Do you know how long we have maintained this system." His voice is different now. Something underneath it that wasn't there before. "How much work. How much — management. Separating Houses. Controlling proximity. Ensuring that certain configurations never —" He stops. Jaw tight.

Starts again.

"Your cluster should not exist." Not the way Silas said it with contempt and disgust. This is something else. Genuine. Almost bewildered. "A cross-House cluster of this size — this composition — we have spent generations ensuring it was not possible. Two Houses at most. Controlled. Documented. Never —" He stops again.

He's just told me something.

He knows he's just told me something.

The mask comes back down. Smooth and immediate.

But I know he's said too much.

"Perhaps some time alone will change your mind about talking."

He's at the door.

"I'd think very carefully about continuing this act of defiance."

He leaves.

I sit on the floor in the too-clean room with my knees gone numb and my wrists burning.

He spent generations making sure a cluster like ours couldn't happen.

He failed.

I'm not sure it matters anymore.

Chapter 9
RANE

I can't sit down.

I've tried. Twice. Both times I lasted about forty seconds before I was back on my feet because sitting down feels like giving up and I'm not giving up, I'm just — there's nowhere to put any of this. There's nothing to do with it. We're in this hall and Nova is gone and Locke is on his back. Kyron is god knows where up in the sky being a dramatic feathered bastard and I want to grab him by the wing and drag him back down here. Then I want to shake Locke until he gets up off his ass. I want to do so many things and I can't and it's bullshit.

Trey said his piece.

He's right. He's completely right. I've known he was right since before he said it and it still didn't give me anywhere to put my hands.

Because I can't think about how she's not here. How they have her.

I open my mouth.

"Don't," she says.

I close it.

Zoe looks at Minerva. Something passes between them — I don't know what, except that Minerva built this town from nothing and she is not someone who steps aside for anyone. She nods.

Zoe turns, looking at all of us.

"I was there," she says. "When they finally left. When Silas and all the shifters he brought walked away and the street cleared." Her voice is steady but her hands aren't. She's got them pressed flat against her thighs. "We got to you as soon as we could. Me and Eli and the others. And you were all on the ground."

I don't want to hear this.

"None of you were moving. No sounds... nothing. All of you, in the dirt." She swallows. "And Nova was already gone. The vehicles were already gone. And the last thing she saw before that bag came down was all of you on the ground not moving."

Beckett's eyes close.

"She doesn't know what those darts were," Zoe says. "She's never been inside the system. She doesn't know the difference between something that puts you down and something that—" She stops. Starts again. "She saw you fall. She heard the rest of you go down right after she agreed. And then she was in the dark."

The hall is very quiet.

"The sound that came out of her..." Zoe shakes her head and I can tell she's trying to hold it together.

"She thinks you're dead."

Locke swears. Low and quiet. We all hear it.

"She's in there right now carrying that," Zoe says. "Thinking she gave herself up and it didn't even work. Thinking she lost all of you anyway." Her voice cracks. Once. She pushes through it. "And you're all in here, doing what... feeling sorry for yourselves?"

She looks at the window. At the sky. "And Kyron is up there deciding she abandoned you when she walked into that vehicle thinking you were already gone."

"Couldn't have said it better myself." Brent interrupts. He's not wrong.

Cal nods.

At least we're all in agreement.

Then Vaelor in the kitchen doorway. Dish towel in his hands. Eyes red.

He looks at Zoe for a long moment.

"What do you suggest?" he says.

I stop moving because what Zoe said actually hits me.

She was there. She saw what Nova saw. And hearing it from someone who was standing on that street makes it real.

Nova thinks we're dead.

She's in there alone. With Silas, and probably Laith too eventually.

And we're the only ones who can tell her she's wrong.

I drag a hand through my hair.

Zoe looks at me. Trying not to show how scared she is.

"Hey," I say.

"Hey," she says back.

"We need a plan," I say because I haven't got a clue what it is.

She grins.

"Damn right we do. Let's get our girl back."

Chapter 10
KYRON

She left us.

She just said yes and walked away. From all of it. All of us.

I know she didn't.

I know she didn't and I still can't stop the feeling that's taken over every part of me. I feel betrayed. I feel like something got ripped out of my chest. I feel like I can't breathe because she's not here. And the fact that she walked away, that she did this — that's what I can't get past. That's the thing my brain keeps landing on no matter how many times I tell it that's not what happened.

The sun is going down. I didn't notice until just now — that shift where the gold bleeds into orange and the shadows start playing over the clouds. I've been up here long enough that the whole sky changed around me.

I keep flying. Lazy pace. Trying to think through all of it — her, the Hollow, the guys, what I said before I left. What I shouldn't have said. What I can't take back now.

I don't want to go back.

I mean — I know they'll probably forgive me eventually. That's not the problem. The problem is I don't want to see their faces when I walk back in. Don't want to see what's in Rane's eyes or the particular set of Locke's jaw or the way Beckett goes very still and quiet when he's decided something about you.

What I've worked out over the last few hours up here is that I didn't just lose my temper and say something wrong. I ran. I actually ran. Shifted and went through those doors and climbed until the Hollow was a small thing below me and told myself I needed air.

I needed to hide. That's what I needed.

And now I'm stuck. Because part of me is hurt and part of me is embarrassed and all of me wants her back and I know we need to do it together.

They can wait.

A sound catches me.

In this form I can hear everything. The wind through my feathers. The creak of branches three hundred feet below. I swear I can hear the clouds moving if I concentrate hard enough.

This is different.

A buzz. Low and steady and mechanical. I turn toward it without deciding to.

There's something on the horizon.

A speck at first. Wrong shape for a bird. Wrong movement for anything I know. I bank toward it and it gets bigger. And bigger. Metal catching the last of the sunset light. Mechanisms I can't make out from here. Something enormous moving through the air like it has every right to be there.

I circle wide, keeping distance.

What the fuck is that.

But more importantly…

It's headed straight for the Hollow.

I don't think. I just go.

I push hard.

My wings ache. I don't care. I track the machine's speed and the direction it's heading and do the math. My stomach drops further with every calculation.

Dawn. Maybe just before. That's when it reaches the Hollow if I'm reading the speed right.

I don't know what it is. I don't know where it came from. I know it's massive and metal and someone is steering it headed straight for the town.

After the bears in the forest, the extraction. After three fucking Houses coordinated to walk into the Hollow like it was nothing.

This isn't happening.

I fly faster.

The Hollow comes into view below me and I don't bother with a clean landing. I come down hard in the back, shift on the way, hit the ground running. It's sloppy and hurts like hell because this is the second time I've shifted.

Brilliant.

I'm through the door before anyone reacts.

"Locke! Trey! Guys! There's something coming—" I'm already talking before I'm fully inside. "A machine. Flying. Enormous. Metal. I've never seen anything like it and it's heading straight for the Hollow. I clocked the speed — it'll reach us around dawn."

Everyone in the room goes still.

Brent is with Rane and Trey at the table, something between them that looks like a map. Locke by the window. Vaelor in the kitchen doorway.

They're planning. They've been planning. I've been gone for hours and they've been down here doing the actual work and I—

Later.

Brent leans forward. "How big?"

"Bigger than this building. Metal. Mechanisms running along the sides. Like a giant... something—" I shake my head. "I don't know. It's like nothing I've ever seen."

"Which direction?"

"From the northeast, coming in faster than something that size should move."

"It's not a threat," he says.

"It's heading straight—"

"It's the Clockwork Order." He's already pushing back from the table, reaching for his jacket. "Minerva's been expecting them. Defensive technology. We just didn't know when." He stands. "I need to find her."

"Kyron," Rane says.

Everyone looks at him.

He's looking at me. Specifically at all of me.

"You're naked."

"I'm aware."

"Just—" He gestures at me. "Wanted to make sure you knew."

"Thank you, Rane."

"Someone had to say it," Beckett says from the corner without looking up.

"First thing he's said in hours," Rane snorts.

Trey bites down on something that might have been a smile.

Brent, deeply unbothered, shakes his head as he walks out the door.

"Here," Locke says, throwing a pair of pants at my face without even looking at me.

I catch them and pull them on.

The door closes behind Brent and the room settles into this weird silence.

I already know what's coming.

"So," Rane says.

"Rane." Locke's voice. Flat.

"No." Rane takes a step forward. "He flew out of here like she was already dead and we were the problem. He said maybe Silas had a point."

"I know what I said."

"Do you? Because from where I was standing it looked like you decided she chose to leave and then you checked out. While the rest of us were trying to figure out how to get her back."

"I came back."

"Because something scared you in the sky."

"I came back." I say it through gritted teeth.

"You said she manipulated us." His voice cracks on it. "You said maybe Silas was right. About her. About everything she is to us."

"I know." Quieter than I mean to. "I was wrong."

"Yeah," Rane laughs but there's nothing in it. "You were."

"What the fuck were you thinking? Taking off like that?"

I try not to flinch because he's right, but another part of me is starting to get really pissed off.

"Rane, knock it off." Locke.

"No. I can't. The things he said — if Nova knew. If she had any idea that this would be his reaction to her sacrificing herself. For the town. For us."

That's it.

"I can't help how I feel." It comes out louder than I mean it to. "I feel it with every fiber of my being. I can't help it. She walked out just like my fucking parents."

Rane stops. Swallows.

"Hey guys, maybe we should—" Trey.

"No." Rane's voice drops. "You don't get to do that. You don't get to pull your parents into this, Kyron. It's not the same and you know it."

"Don't tell me what I—"

"She thinks we're dead."

The room goes quiet.

"She thinks we're fucking dead, Kyron. Don't you get it?"

I can't breathe. For a second everything goes black as I try to process what Rane just said.

"What are you talking about?"

Vaelor comes toward me. Hands empty at his sides. For a minute I think he's going to lay into me too.

"She thinks we're dead." He says it too calm. He looks defeated. "The last thing she saw before they put a bag over her head was all of us shot, lying in the dirt in the middle of the road."

He takes a breath.

"So whatever you needed to work out up there — I hope it's done. Because we don't have time for it anymore."

I don't say anything. There's nothing to say.

"Tell me where we are," I say. "Tell me what we have."

Rane looks at me for a long moment. Then he pulls out the chair beside him.

"Nothing. Fucking nothing."

Chapter 11
Nova

I can't stop shaking.

Another rush of ice cold water hits me from the hose and I scream. I don't know how long it's been. Long enough that I just need it to end.

My legs are shaking so hard I would fall if I wasn't being held up by my bound wrists. Another spray. My right leg gives out. Something pops in my left shoulder and everything goes white.

Cleansing my ass.

When it comes back I'm still standing. Barely. The weight on my wrists is almost unbearable now, pulling at the shoulder that popped, and I can't — I try to get my feet under me and my right leg won't cooperate and the water comes again and I stop trying.

Just breathe.

Just breathe through it.

I think about Rane huddling close showing me my phone. How warm he was, how I wanted him closer. I think about Vaelor's hands around the hot mug of coffee, already adjusted. Setting it down in front of me before I ever asked. I think about the Hollow, all the shifters there. The road...

The water hits my face and something in my chest tears open and the sound that comes out of me doesn't feel like mine. Too raw. Too broken. It keeps coming and I can't stop it and I hate it — I hate that they get this, whoever is watching, whoever is holding the hose, whoever is writing it down in whatever file they have on me—

The water stops.

The silence is worse.

I hang there, shaking, the scream still ricocheting around inside my chest looking for somewhere to go. My shoulder is on fire. My right leg is useless. I'm soaking and freezing and I just gave them something I didn't want to give them and I can't take it back.

One of the women steps forward with a towel. She doesn't look at my face. Neither of them have looked at my face this whole time. Even as I stand here freezing, gasping for air.

I'm not a person in this room. I'm a procedure.

How many others have there been?

I let them dry me off. Let them cut down my wrists and redress them and put something thin and white on me that does nothing for the cold. I don't have the energy to be anything other than what they need me to be right now.

I'm saving it.

I don't know what for yet.

But I'll know.

Chapter 12
NOVA

I don't know how many times I've slept.

It's dark. It's been dark for so long I'm not sure I remember what light looks like. I'm sitting on the cold ground, huddled in the corner. It doesn't keep the cold away.

The tray comes. I don't touch it. The tray disappears. I sleep again. That's the whole concept of time in here — trays and darkness and the particular kind of silence that means no one is coming.

My guess is days. At least a few have gone by since I spent what felt like hours staring at Laith's face and that was before this, so.

Days, then. Maybe more.

It doesn't matter. Time passing doesn't change anything. Time passing just means more of the same dark and the same silence and the same loop of things I don't let myself finish thinking about.

Locke going down in the street.

I stop there. Every time. I stop there and I find something else.

Because I can't...

Vaelor fixing my coffee in the morning like he always did. The way he never made it a thing. Just quietly kept adjusting until it was right.

Rane talking too much at dinner and somehow it was the most comfortable sound I'd ever been inside.

Beckett covered in sawdust, so focused he probably didn't notice me watching.

The house. The blue door at the end of the road, lit from inside because someone was always already home.

I didn't know what that was the first time I saw it. I'd never had it before. I kept waiting for it to stop feeling like something and then one day it just didn't, and I remember being surprised by that. Thinking — oh. This is just what it feels like now.

I thought it would always feel like that.

I survived alone before. Fifteen years. I know how to make myself small and invisible and need nothing and no one. I did it for all those years before they found me and I was fine.

I was fine.

The difference is I didn't know what I was missing.

I'm not sure if I'm awake or still under when I hear it.

Wings.

Somewhere above me or nearby, close enough that I can make it out. I go still and listen. A few moments pass and I hear it again, fading off into the distance. There must be a window nearby.

I don't know what it was.

But something about hearing those wings calms me a little.

Makes me think I'm not alone in here.

Or maybe that's just wishful thinking.

I fall asleep listening for it to come back.

I wake up slow.

Slower than I have since they put me in this fucking box.

My body feels heavy. I can barely see my hands it's so dark, but I can feel them shake.

I sit with my back against the wall and just breathe and let it be enough.

A sound outside the cell and a scrape of metal. The tray slides through.

I don't move for a long time.

Even though I can smell it, still warm enough that I can make out what it is without seeing it. My stomach growls.

I can't keep doing this.

I know I can't and it still doesn't make what I'm about to do any better.

I crawl forward towards the smell in the dark. I don't think I can stand right now. Hell, I'm not sure there's enough room in this box to stand.

I reach out barely making out the tray in front of me. My hand lands on a roll. I take it, turning and settling against the wall. I breathe in.

It smells like bread.

I take a small bite.

I lean my head back, close my eyes and chew, trying to make it last.

"Hello?"

I freeze.

A voice. Quiet and uncertain. Coming from somewhere close— next to me maybe, through the wall, I can't tell, the dark makes distance impossible.

"Hello? Is someone there?"

My throat works around the bread.

"Yeah," I manage. "I'm here."

Silence. Then a breath — shaky, released.

"Oh thank god." A pause. "Why do I know your voice?"

Something moves through me. Cold and wrong.

Because I know her voice too.

"Nova?" It cracks on my name. "Nova, it's Lena."

Something in my chest opens.

"Lena." Her name comes out wrong. Too much in it. "How are you — are you okay? Are you hurt?"

"I'm okay. I'm okay." She sounds like she's been crying for a long time and ran out somewhere in the dark. "Are you? Nova, are you hurt?"

"I'm fine." Not true but not the point. "How long have you been... How did you get here?"

"I don't know. I don't — it's been dark the whole time, I can't —" She stops. Gets herself together. "They came back. Nova, they came back to the Hollow. The crow warned us but it wasn't enough."

I go still.

Why would the crow...

I shake my head. I need to focus.

"The guys?" My voice is steady. I don't know how because I don't want to ask but I need to know. "Lena, the guys —"

"Nova."

The way she says my name makes my stomach clench.

"No."

"I'm so sorry."

"No —"

"They're gone. I watched — Nova, I'm so sorry, they're gone."

The dark doesn't change.

Nothing changes.

I slide down the wall until I'm on the floor and I don't remember deciding to do that.

I roll on my side, bring my knees up to my chest.

I gave myself up so it wouldn't happen and it happened anyway and—

The tears come and I don't try to stop them.

There's no one here to see.

Chapter 13
BECKETT

Nobody slept last night. Not after we all realized she thinks we're dead.

We're sitting in the Community Hall. Maps on the table along with Kyron's relay notes. The bread Vaelor made sits untouched on the counter. I'm on the bench with my laptop, trying to get through Order security again. Same walls. Same dead ends. I've been at this for hours and I'm not any closer to finding where they're keeping her.

I break through another layer. Hit another wall.

I want to throw the laptop across the room.

Rane cracks first.

"Do you think she really believes we're dead?"

"Stop," Locke says.

"We have to talk about it sometime," Vaelor says.

"Yeah," Locke says. "But not right now. What we need is to do something."

I don't say anything. Just keep my eyes on the screen.

Then we hear it.

Low and mechanical. The kind of sound that you can feel vibrate through your body.

Kyron looks up. "They're here."

We're outside before anyone says another word.

The whole town is already gathering in the main street. Darcy with her kid. A couple of the forest shifters at the tree line. I'm not sure where the crow is. I haven't seen it since the morning...

Nope. Not going there.

Minerva is near the front. Hands clasped in front of her. Beaming.

I've never seen Minerva like this before.

Brent stands beside her. He looks excited and wary at the same time. Like he's not entirely sure this is safe but he's committed now.

The sound gets louder.

Then it clears the tree line.

Kyron wasn't exaggerating, the ship is enormous. Metal hull catching the first light. Mechanisms along the sides rotating, adjusting, doing things I might need to figure out later. It descends slow and deliberate, like whoever is steering it has done this a thousand times and finds none of it remarkable.

The whole street goes quiet.

Rane's mouth is open. And it's the first time I've wanted to smile since I woke up in the Community Hall.

Kyron looks at me with an expression that is very carefully neutral.

Locke watches it with his arms crossed.

The ship settles in the field beyond the houses. Something locks into place. A hiss. Then silence.

A few moments go by and then a ramp deploys.

Light spills out — warm, brass-tinted.

Someone drops off the ramp before it finishes extending.

Dark hair in his eyes. Pointed ears with rings along one of them. Soot on his hands. At least six-five, probably more. He's already looking at everything — the houses, the tree line, all of us.

He lands in the grass and spreads his arms, grinning wide.

"What's up, bitches!"

I blink.

Trey makes a sound somewhere behind me.

Two more come down behind him.

The first one is all silver hair and armor and a scar cutting from cheek-bone to temple. He doesn't look around. Just walks straight down the ramp like he already knows where he's going.

The third one is last off. Sleeves rolled. Collar open. Gloves in his back pocket. He's scanning the crowd the same way I do when I'm trying to get a read on a room.

All three of them are massive. Taller than anyone I've ever seen. Broader.

Locke uncrosses his arms and stands up straighter.

I look at Rane. He's still staring with his mouth open.

At this point I'm holding back a laugh.

The three of them walk forward together and stop a few feet away.

Stand there.

Everyone just stares.

Kree looks around. "So who's in charge of this place?"

Minerva steps forward. "I am. Minerva. We've been in contact."

"Right." Kree grins. "I'm Kree. That's Liam." He jerks his thumb at the one with the scar. "And Declan."

Liam gives a single nod.

Declan raises a hand in a half-wave.

Rane, beside me: "Are you guys like... fae? You're fae, right?"

Kree's grin gets wider. "Yeah."

"That's so cool," Rane says. "I've never met—"

"Rane," Locke says.

"—actual fae before, and the ship is—"

"Rane."

"—incredible, by the way, how does it even—"

Kree walks over and puts a hand on Rane's shoulder. Large hand. Rane stops talking immediately.

"You good short stuff?" Kree asks.

Rane nods.

"Cool." Kree pats his shoulder and walks back.

I'm biting the inside of my cheek to keep from laughing.

Liam looks at Minerva. "You don't know how this works, so we'll stay, help you set it up, and show you. Once we're finished, you can provide us with what we've bargained for and we'll be on our way."

I look at the flying machine. Back at them.

I wonder how fast it goes.

Brent steps forward. "I'm Brent. I'll be the one you'll be working with. Probably Cal as well."

Declan looks out at the forest line, the town, back at Brent. "You'll need more than that. This seems like a lot of area to cover."

Brent immediately looks at us.

Fuck.

"Let's get you settled first," Minerva says to the fae. She turns. "Lena!"

She waits.

Nothing.

Minerva looks around. "Where is that girl?"

Brent shrugs.

"Oh very well." Minerva looks at Brent. "Please take them to the available housing." She looks at us. "Take them with you."

"Come on," Brent says to the fae. "Follow me."

Rane immediately falls into step beside Kree. "So how does the ship actually fly? Like what's the mechanism? Is it steam-powered or—"

Kree grins. "Oh, you're gonna love this."

And then he's off, hands gesturing, explaining something that I definitely want to hear more about later while Rane nods enthusiastically and asks follow-up questions.

We follow Brent and the fae down the row of houses. Kree's still talking — something about compression ratios and fuel cells and rotational lift — and Rane's eating it up. Locke walks a few steps behind them, arms crossed but listening. Kyron's doing that thing where he looks like he's not paying attention but is absolutely listening to every word.

Brent stops at the empty house. "This is yours while you're here."

Liam nods once. Declan's already scanning the windows, the door frame, the sight lines. Kree pokes his head inside.

"Not bad," he says. "We've stayed in worse."

"We'll get started after breakfast," Liam says to Brent.

Brent nods. Looks at us. "You too. Minerva wants everyone on this."

We head into our house next door.

"Anyone think this is going to be a nightmare?" Vaelor asks.

"No no, they're from Clockwork Order," Rane says. "Not Nightmare."

Vaelor rolls his eyes. "I know that."

Trey laughs.

"Either way," Kyron says. "We need to get this done quickly and figure out how to get to Nova."

I nod. "I'll keep working on getting into their systems. See what I can find." I turn, heading for the stairs. "I need my signal interceptor. I know I packed it."

I take the steps two at a time, heading straight for Nova's room. The one that's turned into storage because she never slept in it. My bag is where I left it, half unpacked in the corner.

I dig through it. Laptop. Cables. Extra drive. Where the fuck—

My hand lands on fabric.

Soft. Familiar.

I freeze.

I pull it out slowly.

Nova's jacket. The one I grabbed from the bathroom when we were frantically packing to leave the Academy. I don't even remember deciding to take it. I just did.

I bring it to my nose and breathe her in with my eyes closed.

Her scent almost makes my knees buckle.

I stand there for a few minutes just breathing. Trying to calm down. Trying to remember how to function.

I fold the jacket carefully.

Something falls onto the ground.

Weird.

I pick it up.

A card. Plain white. A name and a number printed in simple black text.

Linda Luceran

And a phone number. That's all it says.

Why would Nova have this?

I stare at it for a long moment.

I don't know what it means.

But it's the only lead I've got.

Chapter 14
LOCKE

We're in the house. Unpacking. Repacking. Organizing supplies for when we have a plan.

I'm standing by the window staring at nothing. Outside I can hear Kree explaining something to Brent about placement intervals. His voice carries even when he's not trying.

Inside it's quieter. Someone's moving things around in the kitchen. Footsteps upstairs. The house feels occupied but hollow. We all know why, we just can't say it.

Then Beckett hits the stairs.

Fast.

I turn. Everyone else does too.

Beckett hasn't moved with purpose since we woke up in the Community Hall yesterday morning. He's been here but checked out, sitting with his laptop, breaking through walls that just rebuild themselves.

Now he's taking the stairs two at a time and there's something in his face that wasn't there ten minutes ago.

"Guys." He stops at the bottom. "I found something."

Rane appears from the kitchen. "What?"

Beckett holds up a card. Plain white. Small enough to fit in a pocket.

"It was in Nova's jacket. Inside pocket. I didn't even know it was there." He hands it to Kyron.

Kyron reads it. Looks up. "Who's Linda Luceran?"

"I don't know."

"Why does Nova have her card?"

"I don't know that either."

Vaelor comes over. Takes the card from Kyron. Reads it. Flips it over. Nothing on the back except the phone number.

"Where'd you find the jacket?" Vaelor asks.

"My bag. I grabbed it when we left the Academy. I don't even remember taking it."

Rane looks at the card over Vaelor's shoulder. "Do we call?"

"That's the question," Kyron says.

"What if it's a trap?" Trey's voice from somewhere behind me.

"What if it's not?" Rane says. "What if this is exactly what Nova wanted us to find?"

"She didn't know we'd find it," Beckett says. "She didn't know we'd have the jacket."

"So why keep the card?"

Nobody answers that.

Vaelor sets it on the table. We all stare at it.

"We need to talk to Minerva," Kyron says. "And Brent. See if they recognize the name."

"After the perimeter work," Beckett says. "We finish what we told them we'd do. Then we take this to them tonight."

"Why wait?" Rane asks.

"Because we already agreed to help Clockwork," Kyron says. "And besides, we need to look like we have our shit together. Like we're thinking tactically."

"We are thinking tactically."

"Then we can wait a few hours."

Trey nods. "He's right. We finish the work. Then we move."

The conversation keeps going.

"What if the number's monitored?" Kyron asks.

"Then we're careful," Beckett says.

"What if she doesn't remember Nova?"

"You really think someone isn't going to remember the woman without a mark?"

Rane makes a face as he leans against the counter. "What if she does remember and she's the reason Nova ended up at the Academy in the first place?"

"Then we find out why," Trey says.

Beckett picks up the card again. Stares at it. "We finish the perimeter work. Then we take this to Minerva and Brent tonight."

"Agreed," Kyron says.

They're moving again.

That's what this is. Forward motion. The first real piece of it since she was taken.

I stand.

Nobody looks at me.

I walk toward the door. Past Trey and up the stairs.

Nobody stops me.

I can still hear them talking as I head upstairs. Beckett's voice. Kyron's. The sound of planning instead of sitting.

That's good.

That's what they need.

I'll go back down when I'm ready.

Right now I need something I can finish.

I head to the room at the end of the hall.

The bed frame is leaning against the wall where I left it. Unfinished. Half-sanded. I was going to stain it. Make it look like something she'd want to come home to.

I pick up the sandpaper.

Start working.

The voices downstairs fade into background noise. Planning. Strategy. Hope.

I focus on the wood.

One pass. Then another.

Smooth out the rough edges.

Make something right.

Something she deserves.

Chapter 15
VAELOR

The sun is low by the time we're almost finished.

The shield nodes are glowing faintly along the Hollow's edge. Not bright. Just enough that you can see them if you're looking. Kree's voice carries from somewhere down the line, explaining something to Rane about resonance frequencies. Declan's adjusting spacing on the eastern perimeter. Brent looks thrilled every time one of the devices activates.

The town feels different. Protected in a new way.

People are on their porches watching. A few came out to help earlier. Darcy brought water around midday. Mara checked on us twice. The whole Hollow has been moving today, doing something productive for the first time since Nova was taken.

This is the first day that's felt useful.

Liam is working on the final placement near the northern tree line. I head over to help. He doesn't look up when I approach, just gestures at the device on the ground.

"Hold that steady."

I do.

We work in silence for a few minutes. Comfortable. He adjusts the calibration. I keep it level. Easy rhythm.

"Your town's good," Liam says eventually.

"It is."

"Minerva built something real here."

I glance at him. "She's my grandmother."

His hands stop. Just for a second. Then he looks at me directly.

"Really?"

"Yeah."

"Then you know about the archives."

I nod. "I grew up in them. Memory House. My family's been keeping the records for generations."

Something shifts in Liam's expression. Like a renewed focus.

"Do you know what we traded?" he asks. "What the bargain was?"

I shake my head. "Minerva didn't say."

"The prophecy." He goes back to adjusting the device but his voice stays level. Deliberate. "Some of our legends speak of one. But no such prophecy exists in Clockwork records. Your grandmother has it. That's what we're here for. The defenses in exchange for access."

I go still.

"What prophecy?"

Liam doesn't answer right away. He finishes the calibration. Stands. Looks at me like he's deciding whether to say the next part.

"I think it's about us," he says finally. "I think we're supposed to find someone. Or rather, we're supposed to find the one the prophecy is about."

My chest tightens.

"A woman?"

Liam can't hold back a small smile. "Of course. Wouldn't be fun any other way."

I nod. "We already found ours."

"Oh yeah?" The smile stays. "Well where is she? Why didn't we meet her?"

"She's gone."

The smile drops. "What do you mean gone?"

"She was taken. Three days ago. By the Nightmare Order."

He goes completely still.

"Your government? You can't just let her go."

"We know. We found our first lead this morning."

"Why didn't you say something?"

"Because we promised we'd help. And that's what we're doing. We're helping. So as soon as we're done tonight, we're moving on it."

"What did you find?"

"A card. With a number. It was in her jacket."

Liam nods once. Doesn't push for more. Just looks at me with the same steady focus he's had since he walked off that ship this morning.

"If you need anything, if you need help from us, we're here."

I meet his eyes. "Thank you."

He picks up the next device. Hands it to me.

"Let's finish this."

I nod, a little relieved though I'm not sure why.

We keep working as the sun drops lower. The nodes glow brighter as the light fades. Kree's still talking somewhere down the line. Declan's off triple-checking the eastern edge. Rane's asking questions. Locke's been gone for hours but nobody's said anything about it.

The perimeter is almost done. 64

And when it is, we move.

Chapter 16
TREY

Nobody really slept.

I can tell by the way everyone's moving. Too careful. Too quiet. Like if we make noise we'll break whatever fragile thing is holding us together.

It's early. The sun's barely up and we're all already downstairs. Locke came down sometime before dawn. He didn't say anything. Just sat at the table with his hands wrapped around a mug. He hasn't said anything about where he ran off to yesterday either.

Vaelor made bread. I don't know when. But it's on the counter and it smells like home. Nobody's touched it yet.

Beckett's at the table with his laptop. Kyron's standing by the window looking irritated by Rane's pacing. He keeps moving between the kitchen and the living room like he's looking for something to do with his hands.

The card is on the table.

We talked to Minerva and Brent last night. Showed them the card. Minerva didn't recognize the name but she didn't look surprised either.

Brent set up a secure line. Something that won't ping Order systems if they're monitoring.

Minerva said to call at seven. Before Linda's shift starts but late enough she'd be awake.

It's six forty-five.

"We should eat something," Vaelor says.

Nobody moves.

"I'm serious. We need to eat."

Rane grabs a piece of bread. He doesn't take a bite, just holds it.

I look at Locke. He's staring at the mug in his hands like it's the only thing keeping him grounded.

"You okay?" I ask.

He doesn't look up. "No."

Fair.

Kyron turns from the window. "What do we say when she answers?"

"We ask for Nova," Beckett says. "See how she reacts."

"What if she doesn't remember her?"

"She will."

"How do you know?"

"Because Nova doesn't forget people who help her. And she kept the card."

He's not wrong.

Rane finally takes a bite of the bread. Chews. Swallows.

"This house could actually be good, you know."

I look at him. "What?"

"The house. Once we get her back. It could be good. Like. Home."

Vaelor glances at him. "It already is."

"No I mean really home. All of us. Her. This place." Rane gestures at the walls. "We could be happy here."

Nobody argues with that.

"Too many bedrooms though," I say.

"For now," Rane says.

Kyron looks at him. "You're already thinking about kids?"

"I'm just saying. One day maybe."

"Nobody needs a little Rane running around."

"Fuck you. I'd be a great dad."

Beckett actually smiles at that. Just a little. "You'd let them get away with everything."

"Yeah and you'd teach them to hack before they could walk."

"Better than teaching them to talk people's ears off."

Vaelor's watching us. Not saying anything. But there's a hint of a smile on his face that wasn't there before.

"What?" I ask.

"Just. This." He gestures at all of us. "Talking about it like it's real."

"It is real," Locke says.

We all look at him. He hasn't said much all morning.

"We get her back. We bring her home. And then we build whatever the fuck we want."

Rane grins. "Damn right."

"She'd probably want the room with the window," Vaelor says quietly. "The one that gets morning light."

"She'd want to be near you," I say. "Near all of us."

"She'd take over the kitchen," Beckett says. "Try to cook even though she has no idea what she's doing."

"We'd teach her."

"Yeah but imagine a little Nova."

The room goes quiet.

Kyron's the one who breaks it. "Stubborn as hell."

"Smart," Beckett adds.

"Probably won't eat her vegetables," Rane says.

"She'd have your eyes," Vaelor says to Locke.

Locke's hands tighten around his mug. "And her hair."

"She'd be perfect," I say.

Nobody disagrees.

We sit with that for a while.

I can almost see it. This house full of noise and life and the family we're going to build when we get her back.

Not if.

When.

Beckett checks his laptop. "Six fifty-eight."

The room shifts.

Rane stops pacing. Kyron moves away from the window. Vaelor sets down the bread. Locke finally looks up.

"Everyone ready?" Beckett asks.

We nod.

He picks up the phone at exactly seven.

Dials the number on the card.

It rings.

Once.

Twice.

Three times.

Then a click.

"Linda Luceran."

Beckett doesn't hesitate. "Hello. We're looking for Nova."

Nothing for a few seconds. Then her voice comes back steady.

"I know."

Chapter 17
NOVA

She won't shut the fuck up.

I thought the silence was bad. I thought being alone in the dark with nothing but my own thoughts was the worst thing that could happen in here.

I was wrong.

So fucking wrong.

They brought Lena back maybe an hour ago. I heard the door. The footsteps. The sound of her being shoved into the cell next to mine. I thought maybe we could talk again. Maybe she'd tell me something useful. Maybe just hearing another voice would help.

But something's wrong.

She hasn't stopped talking since they put her back.

Not to me. Not really. Just talking. Rambling. Like someone flipped a switch in her brain and now she can't turn it off.

"Watch for the shifters," she says. Her voice is hoarse like she's been screaming. "The weird ones. Find out how it started. Find out why it's there."

I press my back against the wall and close my eyes.

"Lena."

She doesn't answer. Just keeps going.

"Why would they do that? Why would Clockwork come? Why would Nova come? Why would Vaelor come?"

I don't know what Clockwork is. I don't know why she's saying my name like I'm not right here. I don't know what they did to her while she was gone.

But whatever it was, it broke something.

"Lena," I say again. Louder this time.

Nothing.

"Find out how it started. Watch the shifters. The weird ones. Why would they bargain for the archives? Why does Minerva have it? Why would Clockwork come unless—"

She stops. Just for a second. Then starts again.

"Watch for the shifters."

The pain in my shoulder gets worse as I move, but I grab the piece of bread from the tray they brought earlier. I need to eat. I know I need to eat. But listening to her is making it hard to swallow.

I take a bite anyway.

Chew.

Swallow.

Lena's still talking.

"Find out why it's there. Find out how it started. Why would Nova come? Why would Vaelor come? Watch the shifters. The weird ones."

It's the same things. Over and over. Like she's stuck in a loop she can't get out of.

I wonder what they did to her.

I wonder if they're going to do it to me and if this is what I'll sound like when they're done.

I shudder as I finish the bread. Drink some water. Lean my head back against the wall and try to sleep.

But Lena won't stop.

"Why would Clockwork come? Why would they bargain for the archives? Find out how it started. Watch the shifters."

I close my eyes.

Try to block it out.

I can't.

"Why would Vaelor come? Why would Nova come? Why would Clockwork come unless they found her?"

I sit up.

That one's different.

Clockwork. Archives. Vaelor. And then *unless they found her*.

Found who?

Me?

For half a second something inside me reaches for it. The stupid, broken part that still wants to believe someone is coming.

But I know better.

I watched them fall. Lena confirmed it. *They're gone.*

I stare at the wall between us.

"Lena, stop."

She doesn't answer. Just keeps cycling.

"Watch the shifters. The weird ones. Find out how it started."

That fragment sits in my chest anyway. *Unless they found her.*

And I hate it. I hate that part of me still reacts. I hate that my brain still reaches for the idea that they're coming.

Because they're not.

They're dead.

Lena keeps talking like the world outside this place is still moving. Like people are coming. Like rescue is real.

And every time she does, it feels like losing them all over again.

Chapter 18
KYRON

We're moving five minutes after the call ended.

Boots on wood. Trey's already armed. Beckett has coordinates pulled up on his tablet. Locke's awake — actually awake — for the first time in days.

I'm halfway to the Clockwork house before the others catch up.

Linda knew where she was. Gave us coordinates. Timing window. Everything we need.

Now we just need the ship.

I hit the door hard. Three knocks.

Kree opens it.

Hair everywhere. No shirt. Grinning like he's been waiting for this his whole life.

"Fuck yeah. What do we have?"

"Coordinates," Beckett says. "Location. We know where she is."

Declan appears behind Kree. Fully dressed. Already calculating. "Patrols. Access points. Detection risk."

"We'll figure it out," I say.

Liam steps into view. Looks at us. At our faces.

"Community Hall," he says. "We do this right."

We're moving as a group down the main street. The energy is different now. Urgent. Focused.

Zoe and her cluster are coming from the other direction. She sees us immediately.

Stops.

"You better not be talking about Nova without us."

"Ohh, I like her." Kree grins. "Wouldn't dream of it."

"Good." She falls into step beside us. "Because we're in."

Eli nods. The rest of her cluster follows.

The Community Hall doors are already open. Brent's inside. Cal's moving chairs. Minerva's at the far end watching us file in.

Maps get cleared from the table. Beckett sets down his tablet. Declan's already asking questions about patrol patterns. Kree's bouncing on his heels with dangerous excitement.

Everyone's here.

Now we get her back.

Chapter 19
VAELOR

The people we need are already here.

Brent and Cal near the front table. Minerva standing off to the side watching everything. The Clockwork trio already moving into the space — Kree by the windows gesturing at something, Declan studying the maps Brent already spread out, Liam standing with his arms crossed waiting for the room to settle.

Zoe walks in right behind us. "Let's do this."

Eli squeezes her shoulder. Her guys move toward the table with everyone else.

I take a spot near the table where I can see everything. The maps. The coordinates Beckett got from Linda. The notes Brent's been making since we talked to him last night.

This is it.

We're actually doing this.

"All right," Brent says. He doesn't raise his voice much but the room quiets anyway. "Linda gave us coordinates this morning. Nightmare Order holding facility, eastern sector."

He looks at Kree. "You captain the airship, right?"

Kree grins. "I just keep it from falling out of the sky."

"Noted." Brent points at the map. "How long to get there?"

Kree leans over the table. Declan moves in beside him.

"Four hours if we stay low," Declan says. "Maybe five depending on wind patterns and how much we need to avoid patrol corridors."

"Patrols run every six hours," Brent says. "If we time it right we can slip through during shift change."

"Big if," Kyron mutters.

"It's the best window we've got," Brent says.

Liam looks at the map. "What about entry points once we're there?"

"Three main access corridors," Cal says. "North, east, south. North is most direct but also most watched. East has a service entrance that sees less traffic. South is backup only — it's longer and more exposed."

"So we go east," Rane says.

"Probably," Brent says. "But we need to account for interior layout once we're inside. Linda said she's in a lower holding sector but she didn't have specifics on which wing."

"We'll figure it out when we get there," Locke says.

Liam looks at him. "That's not a plan."

"It's the best we've got."

"Then we make it better."

The room settles into planning mode. Declan asking about guard rotations. Kree sketching approach vectors on a scrap of paper. Cal laying out what the Hollow can supply — ropes, harnesses, tools, backup supplies. Brent filling in gaps about Order protocol and response times.

I'm watching it all come together when Zoe steps forward.

"There's something you need to know."

The room goes quiet.

She looks at Eli. He nods.

"On our way here, we overheard something. Two officials in uniform talking about a testing program."

Beckett looks up from his tablet. "What kind of testing."

"Forced shifts," Zoe says. "On anomalies. People with deformed marks, incomplete bonds, all of it. They're bringing them in and forcing the shift to see if it stabilizes."

"And?" Kyron asks.

Eli's face is grim. "It works. But they don't shift back."

The room goes completely still.

"What do you mean they don't shift back," Kyron says.

"Once the shift is forced, they stay that way," Zoe says. "Permanently. They lose the ability to return to human form."

No one moves as we all try to process that.

Trey's face goes white. "That's what he meant."

Everyone looks at him.

"Silas. At the Academy. He said his father was interested in her. That she was an anomaly and they wanted to understand how she survived fifteen years outside the system." His jaw tightens. "He said when his father came for her, he'd be helping."

"Testing," Beckett says quietly. His voice is flat.

"That's what they called it," Eli confirms.

Locke's hands are fists. "How long."

"Days maybe," Zoe says. "Maybe less. We don't know how far into the process she is. But this is Nova... They'll move quickly."

I look at Liam. He's already looking at me.

"You said you'd help," I say.

"We leave in an hour," Liam says.

Declan doesn't argue. Just nods and starts recalculating the route.

Kree's grin is gone. "I'll prep the ship."

The room shifts. The planning isn't careful anymore. It's fast. Urgent. People moving with purpose.

Brent's already pulling more maps. Cal's moving to find volunteers. Minerva steps forward and says something low to Liam that I can't hear but he nods once.

Mara comes through the door with a bag of supplies. Jonah with older route maps. One of the forest shifters steps inside and says he knows the northern cut if we need it. Darcy appears with climbing harnesses. Someone else with rope.

I watch them drift in. One by one. Two by two. Nobody was asked. They're just... Showing up with the things we're going to need.

By the time Declan says we need a north route scout and something to scramble perimeter detection, Cal's already setting down harnesses. Jonah's saying he knows the route. Kree's grinning again, holding the tech.

Someone from the back of the room lifts a hand. "I can help with whatever else you need."

I don't recognize him. Tall, maybe mid-thirties, he looks like he spends most of his time outside. He steps forward.

"I'm Max. A friend of Lena's." He looks around the room. "Have any of you seen her? She hasn't been around. I checked her place and—"

"She's missing," Brent says quietly.

Max's face goes pale. "Fuck. She wouldn't just disappear like that. Not like the other times."

I catch that. *Not like the other times.* But right now there isn't time.

Max nods. He doesn't look convinced. But he doesn't leave either.

I finally realize what's happening.

The town... They were listening the whole time.

Nova told them this town was amazing. That they'd been welcoming. That it was worth fighting for.

And now the Hollow is proving her right.

They're not waiting to be asked.

They're just here.

Liam looks at me. "We're ready."

I nod.

"Then let's go get her."

Chapter 20
NOVA

I can't feel my toes.

I'm leaning against the wall next to the door because it's the only spot that feels less cold. Or maybe it doesn't. Maybe I just need to believe there's a difference.

Water drips off my hair onto the floor. The shivering won't stop. My teeth keep chattering and I can't make them stop no matter how hard I clench my jaw.

They said it was "time for cleansing" and took me back to that godforsaken shower again. The pain in my shoulder is almost more than I can take. I don't know how to get it back into the socket.

The cold is my only distraction and it's not a good one.

Lena's gone. They took her again. I don't know when. Could've been an hour ago. Could've been five minutes. The silence is worse than her rambling. At least when she was talking I wasn't alone.

Now there's nothing. Just pain and the sound of water hitting stone. My own breathing and the cold seeping into my bones.

I close my eyes and try to stay here. Try to breathe through it.

Footsteps echo in the hallway.

I don't move. Don't open my eyes. Just another guard. Another tray. Another rotation of the same nightmare.

The footsteps stop right outside the door.

Then I hear someone crouch down. Close. So close I can hear them breathing through the bars.

I open my eyes but I don't move. I refuse.

"Still think silence is helping you?"

I know that voice.

Harrick.

My whole body goes rigid.

"You should've talked." His voice is almost pitying. Like he's disappointed in me. "I told them this would happen. That you'd make it worse for yourself."

I don't say anything. Can't. My throat is too dry and I'm shaking too hard.

I don't have the energy to fight him.

"Laith wanted answers before the next phase," Harrick continues. "But you just kept sitting there. Stubborn. Stupid."

The next phase.

My stomach clenches.

"You know what Laith told me?"

I still don't answer.

He leans closer. I can feel it. Feel his breath against my shoulder.

The disgust, the intimacy of it make my body shudder before I can stop it.

"Your parents weren't even your fucking parents."

The words hit like ice water.

No.

No.

He laughs. Sharp and cold. The sound echoes off the walls as he stands. As he walks away.

The door opens. Closes.

Silence.

I'm alone again.

Dripping wet. Freezing. Starving.

And now I can't breathe for a different reason.

Your parents weren't even your fucking parents.

No.

Celeste and Hunter. They were mine. They loved me. They were real.

They were.

...weren't they?

Chapter 21
RANE

"This ship is incredible."

I know I've already said that. Multiple times. Probably out loud. But I don't care because it's true and Kree doesn't seem to mind.

He looks up and grins at me. He's been moving nonstop since we boarded — checking gauges, adjusting brass fittings, tightening something near the wing controls, muttering to himself about calibration and flow ratios and a dozen other things I only half understand.

Okay, fine... I don't understand anything that comes out of his mouth about it.

I'm following him because watching him work is better than sitting still with my own thoughts.

"So this rune here—" I point at one of the glowing symbols etched into the hull. "What does it do?"

Kree doesn't even look up. "Stabilizes the lateral current when we bank. Otherwise the whole thing would spin like a top and we'd all die screaming."

"Cool."

"Very cool. Also that one—" He gestures at another symbol three feet away. "That one keeps the altitude runes from overheating and exploding. Which is also important if you like being alive."

"Noted."

He hops down from the ladder he's been perched on and lands in a crouch, already moving toward the engine housing. "The trick is balancing the magical load across all the primary nodes so nothing gets overworked. Too much stress on one sector and the whole grid collapses. Then we fall. Then we die. Very bad day."

"You say 'then we die' a lot."

"Because it's a very real possibility." He grins over his shoulder. "But that's what makes it fun."

Declan grunts from somewhere near the navigation console. He's been there for the last twenty minutes tightening bolts that probably don't need tightening just so he has an excuse not to participate in this conversation.

"You good over there, Declan?" Kree calls.

"Mm."

"That's a yes," Kree says to me. "He's having a great time."

I grin. "I can tell."

Kree moves to the next panel, fingers flying over switches and dials. "Okay so this gauge measures fuel pressure and this one tracks the resonance frequency and if they don't match within point-three variance we have a problem—"

He stops mid-sentence. Tilts his head.

"Huh."

"What?"

"That's weird." He taps the gauge. The needle flickers. Drops. Comes back up but slower than I'm guessing it should.

"Is that bad?"

"No. Just weird. Probably nothing." He moves on. "Anyway, the wings are self-regulating as long as the primary runes stay active, which they will unless something catastrophic happens, which it won't, so we're fine—"

Another flicker. This time from a rune near the engine. The glow stutters for half a second.

Kree frowns but keeps moving.

I follow him up another ladder to the upper deck where the propulsion array sits. He's explaining something about rotational velocity when one of the brass gears rotates out of sequence. Just once. Then back into rhythm.

"Did you see that?" I ask.

"Yeah." He adjusts a lever. "Magic's acting weird today. Probably atmospheric interference. We're close to the border zones and sometimes the resonance gets choppy."

"Is that normal?"

"Define normal." He grins. "It's not *abnormal*. Just annoying."

Declan climbs the ladder behind us. Doesn't say anything. Just gives Kree a look.

"I know," Kree says. "I'm watching it."

We keep moving. Kree keeps checking things. Adjusting. Recalibrating. The whole time he's talking — to himself, to me, to the ship, sometimes all three at once. I catch maybe sixty percent of it but I don't care. The energy is keeping me from thinking too hard about where we're going and what we're flying into.

Nova's in there. Somewhere in that facility. Alone. Scared. Thinking we're dead.

We're coming.

I focus on Kree instead. On the constant motion. The controlled chaos. The way he moves through the ship like he's part of it.

"So what happens if we lose power mid-flight?" I ask.

"We glide for about eight seconds and then we don't glide anymore and then we become a very expensive hole in the ground."

"Great."

"But that's not going to happen because I'm extremely good at my job."

Another flicker. This time the whole ship gives a wrong vibration. Just for a second. Like a note played off-key.

Kree stops moving.

That's the first time he's stopped moving since we boarded.

He looks at the gauge in front of him. Then at the rune array. Then at Declan.

"That's not supposed to do that," he says.

His grin is gone.

Chapter 22
LOCKE

This is ridiculous.

I know that. I'm aware.

It changes nothing.

I'm in a chair bolted to a floor that's floating.

Breathe.

I'm fine.

Fuck.

I'm not fine. I am one loose bolt away from becoming a cautionary tale.

Don't think about it.

I stare straight ahead. The wall across from me is metal riveted with brass. I focus on the rivets. Count them. Recount them. My hands are gripping the armrests hard enough that my knuckles have gone white.

Unclench.

No.

Rane's voice carries from somewhere below. He's following Kree around asking questions about everything. Kree's answering while moving too fast and talking over himself. The sound of it grates on me but at least it's something to focus on that isn't the fact that we are IN THE AIR.

Breathe.

I breathe. Controlled. In through the nose. Out through the mouth. Like I'm doing something normal. Like I'm fine.

I'm not fine but I refuse to give it the satisfaction of saying so.

Vaelor and Trey are at one of the windows. Of course they are. Both of them looking at the view like it's beautiful. Like we're not held up by *hope* and *brass*.

Kyron's flying alongside in owl form. Apparently some people were built for this nightmare.

Beckett's somewhere quiet.

No one has looked at me. Good. Nobody needs to look at me.

Nova is in a cell.

That's the only reason I'm here. The only reason I got on this ship. The only reason I'm not losing my fucking mind right now.

Actually I am losing my mind. I'm just doing it quietly.

If Rane says one word about how amazing this is I'll throw him off.

The ship banks slightly. My stomach drops. I lock my jaw and don't move and count the rivets again.

Sixteen. Seventeen. Eighteen.

This is not fine. How does everyone else think it is?

We're not dying... That's it.

If we die because of brass runes and magical calibration I'm killing Kree first.

Then I hear it.

"That's not supposed to do that."

Kree's voice. I look and he's no longer grinning.

My chest goes cold.

That is definitely not fine.

The ship gives a wrong vibration. Just for a second. Like something shifted that shouldn't have.

My hands grip harder. I can't stop them. My pulse is in my throat and I'm counting breaths now instead of rivets and my vision is narrowing and I'm not panicking I'm NOT—

The ship dips.

Just a dip. A few feet maybe. A metal groan. A second of wrong.

To anyone else it's probably nothing.

BUT THE FUCKING FLOOR JUST DISAPPEARED.

If we survive this, Kree dies second.

Someone sits down beside me.

I don't look. Don't move. Just keep staring at the wall.

"Turbulence," Beckett says flatly. I can tell he's not looking at me either.

Good. Glad there's a word for dying badly.

I don't answer.

He doesn't push. And thank god because I can't right now.

Then he reaches into his bag and pulls something out. Hands it to me without looking.

It's a strap. Reinforced. The kind you use for cargo.

"Anchor point's there," he says. Nods at the wall. Then goes back to whatever he was doing on his phone like nothing happened.

I take it.

Loop it through the anchor. Pull it tight. Grip it with both hands instead of the armrests.

It helps.

Not much. But it's something.

The ship levels out. The vibration fades. Kree's voice picks back up — still talking, still moving, apparently we're not dying.

Yet.

I keep gripping the strap.

Time passes. I don't know how much. I'm counting breaths and trying not to think about how far we are from the ground.

I hear footsteps on the ladder.

Declan appears. He doesn't look at me as he walks past. Then stops. Turns back.

He doesn't say anything for a second. Just looks at the strap I'm holding. At my hands. At my face.

Then he reaches into his belt and pulls out another strap. Heavier gauge. Tosses it to me.

"Magic interference," Declan says to no one in particular.

Beckett looks up from his phone. "From what?"

"Border zones sometimes—" Declan stops. His expression shifts. "No. This pattern is deliberate. Targeted."

"Meaning?"

"Meaning this realm doesn't use rune magic." Declan's voice goes flat. "But someone here knows how to disrupt it."

Beckett goes still. "Nightmare works with Clockwork."

"Or stole the tech." Declan looks at the wall. "Either way, we're dropping altitude in ten. Can't hold this high or the whole grid fails."

"How low?"

"Tree level. Maybe under."

Beckett nods once. Goes back to his tablet.

Declan leaves.

I grip both straps tighter.

Lower.

Well, at least there's less distance to fall when we crash.

Chapter 23
NOVA

I'm on the floor.

I don't remember deciding to lie down. I'm just here now.

I can't take a full breath. Every inhale catches. The cold has seeped so deep I can't feel my toes. Can't feel my fingers. Just the shoulder. That still screams every time I try to move.

Lena never came back.

I don't know how long it's been. Hours maybe. Days. The silence is absolute. No rambling through the wall. No broken voice. Just me and the dark.

Your parents weren't even your fucking parents.

I can't make the words stop.

It can't be true.

Footsteps in the hallway.

I don't move. Can't.

The door opens. Light floods in. Too bright. I close my eyes.

Someone crouches beside me. Cold fingers against my neck. Checking my pulse.

"Useless," Laith mutters.

Then hands under me. Lifting. My shoulder screams and I can't make a sound. Everything goes white for a second.

When it comes back I'm against his chest. Being carried. My head lolls against his coat because I can't hold it up.

The hallway is too bright. Fluorescent. Clinical. I keep my eyes closed.

His footsteps echo. Steady. Annoyed.

"You're no use to me like this."

His voice is low. Like he's talking to himself.

"I gave you longer than the others. Thought you'd be stronger."

The others.

My stomach clenches but I don't move. Don't open my eyes.

"Why are you resisting what you are?"

A turn. Another corridor. Colder here.

"I needed answers first. About your parents. About how you survived." His grip shifts and my shoulder flares. "But you wouldn't talk."

He keeps walking. Faster now.

"You were separated. Starved. Isolated. It should have faded."

Then his voice drops. Quieter.

"I never forgot those blue eyes. The way they opened and looked at me the day I found you."

We stop.

A door opens. Warmer air. Antiseptic smell. Voices.

"Sir."

"Warm her. Fluids. Reset vitals." His voice is cold again. "I want her conscious for testing by morning."

He sets me down. The table is cold. I can't stop the sound that escapes.

His hand pauses on my arm.

Then he's gone.

Footsteps. Door closing.

Voices around me now. Hands checking vitals. Something being adjusted. A blanket maybe.

I try to open my eyes. Can't. Everything is too heavy.

Someone whispers close. "Testing? She won't survive that."

Another voice. Quieter. "Get the restraints anyway."

Restraints.

I try to move. Try to pull away. My body doesn't respond.

The darkness pulls me under.

Chapter 24
BECKETT

The ship hits ground hard.

Not a landing. A controlled crash through trees and underbrush that rattles my teeth and sends everything not bolted down sliding across the deck.

Locke is losing his fucking mind.

But I don't say anything.

Kree's already moving before we stop. Declan right behind him. Both heading for the hatch.

I'm up. Rane's up. Kyron shifts mid-stride and launches through the open window. Trey and Vaelor are moving toward the exit.

Locke's still gripping both straps but he lets go and stands. His face is pale but his jaw is set.

We're here.

The hatch opens.

Cool air rushes in. Trees everywhere. We're low. Lower than I thought we'd be. The canopy is so close I can see individual branches.

Liam's already on the ground outside. "We've got maybe an hour before patrol circuits loop back. Maybe less."

I move toward the hatch. Rane's right beside me.

"Wait." Kree's voice. Sharp. He's at one of the panels pulling covers off. "Something's still destabilizing the grid. If we don't isolate it the ship won't lift again."

"How long?" Liam asks.

"Ten minutes. Maybe twenty."

"We don't have twenty," I say.

Declan's already pulling tools from a storage compartment. "Then we work fast."

Liam looks at me. "Go. We'll catch up."

I don't wait for him to say it twice.

Down the ramp. Boots hitting the ground. The facility is half a mile north according to the coordinates Linda gave us. Through the trees. Through whatever's between here and there.

Rane's beside me. Trey and Vaelor flanking.

Kyron flying overhead. Scouting. Obvious but then again, so was the ship.

Locke brings up the rear. Still pale. Still moving.

We make it maybe two hundred yards before I hear it.

Growling.

Low. Guttural and wrong.

I stop. Everyone stops.

Then they come through the trees.

Two of them. Then three. Hard to tell because they're not fully shifted. Not fully human either. Limbs too long. Faces distorted. Eyes that don't track right.

Failed experiments.

The kind Zoe warned us about.

One of them lunges.

Kyron drops from the sky and hits it mid-leap. Talons out. The thing screams and goes down.

The second one circles. Faster than it should be. It moves toward Locke.

Vaelor steps between them.

The third one comes at me.

I don't think.

I just move.

My fist connects. Something crunches. It staggers back but doesn't fall.

It comes again.

And something inside me snaps.

No.

Not this thing.

Not today.

Not when she's right there.

Nova is in there and I am getting to her.

Heat slams through my chest. Down my arms. Into my hands.

I look down.

Smoke.

Dark and thick, pouring off my skin.

Rane says my name.

I don't answer.

The thing lunges.
And I let go.

Chapter 25
NOVA

I keep my eyes closed.

I don't want to know.

I'm terrified they're taking me for another fucking cleansing. But if I'm wrong? If this is testing and I come back like Lena—

I can't think about that.

The wheels rattle beneath me. My teeth chatter. They piled blankets on me and I lay there for hours and I'm still freezing.

The room is colder when we stop.

Of course it is.

The smell of metal and antiseptic and something else underneath hits my nose and I almost gag.

I hear footsteps coming closer. I don't mean to hold my breath when they stop right next to me.

"Good."

Laith. I should have known.

Before I know what's happening someone is undoing the restraints, then hands are under me. Lifting. My shoulder screams but I don't make a sound.

They lower me into a chair. The metal is so cold it feels like it burns.

My eyes fly open.

I don't fight.

There's no point. I'm too weak. And fighting didn't help Lena.

The straps tighten. One by one.

I can barely breathe.

Medical staff moves around me. Double checking restraints. Adjusting something. Then they're gone.

And I'm alone in a glass box.

But on the other side, beyond the sheen, stands Laith.

"This could have been easier," he says.

I don't answer.

He turns toward the woman at the panel and nods.

I can't quite make her out.

Then warmth blooms across my wrist.

It's warm. So warm it makes me shiver.

It's spreading from the mark.

I look down.

The mark is darkening. Black smoke curling around my skin.

I gasp.

I don't know how, but watching the smoke move, I don't feel so alone.

"What the..." Laith freezes.

He steps closer, staring at the mark.

"Impossible."

His voice is quiet. Shaken.

"Shadow hasn't—"

He stops.

Laith stares at my mark like he's seen a ghost.

Then his face goes blank again.

He straightens, clears his throat.

Looks at the woman again.

"Begin."

Chapter 26
VAELOR

Beckett shifts.

I watch it happen. Watch the smoke thicken and condense and reshape until he's not Beckett anymore.

He's a wolf.

A massive wolf, black as shadow. Smoke still curling off his fur like he's made of it. Maybe he is. Purple eyes glowing.

I freeze.

That's not—

Shadow wolves are extinct. Everyone knows that. The bloodline died out generations ago.

But he's standing right there.

Just like the phoenix.

I'm still staring at Beckett when I hear Locke shout.

My head snaps toward the sound.

One of the other shifters has him on the ground. Locke's trying to throw it off but the thing is fast. Claws rake across his arm. He blocks the next swipe and...

The shifter gets a hand around his throat.

Locke's eyes go wide. He can't breathe.

No.

I don't think.

I just run.

"Get off him!"

The distance feels impossible. The shifter's claws tighten. Locke's face is turning red.

I'm not going to make it.

Heat explodes through my chest.

My bones crack. Time stands still as pain rips through me.

I leave the ground.

When I land it's not on two feet.

Four paws hit frozen earth. The impact shakes through me.

The shifter looks up.

I roar.

The sound shakes the trees.

The shifter bolts.

Locke's scrambling backward. Gasping. Staring at me.

I look down.

Paws. I have paws.

Golden fur. Claws like knives.

Wings folded against my back.

What?

Kyron drops from the sky and shifts mid-landing. "Vaelor?"

I try to answer. It comes out as a growl.

Trey steps closer. "It's okay. You're okay."

Rane's grinning between Beckett and me. "That is the coolest thing I've ever seen."

Then the heat reverses. Bones crack again and I'm falling forward.

I catch myself on my hands and knees. Human again. And very naked.

Trey tosses me his jacket.

"Everyone good?" Kyron asks.

Locke's on his feet. Bruises forming on his throat. "I'm fine."

Beckett shifts back. Smoke peeling off as he turns human again.

He stumbles once. Catches himself.

Rane doesn't notice. "Okay but can we talk about—"

Kree crashes through the brush carrying clothes. "SAW EVERY-THING. TEN OUT OF TEN."

He tosses pants to Beckett, a shirt to me.

His eyes flick between us.

He catches me watching and smirks.

"What? A guy can appreciate the view."

I pull the shirt on. Beckett drags on the pants. His jaw is tight.

One hand pressed to his chest. I step closer. "Beck?"

No answer.

He looks up at me. Pale.

"Something's seriously wrong."

Chapter 27
NOVA

I can feel the vibration in my bones.

I don't know what it is. Can't see it from this angle.

A hum fills the room. Low. Steady.

Then warmth.

It starts at my wrist. At the mark. Spreads up my arm. Across my chest.

Everything gets hotter with it.

Something reaching inward.

My heart stutters. Speeds up. I can't control it.

The warmth keeps spreading. Down to my stomach. My legs. My fingertips.

I try to move, jerking my arms. The restraints hold.

I try to breathe but I can't fill my lungs all the way.

The hum gets louder.

The warmth turns to pressure. Inside me. Under my ribs. Behind my sternum.

Something is pulling.

No.

No no no.

I force my eyes open.

The room blurs. Lights too bright. Shapes moving beyond the glass.

Then one shape gets closer.

Presses against the glass.

Palms spread flat. Face too close.

Lena.

Her eyes are too wide. Too bright. She's grinning.

But it's not right. Not her, the Lena I know.

She leans closer to the glass. Still grinning.

"Come on," she whispers.

"Let go."

Chapter 28
TREY

I can't ignore the feeling in my chest anymore.

It started as warmth back in the clearing. Just pressure. I recognized it as soon as Beckett said it. But it's getting stronger with every step toward the facility.

We left Kree and the others at the ship to fix the grid. So it's just the six of us now. Walking through the trees toward the building that holds Nova.

Going to get our girl.

I hope.

Beckett's rubbing his sternum again. Has been since his shift. Vaelor keeps glancing at him but doesn't say anything.

"You sure you're good?" Vaelor finally asks.

"I'm fine."

He's not fine. I can see it in the way his jaw is locked.

We make it maybe ten more steps before Beckett stops dead.

We all stop with him.

He's staring at his wrist.

Then he lifts his arm slowly. Turns it so we can see.

"My mark."

It's not Shadow's mark anymore. It's Nova's.

Vaelor lifts his arm. Stares. "Mine too."

Kyron checks his wrist.

Nova's mark sits there. Solid. Complete... Whole.

"Holy shit!" He's grinning. Wide. Then he jumps and I have to stop myself from laughing. "Are you seeing this?"

He's whisper-yelling. Excited but trying to stay quiet.

"Guys. GUYS. Look!"

He's pointing at me.

I look down at my own wrist.

The deformed mark. Half Dream. Half Memory. Fully broken.

Gone.

Her mark is there now.

Clean. Whole. Perfect.

My throat closes up.

I've worn proof I didn't belong anywhere my entire life. Every screening. Every exam. Every time someone looked at my wrist and saw what was wrong with me.

And now it's just... gone.

She did this. Nova. Without even knowing.

She made me hers.

"Everyone," Locke says quietly. "Let's see."

Rane holds his arm out, wrist up and looks around like he's waiting for everyone else to catch up.

Nobody moves for a second.

Then Beckett steps forward. Holds his arm out. Fist closed.

Vaelor moves next to him. Does the same.

Then Kyron. Then Locke.

I step in last. Close the circle.

Six fists. Six marks. All identical.

All hers.

"On three?" Rane asks. His voice is rough.

Nobody answers. We just move.

Our fists touch in the center.

And suddenly heat is everywhere.

So intense I almost can't breathe.

The marks flash white.

Blinding. Hot. A pulse of light that explodes outward from where our skin meets.

Then the marks stay white. Glowing. All of them.

I forget to breathe.

"What the fuck," Kyron whispers.

We pull back. Stare at our wrists.

The marks are still glowing. White light pulsing beneath our skin.

Then it fades. Slowly. Until the marks are dark again.

But it *feels* different now.

Like we're all connected.

"What just happened?" Rane asks.

Nobody answers.

Because I sure as fuck don't know.

But I feel it in my chest. The pressure. The pull.

Stronger now.

Like Nova just grabbed all of us at once and yanked.

"We need to move," Beckett says.

"Now."

Chapter 29
NOVA

The hum is in my teeth.

I don't know when that happened.

The mark is hot. The leather strap is cutting where it's already cut and I can feel the groove. I shouldn't be able to feel the groove from the inside but I can.

Lena hasn't moved.

Cheek on the glass. Palms up pressed into it. Fog where her breath is. The fog isn't going anywhere.

"Let go, Nova."

"It's *easy*."

I don't look at her.

"Output at thirty," the woman at the panel says.

"Hold," Laith says.

The hum gets lower.

Something pushes up under my ribs.

Heat.

Locke on the porch. Bags on the ground. His hand—

The chair shakes.

Coffee. Black. Too bitter. Vaelor taking it back.

Can't breathe.

A donut with sprinkles. He knew.

"Pulse?"

"One-forty-six."

"Track it."

It's hot under my hair. Hot at the corners of my eyes.

Beckett, covered in drywall dust. The hallway. His hands hovering before they—

A sound comes out of me.

Damn it.

"There," Laith says.

Closer to the glass.

"There it is."

I close my eyes.

Kyron's neck. My arms around him. Stumbling toward the porch because—

Ribs.

A roof. A blanket. *You're beautiful, Nova.*

Skin.

Trey on the edge. *Get over here.*

"Output at forty."

"Hold."

"Sir—"

"Hold."

The hum changes.

Something underneath it just—

Laith goes still.

I see it through my lashes. He goes still the way you go still when you hear something you weren't supposed to hear.

"What was that."

"I — I don't have it. The board's not—"

"Then check the board."

The pressure under my ribs *moves.*

Not out.

Something else. Pulling against it. From under the mark. From under that.

It feels like—

No.

No, no, no. Don't.

It feels like hands.

No.

They're gone.

Vaelor's hand on my back. Always. Every time something was hard. Every time.

Stop.

The mattresses on the floor. Soup. Bread. Eating because—

I can hear myself breathing wrong.

Locke at the well. His shirt wet. *I just kissed you next to a well because you wouldn't let me carry a damn bucket.*

The mark flares.

Not warm.

White.

I can see it through my eyelashes. Light around the strap. Light on the chair.

"What—" the woman says.

"Reduce."

"Reducing."

"Reduce *more*."

Beckett's tattoos. My hand on his stomach. *You're covered in them.*

"Sir, it's still climbing—"

"Hold her *down*."

Hands at my shoulders.

The door of the box opens.

Vaelor on the porch. *Happy looks good on you.* My palm flat against his chest because he's too tall and I had to—

The light at my wrist is brighter than the room.

"Get her arm — *get her arm down*—"

Lena's cheek on the glass.

"Yes," she breathes. "Yes, yes. Don't be scared."

"*Sweetheart.* Let go, Nova."

I stop.

Lena's mouth doesn't say *sweetheart*.

That's not Lena's word.

That word is—

Locke saying *sweetheart* with his face in my neck. *I've got you.*

Locke saying *I love it.* Catching it. Going still. Not taking it back.

Never taking it back.

I make a sound.

Broken.

I don't know what it is.

"What did she just do," Laith says.

Lena, the real Lena, with a stupid tiny bottle behind her back. *For courage. Drink it anyway.*

She's right there. Six feet.

She's gone.

"What did she just *do.*"

Heat in my throat.

Rane's restaurant. Maria's arms. *Stunning.* The way nobody had ever—

Skin. Splitting. Or burning. I don't know which.

The button-downs on the porch. Trey on one side. Rane on the other. *Would you do me the honor?*

The light goes through everything.

"Sir — I'm losing the readings—"

"*Stop her.*"

Trey holding the clothes. *It's just clothes. It's not just clothes.*

Beckett's hand on the mattress. Reaching.

Kyron at the window. Hand on his chest.

I can't get enough air.

I miss them.

I miss them so much.

I miss them so much I can't—

Something gives.

Lena says *yes.*

Laith says *no.*

I reach for them.
Everything turns white.

Chapter 30
KYRON

The pain started before Beckett said a word.

A tight band around my ribs that doesn't have a cause. I walk it off. It doesn't walk off. It gets worse. By the time the trees thin and the facility comes into view I'm working harder than I should to keep my breathing even, and the mark on my wrist is hot in a way that has nothing to do with the mark.

I look around at the rest of them. Locke is sweating and the rest of them look some variation of green or pale.

Something is wrong with all of us.

Nobody says it.

We've slowed more than I realize.

Nova is in trouble.

We need to *move* if Nova is in trouble.

"Come on. Faster."

Someone grumbles, but we move.

The facility is set into a low rise. White lights along the perimeter. A side door fifty feet across an open lot, gray, no markings.

Beckett checks his watch and his hands are shaking too hard to read it cleanly.

"Ten seconds," he says.

The door opens.

There's a woman in the gap. Smaller than I expected from the voice. Hair pulled back. Hands already up.

"I'm Linda. *Hurry.*"

We shuffle past her, still moving too slow.

The corridor is too bright. Linda's already past me, walking fast.

"Down two. Left. The door at the end."

I can't get a full breath but I keep moving.

Halfway down the second flight Vaelor stops. Hand against the wall. He's not breathing right.

"Vaelor."

"I'm—" His voice is wrong. "Yeah. Yeah."

He nods, moves again.

The corridor at the bottom is too short and too long at the same time. There's something at the end of it, a brightness leaking around the edges of a door.

That's not right.

Linda stops short of it. She's already turning. Already making herself small against the wall.

"Go. I can't—"

Locke pushes past her.

He grabs the door.

He looks at me. I don't know why he looks at me. Maybe because I'm the one still mostly upright. Maybe because once he opens this door, something changes that we can't take back.

I nod.

Because whatever has changed, it's already happened.

He opens the door.

The light hits us first. So bright I have to fight to open my eyes.

Then she comes into view.

Because the light... It's her.

The room *stops*.

I can't tell if what I'm seeing is real.

She's in the chair but she's not.

There are straps on her wrists and ankles like her body remembers where it was supposed to be. Her hair — silver-white, *floating* — is lifted off her shoulders like there's no gravity in the foot of air around her head.

Light is coming up through her skin. Not from the mark. From *her*.

But she keeps changing like she's shifting through forms between her human body, her phoenix and something... other.

There are wings.

Light shaped like feathers. Lifting from her shoulders and reaching past the chair on either side. Something in the corner of my vision is *bending* where the wings touch it.

She's beautiful.

She's beautiful in a way I'll never recover from.

The sound that comes out of her almost brings me to my knees.

Because it can only mean one thing.

She's dying.

And suddenly the pain is gone.

Gone.

Like it was never there.

My knees hit the ground hard but I can't feel it.

The pain.

It was never mine.

It was hers.

I've been carrying her pain and I didn't know.

She's been carrying it alone.

I can't breathe.

"No!"

Laith yells and I watch his hand cover his mouth. He's looking at her like he can't believe what he's seeing.

Someone is pressed to the glass watching her die. They laugh and my body goes rigid.

Lena.

Locke makes a sound behind me. Not a word.

Beckett is breathing hard. I can hear it.

No one is moving. I don't know if any of us can.

But I *know* Nova is dying.

We have to move.

We have to.

Chapter 31
LOCKE

Why isn't the pain coming back?

I'm braced for the next wave and the next wave doesn't come.

I watch Kyron fall to his knees and it hits me.

Her pain.

Something leaves my mouth I can't stop.

So much pain. And it was hers.

Kyron's mouth is moving and I'm not catching the words because *she's in the chair* and I am looking at her and I cannot get past looking at her.

We don't have time for this.

Move.

My eyes lock on Laith and in three steps he's in front of me.

He's not looking at me. He's looking at her.

His mistake.

I want his throat.

I have wanted it since the day he questioned us in that room back at the Academy. Since he used his son to take her from us. Since he took the only thing that mattered because she didn't fit the fucking system.

But killing him before he answers questions we're all going to need answered is the kind of mistake I don't make.

I drive him into the wall instead.

His head hits concrete. Bounces. His knees start to go.

I hit him.

Once. Hard. Across the jaw. He drops.

It is the most restrained thing I have ever done.

I don't kneel to check him. He's out. I know he's out because Laith would be stupid enough to get up if he wasn't.

I look up and watch Vaelor.

There's only one place he's going.

The fucker is bigger now, like somehow his bear came through just enough.

I move to the glass, where she's still hovering over the chair.

I can't tell if she's breathing.

Then there's a sound.

A screech of metal scraping, giving way.

I turn toward it. Vaelor, partially shifted, his hand is gone, his bear paw in its place.

His claws driving through the steel like it's paper.

I watch him go to her, the sheen of the reinforced glass messing with my eyes.

It takes everything in me not to rush in there and take over.

In three seconds the straps holding Nova are gone.

When the last one parts, she's still suspended over the chair. She's still shifting between forms. Wings of light. Hair still floating.

Vaelor has his other hand — his real hand — under her shoulder.

He doesn't seem to know about the claw.

I'm going to leave that alone.

He's cradling her. His face twisted into something I can't think about right now.

He plucks her from the air slowly. The way a man picks up something he loves to keep it from breaking further.

He brings her down against his chest.

"Sweetheart," he says.

His voice cracks.

"Sweetheart, please."

A click from across the room.

"I've got it," Beckett says. He's at the panel. Smoke around his hands. The hum drops half a step. The lights stutter. "Field's collapsing. She's—"

He stops.

I don't ask why. I can feel it.

The light is fading.

Pulse by pulse. Each one less. Her hair settles on Vaelor's arm. The shifting finally settles.

She's just a small body in Vaelor's arms.

In a hospital gown.

I see the gown. I see the cuts on her wrists. I see the bruises through the fabric of the gown at her shoulders.

Something happens behind my ribs that I am not going to look at right now.

I look around the room.

Beckett's already moving toward Vaelor, fingers reaching for her throat. Kyron's up. Gray-faced but up.

Trey's at the door. Watching the corridor. Looking back at her every two seconds to make sure we're good.

Rane's on the floor with Lena.

She's making sounds. Something garbled I can't make out. Mostly, she's just breathing wrong.

"We bringing her?" Rane says.

"Yes."

He's already lifting her. Doesn't ask twice.

Beckett's hand is on Nova's throat. He's not saying anything, just focused. But the way he's reacting, it means it's not what he wants it to be.

"Vaelor."

He doesn't look up.

"Vaelor. Give her to Beckett."

"I have her."

"I know you have her."

"I have her."

"Vaelor."

He looks at me.

His eyes are not all his. I see his bear at the surface and we do not have time for that.

"Beckett can find a pulse. You can't with that hand. Give her to him. We need you covering."

He looks at the paw like he's surprised to find it there.

I watch him turn back to Nova as his face falls.

He gives her to Beckett.

Beckett takes her like she's precious. He doesn't say anything. Just turns toward the door.

There's a coil of electrical cord on the panel where the woman left it when she ran. I don't know when she ran. I clocked her hands going up and lost her after that.

Bigger fish.

I take the cord. I bind Laith's wrists behind him. Then his ankles. He doesn't move. I check the binding twice because I do not want to deal with this shit.

Kyron is at my shoulder.

"He comes," I say.

"I'll fly him back myself as soon as we're out."

"You take an arm. I'll take the other. He drags if we have to."

"Works for me."

We haul him up. Dead weight. Head lolling. Blood from his nose down his shirt.

I don't feel anything looking at him.

That's not true.

I feel something looking at him. I'm not going to do anything about it right now.

Trey takes point. Beckett behind him with Nova. Vaelor in the middle, hunched, walking like a man trying to fit through a doorway he won't fit through. Probably because he can't without turning sideways right now.

He keeps the claw away from his body. And from all of us.

Rane's behind him with Lena over his shoulder still not forming words. Kyron and I bring up the rear with Laith between us.

The corridor is empty.

Thank fuck.

I don't know how. We've been in the room longer than seven minutes. I clock it and don't have time to be grateful.

Linda is gone too.

Maybe she got out. Maybe she went back to her shift to maintain cover.

We reach outside and don't stop.

Laith is getting heavy. I do not care.

I look at the back of Beckett's head. I look at Nova's hair against his shoulder.

I shake my head.

Focus.

We make it back to the clearing faster than I expect.

I turn to Beckett. He must know because he doesn't move.

I take a second just to look at her. Brush a few strands of hair away from her face.

She hasn't opened her eyes.

She hasn't moved.

But —

I'm not going to say this out loud. I'm not going to say it to anyone.

But her hand has closed.

Just slightly.

Around the front of his shirt.

Like she knows she's being held.

I keep my mouth shut.

We need to keep moving.

We are not out yet. We are not out. We are not out.

But she closed her hand.
It gives me hope.

Chapter 32
BECKETT

Her pulse is wrong.

It's there. I have it. Two fingers on the inside of her wrist.

It's slow. Too shallow. It changes between one breath and the next in a way pulses are not supposed to.

I'm not going to say anything yet. They don't need to worry any more than they already are.

The clearing opens up ahead and I'm two steps into it when something drops out of the tree directly in front of me.

Kree lands and he's already grinning, already talking, already mid-sentence.

"You're back! Did you get your girl—"

The words die in his throat.

His eyes are on Nova. On the hospital gown. The way her hand is closed around my shirt and her face is turned into my shoulder. And probably the fact that she's not awake.

He doesn't move.

The grin is gone like it was switched off. He looks at her for a long moment and something happens on his face that makes me look away.

He steps forward and puts his hand on my shoulder. Squeezes once.

"Let's get her home, Beckett."

"Kree." Liam, from the top of the ramp. Sharp.

Kree nods and steps aside.

Declan sees us come through the hatch and his hands go straight to the panel. The ramp starts rising before Rane's through with Lena.

He knows we need to get the hell out of here.

I find the closest seat and sit with Nova against my chest. One arm around her, the other back on her pulse.

Her breathing is still shallow. I can't help but hold her a little tighter.

Locke sits across from me. His hand goes up to the strap before he's all the way down. I don't make eye contact because his knuckles are already white and we haven't even lifted yet.

Vaelor drops down beside me and his arm presses against mine and I don't think he notices. His right hand sits in his lap, mostly a hand, fur still at the wrist where it hasn't gone all the way back. He keeps looking at it and then at Nova and then at his hand again. He moves over one seat. Giving himself space.

Trey helps Rane shove Lena into a seat and strap her in. She isn't going anywhere. I can hear him talking to her, low, the same words more than once. She doesn't answer.

Kyron doesn't sit. He's at the hatch, like he's checking on all of us one last time. He picks Laith up by the back of his shirt, gets him over one shoulder, and goes out without a word.

It seals. The ship lifts.

A sound from Locke. Small. He'd hate me for naming it. His hand goes white on the strap.

"Easy."

"I'm fine."

"I know."

Kree kneels next to me at some point. He has a cuff, something small with a blinking sensor, and he holds it up. I give him Nova's wrist. He clips it on, the light steadies, and he looks at it for a second.

"Reading. I can give you numbers if you want them."

"Not yet."

He pulls a thermal strap from somewhere and lays it across her shoulders. Adjusts it once. His hand lands on my knee briefly and then he's gone.

"Beckett."

I look up. Trey. His hands are loose in his lap, doing nothing, fingers open like he forgot what they're for.

"How is she."

"Pulse. Breathing. Skin's cool but not cold." I hold his eyes. "She's in there."

He nods once and looks back at her but he doesn't say anything else.

I keep my fingers on her wrist and count.

The engine fills everything. Trees through the window and then more trees and nobody talks. I watched Kyron fly past with Laith shortly after we got in the air.

He's a hell of a lot faster than we are.

Vaelor hasn't moved except to breathe. He's looking at her face like he's afraid she might disappear. His right hand sits in his lap. It's back to normal now. But he keeps checking it. His hand, then Nova, then his hand.

He wants to touch her.

He lifts his hand twice. Gets six inches. Stops both times.

He doesn't trust it yet.

Forty minutes in I notice something I don't want to notice.

That was clean. Too clean. We walked her out of a high-security Order facility while she was lit through the walls and the corridor was empty. Clear lot. Clean lift. Nothing behind us the whole way out.

And where the fuck was Silas?

The only things that showed up were those shifters. And they looked more like strays rather than anything coordinated.

That's not how the system works.

Either Linda is something much more than she looked. Or somebody above the room let us walk. Or whatever happened in that chair went so far past what they were prepared for that they're still standing in it right now trying to understand it.

None of those are good.

We're going to need to talk about that.

Later.

Vaelor's breathing evens out. I hear it before I see it, one long exhale, his shoulders dropping half an inch.

I stand up.

I don't plan it. I just stand with her and step the foot and a half between us and put her in his arms.

He goes still. Doesn't react beyond that. Just sits there suddenly full of her, blinking at what just happened.

I move his right hand under her shoulders where mine was. His left arm so her head is on it. I adjust the thermal strap and check the cuff is still sitting right.

I sit back down beside him.

He starts after a while. Low enough the engine almost takes it. Low enough I shouldn't be able to hear.

"Sweetheart."

Her face doesn't change.

"Sweetheart, wake up."

Nothing.

"Come on." Something underneath the words, a catch he doesn't try to smooth. "Come on. We've got you. You're safe now. Come on."

Nothing.

"Wake up, sweetheart."

I look at the floor.

I'm the one with two fingers on her pulse. I've been counting her breaths against my shirt for forty minutes. I know what this stack means — cool skin, shallow breath, a rate that won't settle — in a body this small.

Vaelor doesn't know what I know.

Vaelor is asking her to wake up.

And if she doesn't wake up he's going to keep asking. Tomorrow. Next week. In the kitchen at four in the morning when the coffee's done. He'll adjust it without making it a thing the way he always does and he'll ask. He'll be one of those people. The kind that never stop.

I've known Vaelor for years. I know his tells, I know his schedule, I know exactly how he goes still when he's trying not to show something.

I don't know what he's going to do with this.

Something gives in my chest. I don't look up.

Wake up, sweetheart, he says.

She doesn't.

Chapter 33
KYRON

I hear the Hollow before I see it.

The tree line opens up and the main street is below me, lit and quiet. Normal from the air. Too normal after what I just saw.

I come down in the back field. Hard landing, sloppy shift — bones cracking the wrong way fast, ground coming up too quick — and I hit the grass on two feet already moving. Laith hitting the dirt a few feet back.

The crow lands on the closest fence post.

It's just there. Watching me with one black eye like it was already waiting. "Yeah," I say. "Me too."

Cal comes around the side of the Community Hall first. Then Brent, half a step behind, wiping his hands with a rag.

They both stop when they see Laith's body on the ground.

Cal reads it fast. His eyes go to Laith's hands, his position, making sure he's bound.

Brent stares like he can't believe what he's seeing.

"Is that—"

"Yes."

The rag stops moving in his hands.

"That fucker." Quiet. Like he didn't mean to say it out loud.

"I know." I look at Laith on the ground. "Where's the bunker?"

Cal's already moving. "This way."

I haul Laith over my shoulder and follow.

The entrance is behind the storage building, set into the ground. The guys from Clockwork reinforced the lock during the perimeter work — I remember Kree crouched over it with tools and Declan telling him not to make it complicated.

The door is heavy. Cal hauls it open.

Brent takes Laith from me without a word.

He's not gentle about it. Probably a little rougher than he needs to be. I don't blame him.

They head down into the dark.

"Kyron."

Max. Coming from the direction of the Community Hall, half-jogging.

He looks at my face and some of the hopefulness in his drops.

"Did you get them," he says. "Nova. Lena. Did you—"

"We got them both."

His exhale is audible. "Okay. Okay, good. Are they—"

"Nova's on the ship." I look at him. "She's not awake as far as I know."

"But she's—"

"She's breathing." I keep my voice even. "That's what matters."

He nods.

"And Lena?"

I don't answer fast enough.

"Kyron."

"She's alive," I say. "She came out of that place and she's — she's somewhere else right now. Not hurt. Just..." I breathe. "We don't know yet."

Max looks at the ground. His jaw works. I know he's not going to fall apart in front of me and I appreciate it more than I can say right now.

"Okay," he says finally. "Okay."

The crow hops from the fence post to the top of the storage building. Settles there. Watching the sky.

I hear it before anyone else does.

Engines.

Low. Getting closer.

"They're here."

Chapter 34
RANE

The ship comes down fast.

Not a bad landing — Declan doesn't do bad landings — but urgent. The ramp drops before we've fully stopped moving and the air hits cool and real.

I'm already on my feet.

Kree's shouting something at Declan. Declan isn't answering.

Nova's still not awake.

I'm not thinking about it.

I am. I just don't want to.

Vaelor has her. Her head against his chest, his arms around her, his face blank because he's using everything he has just to keep moving.

Still. She's so still.

Kyron's at the bottom of the ramp.

He's been here. I don't know how long — long enough that Cal and Max are already behind him, which means he had time to land, to secure Laith, and wait.

His eyes go straight to Nova.

I look away.

I know he doesn't like what he sees.

He moves to Locke, reaches out and takes his bag without a word. Falling into step with the rest of us.

Brent and Cal hang a few steps back with Max.

"Is she—"

"Breathing," I say. "She hasn't woken up."

Brent nods and walks with us.

We get halfway across the field before Kree catches up to me.

His eyes go to Nova first. They always go to Nova first with him. Then they come back to me and whatever he finds there makes him pull me in fast and hard, one hand at the back of my neck like I'm someone he's known for years.

I can't breathe for a second.

When he steps back his hands stay on my shoulders.

"You got her back," he says. "That was the hard part."

I open my mouth.

"Don't," he says, almost gentle. "Don't tell me about the other parts yet. Just — you got her back."

I close my mouth.

He looks at me for another second. Then he nods once, squeezes, and lets go.

"We're heading out after we talk to Minerva." He glances back at the ship. At Liam already at the ramp, at Declan doing something with the rigging that probably has a name I'll never learn. "But Rane."

"Yeah."

"We'll see each other again."

He walks off before I can answer. I watch him go. Watch all three of them move through their goodbyes — Declan easy, Liam saying almost nothing and somehow meaning it, Kree already looking at something past the tree line like he clocked something on the way in.

I don't know what to do with any of them.

I don't think that's an accident.

The guys are already walking but it doesn't take long to catch up.

The Hollow moves around us.

People stop. A few come out of doorways. Nobody gets in the way. Whatever they see in our faces... Nope.

Kyron and Trey hang back close to Vaelor. Eyes on Nova's face like they can't help it.

I know the feeling.

Nobody talks.

We could walk from one end of the Hollow to the other in ten minutes and it feels like we cross the whole world. Not because there's nothing to say.

Because none of it helps her.

Vaelor gets her through the door.

The house is the same. Fire in the grate, the smell of something warm and ready to eat.

Brent I realize.

I look back and he nods, a small smile on his face.

He knew. Before we even touched down... He knew.

I take a moment to really look around because I'm avoiding right now. It's avoidance. I know it is.

Everything exactly where we put it, the same and completely wrong.

Vaelor takes her to the couch. Gets her down slow. Adjusts her head, her shoulders. Sits on the edge beside her and his hand finds hers and stays there.

The rest of us fill the room. Nobody sits. The fire pops once.

I look at her face.

She's here. We got her back. She's breathing and she's here and she's —

Not awake.

"I'm going to fucking kill him."

They all nod.

Locke turns and goes upstairs.

The door slams hard enough the walls feel it.

I stand there and watch her chest rise and fall and I keep waiting for something. A sound. A shift. Her hand closing around Vaelor's the way it closed around Beckett's shirt on the ship.

Anything.

She doesn't move.

Wake up, I think, even though it's useless. *We did the hard part. Wake up now. Come back.*

She doesn't.

The fire pops again.

Come back.

Chapter 35
VAELOR

It's been six days.

I've been counting.

Six mornings of checking her breathing before I do anything else.

She's still on the couch. I tried to move her to the bed upstairs the third night and Locke looked at me like he might kill me. I understood immediately that we weren't doing that yet. The couch is temporary. The couch means she's waking up soon and everything goes back to normal. Whatever that means.

Moving her upstairs means something else.

So she stays on the couch.

I get up before the others. Always. I don't set an alarm — my body just does it now, some internal clock recalibrated around her. I come downstairs and I check her breathing first thing. The rate. The depth. Whether her color is better or the same.

It's been the same.

Until this morning.

I'm crouched beside the couch with two fingers at her wrist when I notice it. Her chest rising. Falling. Rising again.

Slower than it's been. But fuller.

I check again. Keep my fingers where they are and count. Her pulse is still slow but it's steadier. And her breathing — the shallow, wrong quality it's had for six days — is just slightly less wrong this morning. Different from yesterday.

I don't move for a long time because I need to hear it.

I'm still thinking about it as I go make coffee.

Beckett comes down first. He always does, right after me. He doesn't say anything when he comes into the kitchen, just goes for the coffee like it's the only thing keeping him upright. He pours a cup and stands at the counter with his eyes closed.

I wait until he's had half of it.

"Her breathing is better this morning."

He opens his eyes. Looks at me over the rim.

"How much better."

"Not much. But different from yesterday."

He sets the cup down and goes to the couch. Crouches where I was crouching. I watch him check the same things I checked, in the same order, and come to the same conclusion.

He comes back to the kitchen.

"Yeah," he says. That's all.

We stand there and drink our coffee.

It might be a different kitchen now, but it's the same Beckett.

For some reason that gives me hope.

Upstairs, the hammering starts around mid-morning.

It's been the rhythm of the house since we got back — Locke up there with Cal, occasionally Brent, sometimes Rane when Locke will tolerate it, which isn't always. Nobody asked him to build anything. He just started. Nobody said anything about it because we all get it.

I look over at the nine loaves of bread on the counter.

Just in case she wants some when she wakes up.

Trey helps when Locke lets him. He comes downstairs around two, sawdust in his hair, and drops into a chair at the kitchen table.

"Cal says the frame's done," he tells me.

"Good."

"Locke wants to finish it today."

I glance at the ceiling. The hammering has a particular quality right now — focused, rhythmic. Locke in his version of prayer.

"He will," I say.

Trey looks at Nova. He does this — comes in from upstairs and immediately looks at her, like he needs to confirm she's still there before he can settle.

She is. Still. The thermal blanket Kree left is pulled up to her chin because her temperature keeps dropping at night and going back up during the day. Small. Her silver hair spread across the pillow Rane repositioned four times yesterday until he found the angle that looked right.

Trey looks at her for a long moment. Then he looks at his wrist. Her mark there, clean and whole on his skin.

He does that too. Both things, always in that order.

I put a bowl of soup in front of him and he eats it without asking what it is.

We've been sitting like that for a few minutes when I say it.

"He's still not talking."

Trey looks up.

"Laith." I don't know why I need to clarify. There's only one he. "Six days and nothing. I bring water. Food he doesn't touch. He just sits there."

"He's waiting," Trey says.

"For what."

"I don't know. But that's what it looks like."

The back door opens and Rane comes in, mug in hand. He looks at us and already knows.

He sets the mug down and pulls out a chair.

"He has answers," Rane says. Not a question.

"He has to." The words come out harder than I intend. "He ran that facility. Whatever they did to her in that chair — he knows what it was. He knows what she needs. And he's just—" I stop.

"Sitting there," Trey finishes.

"Yeah."

Rane's jaw is tight. "So we make him talk."

"Locke's already suggested that."

"I'm not suggesting what Locke suggested."

"Then what are you suggesting?"

He doesn't answer. He picks up his mug and puts it down again without drinking from it.

The thing nobody's saying is sitting in the middle of the table between us. We have him. We actually have him. We did the impossible and we got her out and we got him and he's forty feet away in a bunker and Nova is still on that fucking couch. He won't say a single word and there is nothing — nothing — we can do about it.

"Kyron's working on something," Trey says quietly.

"I know."

"He'll figure it out."

"I know that too."

Rane looks at the nine loaves of bread on the counter. Looks back at me. Doesn't say anything.

He doesn't have to.

The hammering stops around late afternoon.

The silence of it is louder than the sound was.

I look up from the counter. Trey looks up from the table.

Footsteps on the stairs. Then Locke in the doorway, sawdust on his shirt, knuckles abraded in that new way they have from the work.

"It's done," he says.

Nobody moves for a second.

Then we all move.

Up the stairs, nearly shoving into one another.

I get an elbow to my side. "Fuck."

"Sorry!"

Rane is not sorry.

We shove in and stop.

The room is ours.

I don't mean that in a small way. I mean Locke looked at what we had — walls, a floor, a ceiling — and made it into something that couldn't be anything but ours. The bed takes up most of the space and it should feel like too much but it doesn't. Cal helped him build the frame and you can see where the wood is different, where two people with different hands worked the same piece, and it doesn't look wrong. It looks right because he made it.

For her.

For us.

There's enough room for all of us.

Rane has his hand on the frame like he's checking it's real. Locke is watching us look at it. I don't miss the hope in his eyes. What this means.

The room smells like sawdust and wood and the window is cracked and the last of the day's light is coming through.

Nobody says anything for a long time.

Then Rane says, quietly, "She's going to love it."

Locke looks at the floor.

I put my hand on the frame beside Rane's.

The wood is solid. It doesn't give.

"Yeah, she is."

Chapter 36
NOVA

I wake up and something's wrong.

My body doesn't feel like mine. Breathing hurts. I try to move my fingers and they won't respond.

I don't open my eyes yet.

Woodsmoke. Bread. Clean fabric against my face.

Not the cell. Not the chair.

Thank fuck.

My heart kicks and immediately I regret it because my chest aches in a way that makes every breath feel impossible.

I force my eyes open.

Ceiling. Wood beams. Window with pale light coming through.

I know this ceiling.

No.

I try to sit up. My arms shake. My shoulder—

The sound that rips out of me isn't something I can control. My shoulder is still wrong. Still out. White-hot pain and I can't breathe through it.

The Hollow.

I'm in the house. On the couch.

How am I—

They're dead.

The thought sits there. Flat and certain and unbearable.

I left. I walked away and Silas said they'd live if I went and I believed him because I'm so fucking stupid and now they're—

I can't think about that. I can't be here.

I get my elbow under me. Push. My arm gives out halfway and I collapse back down.

Try again.

This time I make it to sitting. Barely. The room spins and I have to put my head between my knees and wait for it to stop.

When I look up, the room comes into focus in pieces.

The fireplace. Beckett's shoulder against mine. Just sitting.

The kitchen doorway. Vaelor at three AM making bread.

The floor. Clean now but I can still see it. All the mattresses they dragged down. Rane on one side. Kyron on the other. Locke's arm across my waist. Beckett's hand in my hair. Vaelor breathing steady. Trey's fingers in mine.

All of them. Here. With me.

The sound that comes out is worse than the first one.

I can't be here.

I get my feet under me. Stand. My legs shake but I force them to hold me because I need out.

Three steps and I catch myself on the wall. My legs are shaking so hard I don't know how I'm upright. I push off. Make it to the door. My hand closes around the handle and I stop because I don't know what's out there. I don't know if this is real or—

I open it anyway.

The air hits my face and I gasp.

Two steps onto the porch and my legs give out. I catch the railing, then the post, then I'm lowering myself down because falling seems worse.

I end up on the top step.

I can't go back inside. Can't look at that living room again. But I can't walk any farther than this.

So I sit.

The Hollow is quiet. Morning quiet. Birds. The house settling. My own breathing still too fast.

My shoulder throbs with every heartbeat.

I should—I don't know what I should do.

They're dead and I left them and—

In the chair, in the light, for one second I swear I felt them. All of them. Like they were right there.

But that wasn't real.

This is real. This porch. This exhaustion. This pain.

This emptiness.

I pull my knees up. Rest my forehead against them. Close my eyes.

Don't think about Locke saying *sweetheart* with his face in my neck. The way he kissed me on those steps.

Don't think about Kyron's blue eyes. The way he smirked at me that first day. The roof under the stars. The way he felt that first time.

Don't think about Rane's smile. The way he called me beautiful and turned red. Our date. The way he shifted and looked at me through the window.

Don't think about Vaelor running into the fire. The bread. Holding my hand.

Don't think about Beckett. The plate. The way he just sat with me.

Don't think about Trey. His smile. The clothes. The way he...

Stop stop stop—

I'm crying. I don't know when I started but I can't stop. Face pressed against my knees. My good arm wrapped around my legs like I can hold myself together if I just squeeze hard enough.

They're gone and I'm here and I don't know how or why but they're—

"Nova?"

I stop breathing.

That voice.

No.

That's not possible. I'm hearing things. The testing broke something. I'm broken. That's what this is.

"Nova."

Closer now.

I don't look up. If I look up and no one's there then I'll know for sure that I've lost it.

"*Nova.*"

I lift my head.

Trey is standing in the street. Just standing there. Twenty feet away. Staring at me.

Same clothes. Same hair. Same face.

"Trey?"

The word comes out broken.

He takes a step toward me.

"Oh my god. Trey?"

He's moving now. Fast.

I'm trying to stand. My legs don't work. I get halfway up and stumble and he's already there, already catching me, and then I'm in his arms.

I'm kissing him. His face, his jaw, his mouth, his neck—everywhere I can reach. My hands in his hair, on his face, confirming he's solid, he's real, he's *here.*

"You died." I'm sobbing between kisses. "You died, you fucking died, how are you—"

"I'm here." His arms are so tight around me I can barely breathe. "I'm here, Nova, I'm here."

"You're alive." I pull back just far enough to see his face. To look at him. "You're— you died, I saw—"

"I'm okay." His hand is on my face now. His thumb wiping at tears I can't stop. "We're okay. We're all okay."

The world stops.

"What?"

"We're all here." He's smiling through his own tears. "All of us. We got you out."

I can't process that. I can't—

"They're alive?" My voice breaks. "They're all—"

"They're alive. They're here. They're—"

I don't hear the rest. Just the rushing in my ears and Trey saying *they're alive* over and over.

I'm laughing. Or crying. Both.

I bury my face in his neck and hold on.

They're alive.

Chapter 37
TREY

I'm still holding her.

She's shaking so hard I can feel it through my chest. Her face is buried in my neck and she's crying and laughing at the same time and I don't think she's even aware she's doing it.

"They're alive," she keeps saying. "They're alive, they're alive—"

"Yeah." My voice cracks. "We're all here."

She pulls back just enough to look at me. Her eyes are red and swollen and she's searching my face like she's still not sure I'm real.

"I need—" She looks toward the house. "I need to see them. I need—"

I set her down.

Her legs fold immediately.

I catch her before she hits the ground. "Okay. Not walking."

"I'm fine." She's not fine. "I just need to—"

"You can't walk."

"I can—"

"Nova." I shift my grip. Get one arm under her knees. "I'm carrying you."

"Trey—"

I lift her before she can finish. She makes a sound—half protest, half something else—and then her arms go around my neck and she's holding on.

She's so light it makes my chest hurt.

I head for the house. Up the steps. Through the door.

She's not looking around. Her face is pressed against my shoulder and I can feel her breathing—fast and uneven.

The stairs are narrow. I take them slow. She doesn't say anything. Just holds on.

At the top I turn left. Down the hall. Last door.

The room is dim. Early morning light through the window. The bed takes up most of the space—massive, solid, built for all of us.

They're all there.

Locke on one side. Kyron next to him. Vaelor sprawled out. Rane half on top of Beckett. All of them still asleep.

I walk to the bed. Lower myself down carefully. The mattress dips.

I put her in the middle.

Right in the center.

She doesn't let go of me at first. Her hands are fisted in my shirt and she's still shaking.

"They're here," I say quietly. "Right here."

She turns her head.

I watch her see them. One by one. Her breath catches.

And then—

The sound that comes out of her is raw and broken and it cuts through everything.

Locke jerks awake first. His eyes snap open and he's already moving—sitting up, scanning—and then he sees her.

He goes completely still.

"Nova?"

She sobs harder.

Kyron's awake now. Rolling toward us. His eyes land on her and his whole face changes.

Vaelor sits up so fast he nearly falls off the bed. "What—"

He stops.

Rane's blinking awake. Confused. "What's—"

Then he sees her too.

Beckett's the last. He opens his eyes and looks at her and doesn't move.

Nobody moves.

Nobody says anything.

Nova is crying so hard she can't breathe. One arm wrapped around herself as her shoulders shake. She's making sounds that shouldn't come out of a person.

"I don't understand." She can't get the words out. "I saw—I heard—"

Locke moves first.

He's across the bed in half a second. His hands on her face, tilting her head up, looking at her like she might disappear.

"Sweetheart." His voice breaks. "It's okay. We're here."

"Silas said—" She's looking at him but I don't think she's seeing him. "He said if I went with him—"

"We know." Kyron's beside her now too. His hand on her shoulder. Gentle. "We came for you. We got you out."

She shakes her head. "But I heard—"

Vaelor makes a sound. Low and wrecked. Then he's moving. Pulling her against his chest. Just holding her.

She collapses into him. Completely.

Rane's on her other side. His hand in her hair. Not saying anything. Just there.

Beckett's at the foot of the bed now. Watching. His hands are shaking.

I stay where I am. Right beside her. My hand on her back.

She's still crying. Harder now. Her face pressed against Vaelor's chest and her whole body shaking with it.

Nobody tries to stop her.

Nobody tells her it's okay.

Chapter 38
NOVA

I don't know how long we've been lying here.

Hours maybe. Long enough that the light through the window has shifted. My face feels swollen and raw from crying. But at least I'm not shaking anymore.

Vaelor left a while ago. He insisted on making food even though I don't think anyone's hungry.

My stomach growls.

Of course.

Beckett's still here. Sitting at the end of the bed. Just watching.

Rane's beside me. His arm around my waist. His chin resting on top of my head. He hasn't said much. He can't seem to let me go.

I shift slightly. Try to get more comfortable.

Pain shoots through my shoulder and I can't stop the sound that comes out.

"Nova."

Beckett. His voice sharp.

I press my face against Rane's chest and breathe through it.

"What was that?" Beckett's moving. I can feel the mattress shift. "Nova, what's wrong?"

"Nothing. I'm fine."

"Bullshit."

I don't answer.

"Nova." His hand on my arm now. Gentle but firm. "What's going on?"

I pull back from Rane just enough to sit up. My shoulder screams and I have to bite down on my lip to keep quiet.

Beckett's eyes narrow. "How long has it been like that?"

"Like what?"

"Don't."

I look away. "It's fine."

"It's not fine. You just—" He stops. Takes a breath. "What happened?"

I don't want to say it. Don't want to go back there. But he's looking at me like he's not going to let this go and I'm too tired to fight.

"The first day." My voice comes out flat. "Before they—before everything. They took me to the showers. Had my hands tied above my head and I—" I stop. Swallow. "I lost my footing. My shoulder went out. I couldn't get it back in."

Silence.

Beckett doesn't move. Doesn't speak. His jaw is tight and his hands are clenched at his sides.

"I tried," I add. Like it matters. "I tried to fix it but I couldn't—"

"Can I see it?"

I nod.

He moves slowly. Sits beside me. His fingers at the collar of the shirt I'm wearing—one of theirs, I don't even know whose—and he pulls it down just enough to expose my shoulder.

He goes completely still.

I don't look. I don't need to. I know what it looks like. Black and purple and swollen. Wrong.

"Nova." His voice is barely above a whisper.

"I know."

"How long have you—"

"I told you, since the first day."

"But that's almost two weeks."

I can hear his voice almost crack.

"I know."

He doesn't say anything for a long moment. Just looks at my shoulder. Then into my eyes and I don't like the look he's giving me.

"We need to reset it."

I shake my head.

"Nova—"

"I know." The words come out sharp. "I know we have to. Doesn't mean I want you to."

His hand is on my good shoulder now. Steady. "I know you don't. But it's been too long. If we don't—"

"I said I know."

Rane's sitting up now. His hand on my back. Not saying anything. Just there.

Beckett looks at me for a long moment. Then he stands.

"I'm getting Locke."

"What? No—"

"He's stronger than me. If we're doing this, we're doing it right." He's already heading for the door. "Don't move."

He's gone before I can argue.

I sit there with Rane's hand on my back and my shoulder throbbing and the weight of what's about to happen sitting heavy in my chest.

"It's going to suck," Rane says quietly.

"I know."

"But then it'll be better."

"I know that too."

He presses a kiss to the top of my head. "You're stronger than you give yourself credit for."

I close my eyes.

I know.

Footsteps on the stairs. More than one set.

My stomach drops.

The door opens and Locke walks in. Beckett right behind him. Then Kyron. Trey.

"What—" I look at Beckett. "I thought you were just getting Locke."

"I got everyone."

"Why?"

Locke's already crossing to the bed. He sits in front of me. His eyes go to my shoulder and something in his face hardens.

"Because you need to be held still," he says. His voice is calm. Too calm. "And you're going to fight."

"I'm not—"

"You will." He looks at me. "It's going to hurt. A lot. And your instinct is going to be to pull away. So we're making sure you can't."

I want to argue. Want to tell him I can handle it. But the way he's looking at me—the way they're all looking at me—makes the words die in my throat.

"Okay," I say instead.

Kyron moves to sit behind me. His legs on either side of mine. His chest against my back. "Lean into me."

I do.

His arms come around my waist. Not tight. But I can feel the strength in them.

Trey sits on my left. Takes my good hand in both of his. "Squeeze as hard as you need to."

Rane's still on my right. His hand on my thigh now. Anchoring me.

Beckett's at the foot of the bed again. Watching. His hands are shaking.

Locke is directly in front of me. Close enough that our knees are touching.

"I need you to relax," he says.

"I can't."

His lips tilt up. "I know. But try anyway."

I take a breath. Try to let the tension out of my shoulders. It doesn't work.

Locke's hand goes to my bad shoulder. Just resting there. Warm and steady.

"On three," he says.

My heart is pounding so hard I can feel it in my throat.

"One."

I squeeze Trey's hand. He squeezes back.

"Two."

Kyron's arms tighten around my waist.

Locke doesn't say three.

He just moves.

The pain is—

I can't—

I scream.

The sound rips out of me and I'm trying to pull away but Kyron's holding me and Rane's got my leg and Trey won't let go of my hand and Locke is still moving, still adjusting, and the pain is white-hot and everywhere and I can't breathe—

Then something pops.

The pain doesn't stop. But it changes. Shifts from sharp and wrong to just—

Wrong.

I'm gasping. Tears streaming down my face. Kyron's arms are so tight around me I can barely move.

"Done," Locke says. His voice rough. "It's done, sweetheart. It's back."

I can't answer. Can't do anything except shake and try to remember how to breathe.

Locke's hand is still on my shoulder. Gentle now. "I know. I know it hurts. But it's going to get better now."

I nod. Or I think I do. I can't tell.

Kyron's loosening his grip. Just slightly. His mouth is against my hair. "You're okay. You're okay."

Trey's still holding my hand. I look down and realize I've left marks. Deep red crescents where my nails dug in.

"Sorry," I manage.

"Don't." His voice is tight. "Don't apologize."

Rane's hand is still on my thigh. He hasn't moved. Hasn't said anything. But when I look at him his face is wet.

Beckett's standing now. He looks like he might be sick.

Locke is still in front of me. Still close. His hand moves from my shoulder to my face. He's gentle. His thumb wiping at tears I didn't know I was still crying.

"Worst part's over," he says.

I want to believe him, but I'm not sure I do.

I nod anyway.

He pulls me forward. Carefully. His arms around me and my face against his chest and I just—

I let him hold me.

Because I can't do anything else.

Chapter 39
LOCKE

She's so small in the middle of the bed.

Right where we left her after Vaelor brought her food. An hour ago. Maybe two. I've lost track.

I stand in the doorway and count her breaths. In and out. Steady.

Good. That's good.

She's here. She's alive. We got her back.

It doesn't feel like enough.

I cross to the bed. Sit on the edge carefully. The mattress barely dips.

Her face is turned toward the window, late afternoon light coming through. Her hair spreads across the pillow and I can see the bruising on her shoulder even through the shirt she's wearing. The dark purple bleeding down her arm.

Two weeks with a dislocated shoulder.

I keep turning that over. Trying to make it make sense.

It doesn't.

I hear footsteps behind me. I don't turn.

"How is she?" Beckett.

"Still asleep."

"Good."

He doesn't leave. Just stands there. After a minute Kyron shows up beside him. Then the rest of them. Vaelor is last, wiping his hands on a towel like he's been scrubbing something. Whatever it was probably didn't need scrubbing.

We're all here. All of us staring at her like lovesick idiots.

"We need to talk," Beckett says.

I look at Nova. At the way her hand curls against her chest.

"I know."

Nobody moves because none of us want to leave her.

"Downstairs," Rane says quietly. "I don't want to wake her."

We end up in the kitchen. It's dark outside now. Later than I thought. The clock on the wall says just after eight.

Kyron leans against the counter. Beckett moves to stand beside him, close enough their shoulders almost touch. Trey's near the door.

Nobody sits.

Rane and Vaelor end up on either side of me.

The silence stretches.

Then Kyron breaks it.

"It's different."

We all look at him.

"The bond." He's staring at the floor. "It feels different. Stronger."

"Yeah." Beckett's voice is flat. "I noticed."

Trey shifts. "I thought it was just... relief. Having her back."

"It's not relief," Kyron says.

I look at him and he meets my eyes. He's not wrong.

Nobody argues.

I feel it too. Since the facility. Since we walked into that room and saw her in the chair. Something changed. I don't know what.

It should feel good.

It doesn't.

"What did we actually see in there?" Rane asks.

"Light," Beckett says. "From her. Not the mark."

"Wings," Trey adds. "Made of light. They—" He looks at me. "You saw what they did to the air."

"I saw."

Kyron's jaw tightens. "She was shifting. Into her phoenix. But it kept flickering. Like it couldn't hold."

"There was something else too," Beckett says. His voice is careful. "Between forms. I don't know what it was."

"The wings," Trey adds. "Weren't always phoenix wings."

Vaelor makes a sound. Low. Almost a growl.

"And Laith looked surprised," I say.

Silence.

"We don't know what it means," Beckett says finally.

"No." I push off the counter. "We don't."

"Laith does," Rane says.

"And he's not talking."

Trey's hands curl into fists. Kyron notices. Shifts slightly closer without looking at him.

"We could make him," Trey says.

"We could try." I look at him. "But he's been down there six days. You really think he's breaking now?"

Somebody curses.

Because we all know he won't.

"So what do we do?" Rane asks.

I don't have an answer. We're standing in the kitchen and Nova is asleep upstairs. Laith is in the bunker and we still don't know what they did to her.

Or why.

We're stuck.

"We talk to him," I say finally. "Tomorrow morning."

"And if he still won't—"

"Then we make him understand what happens if he doesn't."

Kyron looks at me. His eyes sharpen. The corner of his mouth twitches.

"Nova should be there," Trey says.

We all turn to look at him.

"If she wants to be," he adds. "It's her choice. But she should have the option."

Rane nods. "He's right."

"She'll want to be there," Beckett says quietly.

"Then we wait until she's ready," Vaelor says. "Tomorrow. We do this together."

I look around the room. At all of them. Beckett and Kyron side by side. Rane and Vaelor flanking me. Trey near the door but not leaving.

"Tomorrow," I say.

Nobody argues.

Nobody says anything else.

Vaelor shifts first. "I'm gonna go check on her."

He's already heading for the stairs when Trey speaks.

"I'll come with you."

Vaelor stops. Looks back. Nods once.

They leave together.

Chapter 40
VAELOR

The door is open a few inches.

I push it the rest of the way and she's there — middle of the bed, hair across the pillow, the thermal blanket pulled up to her shoulder. Breathing slow and even.

She's beautiful, even like this.

I stand there longer than I mean to.

Trey stops beside me. Doesn't say anything. He doesn't need to.

We kick off our boots. I go first, careful, and the mattress dips and she shifts — just slightly — and presses back toward me before I've even settled.

My arm ends up across her waist. I notice it after the fact.

Trey takes the other side. He sits on the very edge and leaves more room than he needs to. I watch him slowly lay down like he's afraid he's going to break her.

If anyone is going to break her, it's me.

Her hand finds his in the dark.

She needs us close, even unconscious.

Trey stops breathing.

When he finally exhales it's long, wrecked. I stare at the ceiling and try to think about anything else besides her pressed against me.

I nearly doze off.

The room is darker. The house is quiet. Her breathing has shifted — a fraction too fast, a fraction too deliberate — and my arm tightens across her waist before I'm fully awake.

Her hips roll back. Once. Twice.

Oh. Oh no.

I try to create space, shifting back an inch.

She follows still asleep. Her back finds my chest and I press my forehead to her shoulder and think about bread.

It doesn't work.

She does it again and this time a sound comes with it — soft, breathy — and my grip tightens.

I make myself relax.

Trey says my name. So quiet I almost miss it.

"Yeah?"

"What do we—"

"I don't know."

His hand, still caught in hers, is being pressed now. Against her chest.

I don't miss the groan that comes out of Trey.

I try two inches of space.

She makes a noise in protest. Her body follows mine.

Trey muffles a laugh and I want to kill him right now.

"She's asleep," I say frustrated.

He's laughing so hard the bed shakes.

"Vaelor."

"Yeah."

"She's really not—"

"*I know.*"

My thumb moves at the curve of her hip without permission. She arches into it and I bite down on my lip.

The room gets very quiet.

"We're in trouble," Trey says.

"Yeah."

"Both of us."

"Apparently."

"At the same—"

"Trey."

"Right."

I look at her face.

The line between her brows. Her mouth parted. Her fingers moving against Trey's wrist like she can't help herself.

"Nova."

Nothing.

"*Nova.*"

Her eyes flutter open.

She blinks at the ceiling. Then she turns her head and looks at me. The smile is soft, comfortable. And we put it there.

"Your ears are red," she whispers.

"They're not."

"They really are."

Behind her, Trey makes a sound. Strangled.

"Go back to sleep," I tell her.

"I don't want to sleep."

"Sweetheart—"

"If you say sleep again," she says, "I'll go find Rane."

Trey loses the fight. The laugh comes out real — startled, warm — and it's the first unguarded thing I've heard from him in a long time.

Nova's hand reaches back without her looking. Finds his arm. Squeezes once.

His jaw shifts and his whole body settles on one breath.

She turns back to me and I can't stop what I'm feeling.

Six days of watching over her, making sure she's still breathing. After we lost her. After they took her from us.

I lean down and let all of it go at once.

Her mouth opens before I get there.

She tastes like sleep.

The warmth of her mouth, the way she opens immediately, no hesitation, like she's been waiting and she's done being patient about it. Her hand finds the back of my neck.

I pull back half an inch.

She makes a sound.

"Trey," I say.

He's already closer than he was. I don't know when he moved. His forehead is at her shoulder, his hand still caught in hers.

She turns her head.

Looks at him.

He goes still.

She sees exactly what I see. Trey is hers.

She reaches up and touches his jaw with her free hand. Runs her thumb along it. Trey's eyes close.

"Hey," she says softly.

His throat moves.

She pulls him down.

The sound he makes when their mouths meet — something low and broken that only confirms what she already knows. She makes one back and his whole hand splays against her ribs like he's making sure she's real.

When he pulls back his eyes are wet.

He blinks it away fast, jaw working. She cups his face and holds it.

"Hey," she says again. Firmer.

He exhales. Gives her a small smile. She nods back.

His hands start moving and she lets out a breathy moan.

Her hands on my chest move slightly, nails digging in.

I don't hate it.

The shimmer starts where her hands are. Pale. Iridescent. Warmth that I feel before I see it.

She makes a low sound.

"Vaelor."

"Yeah."

Her hands slow. She's looking at the shimmer moving under her palms.

"Is this—"

"You." I cover her hands with mine and the warmth doubles. "Just you."

She looks at it for a second. Then her hands move to my waistband.

"Nova—"

"Let me." Her fingers curl into the fabric. "I've never... But I want to."

"Your shoulder—"

"Is *fine*."

"Sweetheart—"

She pulls.

"Shut up, Vaelor."

I let her.

The sound that comes out of me when her hand wraps around me goes somewhere past dignified and she knows it immediately.

"Oh," she says.

"Don't."

Her hand moves.

My forehead drops to her shoulder.

"*Nova.*"

"Hmm?" Entirely too pleased with herself.

Adorable little shit.

She does it again. Slow. Deliberate.

The sound that comes out of me this time has some bear in it and she goes still for half a second — staring into my eyes like she sees something — and then her grip tightens.

"That was different," she says.

"Yeah."

"Do it again."

"That's not — that's not how it—"

She laughs and moves her hand and the growl happens before I can stop it. She makes a sound against my throat that is genuinely delighted and I am going to lose my mind.

Trey makes a noise. Trying very hard not to be a laugh.

"Don't you dare," I tell him.

"I didn't say anything."

"Damn right."

Nova pulls back just enough to look at me. Face flushed, eyes dark, wearing the expression that means she has decided something and the rest of the room is going to find out when she's ready.

"Trey, come here," she says.

She reaches back without looking. Finds his hand. Brings it to her waist.

"I want—" She stops. Her hips press back into Trey. He makes a sound against her hair. "I want—"

"Tell me," Trey says. Low. His mouth at her ear.

Her breath catches.

Trey's hand slides down her stomach.

She grabs my wrist.

The sound she makes when his fingers find her is real. Unguarded and loud and she doesn't try to stop it — just tips her head back against his shoulder and lets it out. Trey makes a sound against her temple like it wrecked him to hear it.

"*Trey—*"

"Shhh." His voice is already gone. "I've got you."

She's still holding my wrist. Her grip tightens each time he moves. I watch her face — the flushing, the way her mouth stays open, the shimmer moving in waves across her chest and stomach, brightest where his hand is.

He looks up at me over her shoulder.

His eyes are glowing gold.

He looks like a man who just realized the edge he's been standing on for months has ground under it after all.

I lean in and put my mouth to her jaw and she turns toward it immediately and the three of us find a rhythm.

"I said I've never... and I want to," she breathes.

I pause, trying to figure out what she...

"Get on your knees Vaelor."

Oh. Shit.

I don't move fast enough.

She pushes at my shoulder and I go — down, back, whatever she wants — and she follows me, leaning on her good arm, and I realize what she's doing about two seconds before she does it.

"Nova—"

"I said I've never." Her mouth close. Too close. "Doesn't mean I don't want to."

I open my mouth.

"Vaelor." She looks up at me. "Let me."

I let her.

She licks across the tip and the sound that comes out of me sounds more bear than man.

She does it again.

I grab the headboard.

She looks up at me — holds it — and then her lips wrap around me and my free hand goes to her hair and I stop thinking in complete sentences.

I barely catch Trey reaching for her underwear. The small lift of her hips as she lets him slip it off. His hand moving back between her legs.

She takes me deeper.

I watch as he pushes two fingers inside her and the moan she makes around me goes straight down my spine. Trey makes a sound above her like he felt it too — felt what it did to her, what it did to me — and his fingers move.

She moans again.

Her mouth finds a rhythm and every time his fingers curl her mouth on me tightens. The shimmer rolls off her in slow waves — gold where Trey's hand is, brightest at her wrist — and I am holding the headboard with everything I have.

"*Nova.*" Warning.

She hums.

The vibration goes everywhere and my hips move without permission and I tighten my hand in her hair.

"*Sweetheart—*"

She does something with her tongue.

The growl that comes out of me shakes the bed. His fingers move and she breaks around them — loud even muffled, shaking — and I don't know how I hold on.

She pulls back. Forehead to my thigh.

"Okay," she says breathing hard.

She turns towards Trey as he slips his wet fingers into his mouth and groans.

She gasps, swats at him with her good hand as she sits up.

"What?!"

"You know what."

He shrugs. "I can't help it you taste so good."

She turns red but moves forward, forcing him flat on his back. She straddles him carefully and I don't know how I'm going to get through this without coming like an inexperienced teenager.

She settles her weight over him and reaches down between them. Trey's jaw drops and he makes a sound that is not a word in any language.

She laughs as she starts to sink down. Gasping suddenly as she takes him in slowly.

Her right hand braced on his chest, her eyes on him while completely overwhelmed. I can see it, the effort she makes trying to stay present through both at once.

Trey's hands go to her thighs. He's just barely holding on.

"*Nova.*" His voice is gone.

"I know." Breathless. "Just—"

She rolls her hips and he chokes and his head goes back.

She starts to move.

It works for a minute. Maybe two. She finds a rhythm and Trey finds it with her and the sounds coming out of both of them are loud and I do not give a shit anymore. The shimmer flows across her body and she's the most breathtaking thing I've ever seen. The bear in my chest runs a single long note underneath all of it.

Then she reaches forward.

Her left arm comes up to brace on his chest and I see it — the fraction of a second where her shoulder catches, and pain shoots through her. She tries to find another way to hold herself and can't.

But she doesn't stop.

Trey feels it. His hands come up to her hips immediately, trying to take the weight — and I can see from his face that he wants to fix it. He tries, but nothing is working and she's determined not to slow down.

So fucking stubborn. I love it.

I move.

My hands go to her hips from behind. She goes still for one second when she feels me — then presses back into my hands. She makes a sound that I swear is only for me.

"You okay?" I whisper in her ear.

"*Yes.*" Already moving faster. "Don't stop."

Trey looks up at me over her shoulder. Smirks.

His legs shift, making more room for me but then she rolls her hips and we both stop thinking.

The shimmer is everywhere.

Trey's eyes keep closing and snapping back open like he refuses to miss a second of this. His hands are white-knuckled at her hips. He's saying her name — *Love, Love, Love* — like he can't stop.

She reaches back for me with her right hand. Finds my hip. Pulls.

I lean forward and my mouth finds her neck. My hands still taking the weight her shoulder can't.

"*Vaelor.*" Barely there.

"You gonna come for him?"

"Yes."

Trey groans and his eyes find mine over her shoulder. Fully gold. He nods.

She tips her head back onto my shoulder.

My hands slide up to her breasts as Trey takes over.

She grips my forearms where they're crossed over her chest. Her nails dig in. I keep my hands on her breasts and she makes a sound that bounces off every wall in the room.

The shimmer is constant. Gold at her wrist.

Trey's watching her face — his eyes fully gold and locked on her like that's the only thing keeping him inside himself.

I shift my weight. Take more of hers. I can feel it in the way she's holding herself — the slight lean, the way she's stopped using her left arm entirely. I pull her back against my chest fully and my hands move to her hips alongside his, not taking over, just adding. Helping him move her.

"*Vaelor.*" Trey's voice is three syllables of warning.

"I know."

"I swear to god if you—"

"I'm not doing anything."

"You're doing something—"

"*If either of you stop—*"

She cuts herself off because Trey moves faster.

The sound she makes goes straight to my cock. Her nails break skin on my forearms as she arches back into me. Trey groans and his hands go white-knuckled.

He is barely holding on.

"*Nova—*"

"*Don't stop—*"

"Never."

I pull her hips a little higher and Trey chases her thrusting harder. She cries out as she comes, her whole body locking as the mark on her wrist blazes. The shimmer spiking everywhere at once.

"*Fuck—*" Trey's voice cracks.

I pull her up.

Off him, back against my chest, and he goes over — his hand wrapping around himself, one stroke, two — and he groans her name and spills across her stomach and his arm goes over his face.

Nova is breathing hard against my chest. She looks down at herself. Then at his arm over his face.

"Trey," she says.

Nothing.

"*Trey.*"

"Give me a minute." Muffled. "I need a minute."

The laugh startles out of her. She claps her hand over her mouth and her shoulders shake and I press my lips together and look at the ceiling.

"You're fine," I tell him.

"I'm not fine."

"You're fine."

"Vaelor I'm going to need you to not talk to me right now."

Nova laughs harder.

She's still laughing when Trey sits up.

He reaches over the side of the bed, grabs his shirt off the floor, and cleans her stomach without making it a thing. Then he pulls her down onto his chest and wraps his arms around her. She's still breathing hard, her cheek finding the place on his chest that is apparently specifically hers.

I move to give them room.

Starting to reach for my shirt. Figuring this is the part where I—

Her hand finds my wrist.

I go still.

She doesn't look back. Just holds it. Her fingers curled around my wrist in the dark.

Trey looks at me over the top of her head.

"Really?" he says like this can't be happening.

She lifts her head.

"Really," she says.

He looks at me for a moment. His jaw shifts. He practically rolls his eyes.

"I've got her," he says.

I don't hesitate.

She's warm and close and already sensitive.

I move between both their legs. She arches up instinctively — her hips lifting, her ass higher — and Trey's hands spread across her lower back and hold her there.

I take myself in hand and press against her entrance and she gasps at the pressure. Her whole body goes tense.

"Vaelor—"

I push in.

Just the head. She chokes on a sound and her hand slaps onto Trey's forearm and grips. I'm gritting my teeth. She's so wet and so tight and I am going to embarrass myself completely if I move right now.

"*Vaelor.*" Strained. Overwhelmed.

"Fuck." Barely getting it out. "Give me a second."

"You're so—" She stops. Swallows. "*God.*"

"Yeah."

Trey's mouth is at her hair. His hands stroking slow up and down her back, steadying her, steadying both of us probably. She's trembling. I can feel it everywhere we're connected.

I push deeper.

She cries out. Her back arches harder and Trey holds her and I groan from somewhere low in my chest and keep going — slow, inch by inch — until I bottom out and we both go completely still.

The bear in my chest hums like a happy fucking bastard.

"*Fuck.*" My voice is gone. "Don't move."

"I can't—"

"*Don't move.*"

She laughs. Breathless and wrecked and laughing. And then she moves anyway — just barely, just her hips — and the sound that comes out of me isn't human and she does it again.

I take a breath, because I can't think straight.

Then I go slow.

"*Vaelor.*"

I don't go slow.

Her hand white-knuckled on Trey's forearm. His mouth at her temple, his arms pulling her back against his chest every time I push forward. The sound he makes when I move is low and wrecked like he can feel it too — the bond running it through all three of us, the shimmer rolling off her in waves.

The mark blazes gold.

All three wrists at once. The shimmer across her skin, across both of ours where we're touching her. The bear cresting and I stop holding it back.

She tips her head back.

"Vaelor." Barely there.

"Mmhmm. I want to feel you come around my cock."

She shudders.

Trey's arms tighten.

She comes first — loud, shaking, the mark spiking white — and I follow her with my head thrown back and Trey holding her through all of it.

The room goes quiet.

She doesn't move for a long time.

None of us do.

Her cheek on Trey's chest. His arms still around her. My hand on her back, feeling her heartbeat slow, feeling his underneath it.

The mark is warm. Just resting.

"Trey," she says. Eventually.

"Mm."

"You called me Love."

His hands stop moving.

"Yeah."

"You've been calling me Love."

"Uhhuh."

"I like it," she whispers.

His whole body loosens on one breath. His arms pull her closer. His mouth at the top of her head.

My hand moves up her spine without deciding to.

I realize the house is too quiet below us.

The door opens.

Locke stops in the doorway, looking at the three of us.

At the marks, still glowing. At the three of us tangled together.

His jaw shifts.

"Really?"

I can't quite read him.

"Door was closed," I say.

"Was it?"

"I thought it was."

"You thought a lot of things tonight."

Kyron appears behind him. Hides his smirk, but I catch it.

"We were all thinking it, Locke," he says. "You just weren't fast enough."

Beckett moves past them, staring at us.

Rane shoves his way into the room. He grins, slow and wide.

"So, you're feeling better?"

Nova starts laughing. Shaking against my chest.

"Get in here," she says when she can breathe. "All of you."

Locke doesn't hesitate.

Nobody does.

Chapter 41
NOVA

I wake up under Rane.

His head is on my stomach. Face turned in. Hand fisted in the sheet by my hip. He must have slid down sometime in the night because that's not where he started.

I lift my head an inch.

There are men everywhere. Locke closest to the door, arm over his face. Vaelor next to him, taking up too much space even asleep. Beckett curled at the far edge. Kyron half-up against the headboard like he tried to stay on watch. Trey on my other side.

Six men. And this enormous bed.

I let my head fall back.

Trey wakes the way he always does. Fingers twitching while his breathing changes. His hand finds my hair without him opening his eyes.

"Why is Rane on you," he says into the pillow.

"I don't know."

"Rane."

Rane mumbles into my stomach.

"You're on Nova."

"Comfortable."

"She has a bruise where your face is."

Rane lifts his head. Squints at Trey over my body. Looks at my stomach. Looks back at Trey.

He frowns.

"Wait…"

I try to look innocent.

I feel Vaelor stir on the other side of Locke. He's awake. I bet he's been awake. I can feel the suppressed shake of him through the mattress.

"Trey?"

"Hmm?"

"On her stomach."

"Mhm."

"Last night."

"Yep."

"Are you serious?"

"Vaelor cleaned me up," I say.

Vaelor makes a sound into his pillow that he absolutely tried to keep in.

Trey is shaking harder. I'm biting the inside of my cheek and it isn't working.

"It's fine," I manage.

Rane closes his eyes. Lets his head fall back to my stomach.

"I've been here a while," he mumbles. "I'm not moving."

Trey loses it. Out loud this time.

I thought they were dead. Now Rane's lying in... that. On top of me.

"Hey," I say.

Rane grunts.

"Up. All of you."

Beckett opens his eyes first. He's the only one who doesn't pretend.

"What?"

I look at him. He sees something on my face and sits up. Pushes that pink hair back. He looks at the others, then at me.

"You should know," he says like he's being careful. "Laith's in the bunker."

I stop breathing.

I sit up too fast. My shoulder protests. I ignore it.

"What?"

"Kyron brought him back the night we got you out. It's behind the storage building. Kree reinforced the door."

"Who's Kree?"

Beckett's mouth opens. Closes. Looks at Rane.

"Right," Rane says. "You haven't—"

"Clockwork," Vaelor says, into his pillow. "The guys that flew the ship. Three of them. Liam, Declan, Kree."

"They're the reason we got you out," Kyron adds. Too quiet. "Kree's the engineer. Worse than Rane. You'd like him."

Maybe it's better that I didn't meet him.

A whole rescue I wasn't conscious for. A crew from Clockwork Order I never met. Reinforcing a door for the asshole I didn't know was in there.

"Okay... And Laith's been here the whole time?"

"Yeah."

"And nobody told me?"

"You were healing." Locke. Arm finally down from his face. "We were going to tell you this morning."

"We talked about it last night," Beckett says. "Didn't want to do it without you."

Trey looks at him. Beckett nods.

I look around the bed. Nobody is laughing anymore.

"Has he talked?" I ask.

"No," Vaelor says. "Nothing. He doesn't eat. Doesn't speak. Just sits there."

"Waiting," Trey adds.

"For what?"

Nobody answers. Because we all know.

I'm already pushing the blanket back. Swinging my legs over.

"I want to talk to him."

They're quiet. Too quiet.

If they try to talk me out of this...

Then Trey, very softly: "See?"

"See what?" Locke says.

"Nothing."

"Sweetheart." Locke ignores him. Looks at me. "You don't have to do this today."

"I'm ready."

"Your shoulder—"

"Locke."

He stops.

"He's not going to crack on his own. I'm the thing he was after. I need to be the thing in the room."

Kyron's mouth twitches.

"What?"

"Sassy..." he says. "I like it."

I snort and try to hide my grin. "Get used to it."

"Yes ma'am."

Beckett is watching me with a small smile. He likes it too.

"She's right. He's waiting. The only thing that changes the room is her in it."

Locke closes his eyes for a second. When he opens them again I can tell he's about to get...

"If it gets bad—"

"I'll tell you."

"If your shoulder—"

"I'll tell you."

"If he says—"

"Locke."

He groans.

"I'll tell you," I say. "I promise. I'm not going alone. I'm going with you."

Vaelor exhales. "Come on man, she'll be with us."

"Okay," Locke says.

Rane catches my elbow before I'm all the way up.

"We're proud of you."

"Don't."

"Too bad."

I lean down and press my forehead to his for a second and then push myself up before this gets harder.

"Get the fuck up, guys. Come on, let's go." I'm already heading for the door. "I'm jumping in the shower. Five minutes."

Behind me, Locke laughs.

"Yeah," he says. "Okay."

I make it downstairs before any of them are even out of the room.

"Guys! I'm going!"

Someone yells but my hand is already opening the door.

I almost crash into her.

Zoe is standing on the porch with her hand up like she was about to knock.

Her eyes go wide.

"Nova."

"Hi." I grin.

"You're—"

She's already crying. I'm nodding, already moving. My shoulder protests when she gets her arms around me. I don't care.

"I missed you so much," I say into her hair.

She nods against me. Shaking.

"Where are you going," she says, as she pulls back. Her eyes flick past me to the guys. I can feel them standing behind me.

"To talk to Laith."

Her eyes go wide and she takes a breath.

"Okay."

"Walk with us?"

She tucks her hand into my good elbow.

The Hollow is awake but quiet.

I missed this.

It's just people... living.

There's a door open across the way. Someone shaking out a rug a few houses down. Two kids running barefoot across the road without a care in the world.

Cal is on a porch, talking to Mara. Darcy walks by carrying her little one.

Cal looks up as we pass.

"Morning, Cal."

"Morning, Nova. It's good to have you back."

I smile, because it is good to be back.

We keep walking.

As we do, I hear her say quietly "See? I told you she was okay."

I don't look back.

"This is weird," Zoe murmurs.

"What is?"

"They're acting like nothing happened."

"No," I say. "They're acting like *I* happened. And I did."

She looks at me and laughs. Bumps my hip with hers.

We're halfway across the main road when I hear small footsteps coming fast.

A kid comes around the side of the Community Hall like a shot. Brown hair sticking up everywhere. Jam on his face.

He stops in front of me. Eyes wide, breathing hard.

He swallows. "Are you still a phoenix?"

Behind me Rane chokes on something.

I crouch down. Slowly. My shoulder doesn't love it.

"Yeah. I'm still a phoenix."

"Can I see?"

A woman is hurrying around the corner. "I'm sorry, sorry. I told him not to —"

"It's okay," I say.

"Just the wings," the kid says. Negotiating and I hold back a smile. "You don't have to do the fire. My mom said you can."

I look up at his mom. She's mouthing *sorry*.

I grin at the kid.

"I've never tried it. Let's see if I can."

I straighten up.

He's grinning like I'm his new favorite person.

I don't hate it.

I close my eyes.

Just the wings.

Right Nova, like that's going to work.

The mark warms suddenly. I hold in the gasp that tries to come out. I feel heat in my back. I brace for the rest of it — for the bones, the world going hot — and it doesn't come.

Just my back.

There's a pull and the wings come out.

I can see them on either side. Gold and red. Big enough to throw a shadow across the kid and his mom too.

His mouth falls open.

"They're the coolest!"

I start to smile but something feels different. Something...

The tests...

The feeling of being in that chair...

Of that hum...

I desperately try not to show it.

And then there's white.

Just light everywhere. My wings iridescent. Glowing.

But then everything seems to just stop. The feeling, the hum. Everything gone and I feel my body relax.

The glow fades slightly reminding me of last night. Trey and Vaelor, because when they touched me...

I look over at my right wing.

It looks like that now.

The kid says "*whoa*" so quiet I almost don't hear him.

I'm suddenly too aware of how quiet it is around us.

"Are you still hot?" he says.

"Try."

He reaches up and runs his fingers against my wing.

He grins.

"Just warm!" he announces.

I laugh, I can't help it.

"So cool!"

He turns and runs back to his mom.

"Mom!"

"MOM!"

"Did you see?"

"I TOUCHED IT!"

She catches him. Looks at me over his head with her eyes wet.

I let the wings go. They pull back into me and I'm surprised by how natural it feels.

Someone clears their throat.

I turn around.

They're all looking at me.

"What?"

Locke shakes his head.

"Nothing, sweetheart."

Zoe is holding back a laugh beside me.

Trey is grinning.

"You love it," he says.

"Shut up."

The squawk of the crow startles me enough I jump.

Dammit.

I look across the road.

The Community Hall looks the same as I remember.

But the bunker... It's time.

I make it five steps before Brent runs up.

"Hey Nova, guys." He nods. "Zoe."

He bends at his knees breathing hard.

"I wanted to catch you before..."

He swallows. Stands.

"Minerva wants to see all of us. Now."

Chapter 42
NOVA

Brent walks like there's somewhere he has to be and none of the rest of us are moving fast enough.

I'm trying. My shoulder has opinions about pace and I'm overruling them, but Trey keeps slowing to match me and then speeding up and then slowing again, which is somehow more annoying than just being slow.

"Stop," I say.

"I'm not doing anything."

"You're hovering."

"I'm walking."

"You're walking *at* me."

Zoe laughs from my other side. She has my good arm and she's not letting go, which I've stopped arguing about. The crow drops from somewhere above and lands on a fence post as we pass. Zoe looks at it. Looks at me.

"Is that the bird that warned you?" she says. "Before they came?"

"Yeah."

"So it's—"

"I don't know what it is."

She watches it over her shoulder as we pass. "Do we think that's weird?"

"Probably."

She snorts.

I hate that I smile.

Rane appears from somewhere in the back of the group and squeezes up beside Trey. "What are we talking about?"

"The crow," Trey says.

"Love that crow."

Behind us Vaelor says something that makes Kyron snort and I don't catch the rest because Brent rounds the corner ahead of us and I have to keep up. I want the bunker. I've been wanting the bunker since I woke up this morning and I am being very patient about it.

Minerva's door is open.

She's standing when we come in. The room has tea on the low table that nobody's touched. Books stacked with a folded piece of paper on top. A chair angled like she sat down and stood back up at least twice before we got here.

She's nervous. Huh.

Vaelor crosses to her. Locke finds the doorway. Brent goes to the far wall and stays there.

Trey is close on my left. Zoe keeps my arm.

We talk about the shoulder. The wings — the kid this morning, the partial shift, just warm. Minerva says the Hollow has been steadier since I came back, the forest closer, something about the garden.

I let it run maybe two minutes.

"Why are we here?" I say.

Minerva stops.

"Because there are things you should hear from me," she says, "before you hear them from him."

Her eyes change for a moment and go from Vaelor to me.

"But first, are you alright?"

I blink because I was not expecting that from her of all people. I didn't think she cared. Not like that anyway.

I nod. "Yeah, thank you."

She doesn't say anything. Just nods and moves on.

"Your parents came to me once."

"They aren't my parents."

It comes out before I decide it. It's the first time I've said it out loud anywhere except inside my own head. It feels wrong admitting it, like it's real now.

Zoe's grip tightens.

I can't look at the guys. I just stay focused on Minerva.

"Harrick said—" His name is wrong in my mouth. I can't.

Minerva doesn't say *that's not true.* She doesn't say anything.

"Nova, whoever they were," she says, "they loved you."

I nod, barely. Keep my eyes on her. "Tell me what you know."

She sits. Folds her hands the way she always does.

"They came when you were an infant," she says. "Frightened. They didn't understand what you were because the mark hadn't appeared. They wanted answers." She takes a breath. "I didn't have the ones they needed."

I stay quiet.

"But I couldn't stop thinking about it after they left. That if they existed — a child outside the system's categories, people the system hadn't accounted for — there had to be others." She looks at her hands. "A few months later, a woman came. Her mark had split, half Shadow, half Memory. The system called her unstable. She had two small children and nowhere to go." She smooths her shirt. "I couldn't very well send her away. So I told her she could stay while I figured out where to send her."

"And?"

"I never figured out where to send her. Because then a man came whose shift was only partial and the system had labeled him defective. Then a cluster whose Order records said they weren't one." She opens her hands. "They just kept coming and I stopped trying to figure out where to put people."

Something climbs through my chest.

"You built a whole town of people the system threw away."

"They built it," she says. "I just stopped closing the door."

I look at Locke in the doorway. At Vaelor beside his grandmother.

Two scared people showed up with me and she couldn't help them. And then she spent decades building the place she wished she'd had to send them.

"Obviously the Order knows about this place now," I say. "Why didn't they shut it down?"

Minerva goes quiet.

"I don't know," she says finally. "I told myself we were careful. Hidden. That we'd built far enough outside the system's attention that they simply hadn't found us." She smooths her shirt again. "But after what happened

— after they walked in here like they'd always known where the door was — I'm no longer sure that was true."

My breath catches.

Not hidden.

Allowed.

The thought makes my stomach turn.

"When word came out that they were looking for an anomaly," she says, "for you, I tried to get Clockwork here faster. Hoping we had everything in place before you arrived."

She purses her lips.

"We had incursions. Patrols at the border. But nothing coordinated. Nothing like what came for you." She looks at me. "And the help came too late."

I look at Locke. He's already looking at me.

"But it's here now." Locke says quietly. "We helped them set it up just before coming to get you."

I nod, thank fuck for that.

I turn back to Minerva. "You're afraid."

"Yes," she says with no hesitation.

Minerva, who built all of this and held it together all this time — sitting here afraid and not pretending otherwise.

Vaelor's eyes find mine. He doesn't say anything.

"Did they know," I ask. "Celeste and Hunter. What I was?"

Minerva's hands fold tighter.

"I don't know," she says. "They didn't tell me. I'm not sure anyone told them anything. They were scared. They wanted answers. I didn't have them."

The words hit harder than an answer would have.

"So no answers there. Fantastic."

I breathe.

"Did you love them?" Zoe asks.

"Yeah," I say. "I did."

"Then they were your parents. That's all it takes."

I don't have anything to say to that.

I look at Brent.

He's been at the far wall the entire conversation. He looks anxious. That's not like him.

He catches me looking and looks away.

Minerva doesn't have all the answers. But I know someone who does.

I'm already standing, turning for the door.

"Nova?"

I stop. Don't turn around.

"Be careful with what you're carrying when you walk in there," Minerva says. "He'll use it."

I look at her over my shoulder.

"Good."

Chapter 43
NOVA

The morning air makes me shiver after the warmth of the room.

I'm moving before the door finishes closing behind me. Down the porch steps and onto the road. My shoulder aching, my heart beating too fast. I don't know if I'm walking toward the bunker or just walking.

Both, maybe.

I need the answers sitting behind a reinforced door and I need them now. Everything Minerva just said is sitting in my chest and it... hurts.

My parents. But not.

Knowing I'm the reason the Order finally came to the Hollow.

They left us alone.

I get maybe halfway down the road before the door opens behind me.

"Nova—"

"Nova, wait—"

Footsteps. Multiple sets. They spill out after me, down the steps. Then they're around me and they're all talking at once and I can't—

"Are you okay—"

"You don't have to go in today, you could wait—"

"What happened with Harrick—"

"What are you thinking right now—"

"Nova." Trey, trying to slow it down.

I stop walking. I'm standing in the middle of the road with all of them around me and my shoulder is screaming.

I catch a glimpse of Zoe heading towards us. Look back at the guys, try to focus.

I open my mouth but nothing comes out.

"Nova."

Brent's voice.

Everyone goes quiet.

He's just standing there. He looks — not right.

"There's something I need to tell you," he says. He looks at the group. "Something all of you deserve to know."

I take a few steps toward him.

He comes down the steps slowly. Stops at the bottom.

"I was young when I joined the Order," he says. "Laith took notice of me early. I ran errands, carried files. I was at his residence often enough that it felt routine." His jaw works. "One night I was there late. Filing something. There was a knock at the door and I answered it."

He looks at the ground.

"No one was there. Just a basket. A blanket." He pauses. "And a baby."

Why would someone leave a baby with Laith?

"It stared right up at me. Like I was its whole world," he says quietly.

Oh.

"Laith heard the door. He came out and I stepped back. He looked down and stared for a long time. I'd never seen him do that. Not before or since." Brent's voice has gone rough. "He picked the baby up, carefully. And he said something — it was so quiet I almost didn't catch it."

"What did he say?" Locke says.

"*They're so blue.*" Brent looks at me. "That's what he said. Looking at her eyes."

No.

"And then he pulled back the blanket. Checked one wrist. Then the other." His jaw tightens. "His face — I can't describe it. I'd never seen that on him before either. He said — *it can't be. This can't be right.*"

Zoe makes a sound beside me. I don't look at her.

"Then he looked up and saw me. Like he just realized I was there." I can see the guilt on his face. "He said *get out.* Just like that. No explanation. The way he said it—" He stops. "I left. I didn't ask questions."

"Why not?" Kyron asks.

"Because it was the first time Laith ever scared me." He's quiet for a moment. "I told myself it wasn't my business. That there was nothing I could do anyway. I kept working for him for years after that."

He looks at me. "I should have asked questions. I should have done... something. Anything."

Brent was there and *I* was that baby.

Laith held me.

Checked my wrists.

He knew.

He's known all this time.

Just like he knew about me.

About my mark.

About the Hollow.

My breath catches. I don't know what to do with any of this.

"Nova." Rane's voice. Close.

"I'm fine," I say. I don't sound fine.

"You don't have to be—"

The pulse hits before he finishes the sentence.

I feel it through the ground first. Then in my chest. Then in my mark — gold and red flaring hot under my skin — and every person in a ten foot radius reacts at the same time. Locke's hands curl. Vaelor goes rigid. Kyron's eyes snap to the tree line.

Then the screaming starts. Not people. The wards.

Zoe steps back.

"That's the perimeter," Brent says. He's already moving. "East side."

They're here.

Chapter 44
BECKETT

The wards are still screaming when the Hollow loses its mind.

Half of them move toward the perimeter. Brent already gone, Cal right behind him, Jonah calling out positions to whoever's listening. The forest shifters are already changing, shapes pulling and stretching at the tree line. Marcus at the front. It's fast. Practiced. This town has done this before.

The rest of us are torn between Nova and the town.

"She can't go down there alone—"

"Someone needs to stay with her—"

"We should all—"

"The perimeter needs—"

Rane and Kyron are both talking at once and Trey's caught between them. Vaelor's looking at the tree line and then back at Nova. Nobody's moving in any particular direction and Nova is.

Walking.

Not toward the perimeter. Away from it.

Toward the bunker access behind the storage building.

I watch her for exactly two seconds.

"I've got her," I say.

Nobody argues. That's the thing about these guys — when one of us says *I've got her*, everybody believes it. Locke's already turned back toward the tree line. Rane stops mid-sentence. Kyron nods once.

I go after her.

She hears me coming but she doesn't stop.

"I swear to God, Beckett, if you try and—"

I catch her hand.

She stops.

I turn her around and she's already braced for the argument, chin up, eyes hard. I look at her for a second and then I kiss her. My hand comes up to her jaw and she makes a small surprised sound against my mouth and then she's kissing me back. Her lips soft against mine. It's warm and certain and I feel it everywhere. Because I'm hers. Always.

When I pull back we're both breathing differently.

She's staring at me like she's trying to remember what she was mad about.

"I would never," I say.

She gives me a small smile because she knows.

"Okay," she says.

"Go do what you gotta do."

She turns. I follow.

The Hollow is loud behind us but they'll manage. Nova doesn't hesitate. Doesn't look back. She knows exactly where she's going.

This is not the same woman from that first night.

She's done being afraid.

I don't know exactly when it happened. But it did.

It looks damn good on her.

We reach the hatch. Heavy steel set into the ground, Kree's lock and reinforcement still visible at the seams.

I know how to unlock it.

I crouch down and work it. The lock clicks. I pull the hatch open and look up at her.

She's already looking at me. Completely ready for this. For him.

I hold the door.

She goes first.

I watch her disappear down into the dark. Determined and steady. It's breathtaking.

I fucking love it.

I follow her down. Pull the hatch closed above us.

Take him down, Nova.

Chapter 45
NOVA

The stairs hurt.

Each step jars my shoulder and by the third turn I'm breathing through my teeth but I'm not stopping. Beckett's behind me. I can hear him. Feel him there without looking.

The wards are muffled down here but they're still screaming.

I should care more about that.

I don't.

The stairs end at a heavy steel door. I stop in front of it and my hand goes to the handle before I decide to.

Beckett's two steps up. I feel better that he's here.

"You good?" he says.

"No."

He doesn't try to talk me out of it. He just squeezes my good shoulder once and lets go.

"Stay at the stairs," I say. "If this goes bad I need you to hear it."

"I'm not going anywhere, Nova. I promise."

I nod and pull the door open.

The room is smaller than I thought.

Concrete everywhere and a single light overhead that buzzes quietly. A chair bolted to the floor in the center.

Laith is in it.

Wrists, ankles, a strap across his chest. He's not fighting any of it. Just sitting there like he's been waiting a long time and he made himself comfortable. His head comes up when I step inside.

He looks like shit.

Good.

His eyes find me.

And he *stops.*

"You," he says.

Not a fan of that.

The door swings shut behind me and it's just us.

I hope Beckett can hear through the door.

Laith is still staring at me like I'm a puzzle. Like each time he blinks he's expecting me to be something else.

"You're not supposed to exist," he says.

It doesn't sound like an accusation. That's the thing. It sounds like a fact he's been carrying. Except here I am, existing.

"Yeah, well." My voice comes out steadier than I feel. "Too bad."

His eyes drop to my wrist. To the mark.

He keeps his face still but I watch his jaw move until his eyes widen just a little.

"It finalized," he says quietly. Almost to himself. "The bond. It actual-ly—"

The wards get louder for a second. He hears it. Looks at the ceiling. Back at me.

"You should go," he says. "They're coming for you."

"I know."

"Then what are you doing down here?"

"Getting answers."

"There's no time—"

"Yet here we are."

He glares at me.

"You're angry."

"You think?"

"Good." He settles back against the chair as much as the restraints let him. "Angry is better than afraid."

I don't tell him I stopped being afraid a long time ago. It's not his to know.

"What were you doing to me?" I say. "In the chair."

He doesn't pretend not to know what I mean.

"Isolating the variable."

"Which variable?"

"You." He says it like it's the most obvious answer in the room. "That cluster of yours has been together for years. No shift from any of them. Then you arrive and within weeks—" He stops. His jaw tightens frac-tionally. "I knew what I was seeing. But it couldn't be. So I needed to be certain."

"So you strapped me down."

"Yes."

"That's your version of science."

"Yes."

I wait for the qualifier. The context. The *but you have to understand.* Something. Anything.

It doesn't come.

"Your clusters aren't shifting anymore," I say. "Are they, Laith."

He goes still.

Won't meet my eyes.

"How do you know that," he says.

"I know a lot of things."

He looks at me like he's trying to see through me.

"Every generation," he says finally. "Fewer people can do it. System assigned clusters form and maybe a few shift. Sometimes nothing happens. Bonds finalize with the secondary mark from the System and the shift never comes."

"How do you... Oh. The Academy."

I shift my weight trying to make it make sense.

"You're using the Academy to track shifting." I step forward. "That's why no one even knows about shifting before they go."

"It was necessary."

"It's wrong."

"I was giving them hope."

"Hope for what?"

"A final mark. A cluster. Something to belong to."

I think about Zoe the day I first met her at the Academy. About the second mark she has.

My attention moves back to him as he shifts in his chair like he doesn't want to say whatever he's about to.

He opens his mouth and closes it again.

I hold my wrist with my other hand. Rub my thumb over my mark.

I don't know why but...

Oh.

Eli's mark. Zoe's mark. I think I might be sick.

"They're not real."

"Excuse me?"

I swallow trying to settle myself.

"The system assigned clusters... The second small marks that are supposed to show a finalized bond... None of it's real. Not a real bond."

He doesn't say I'm wrong. Just sits there not meeting my eyes.

"But mine is."

"Yes."

My head spins but I will not let this man see me vulnerable ever again.

"We've been watching for decades. Waiting." He looks at the mark on my wrist. "And then someone dumped you on my doorstep."

The room is very quiet underneath the buzzing of the light.

"And you thought I was the missing piece," I say.

"A baby without a mark... Removed from the system. Do you realize how rare that is?"

"Yeah." The word comes out flat. "Pretty sure I lived it."

He doesn't deny it.

"What even is it," I say. "The thing on my wrist. It's not a House mark."

"No."

"So what is it?"

He's quiet for a moment.

"It predates the Houses," he says. "It predates the system."

The wards outside scream louder.

Neither of us looks up.

And I have had *enough of his bullshit.*

I step forward until I'm right in front of him.

"Then what the fuck is it?"

He swallows and for one second he looks like he might fight me. But then his shoulders sag.

"It's the mark of the Fourth."

I blink.

What the hell?

"And you knew what that meant."

"I suspected," he says. "What I knew is that it was impossible. When you showed up on my doorstep without a mark something was different." He looks at me. "And yet..."

"And yet," I say. "So what did you do."

"I identified you as an anomaly," he says. "And I made a decision about how to handle it."

I hate that fucking word.

"You assigned my parents," I say. "Celeste and Hunter."

"Yes."

"They were Order personnel."

He nods. "A system bonded pair. Highest clearance. The assignment was straightforward — raise you, keep you close..."

He stops when the door opens behind me.

My body goes rigid.

"Well," Silas says. "Isn't this cozy."

The room fills fast. Silas. Harrick. Three others I don't recognize, spreading along the walls like they've done this before.

Harrick's eyes find me and he grins.

I look at Laith.

He's already watching me.

"I told you," he says, very quietly. "You ran out of time."

Chapter 46
KYRON

The Hollow is not a battle anymore.

It's collapse.

I bank hard left and take out the dart operative before he clears the tree line — drop him face-first into the dirt, I'm climbing before he stops moving. Below me the smoke is wrong. Too thick. Coming from three directions at once.

I've been up here long enough that my wings ache.

The crow has been up here with me. I've noticed it between passes, moving differently than it usually does. It keeps circling back toward the bunker entrance.

I know how that feels.

I circle wide and find them through the chaos.

Locke is northwest in his panther form. I don't look too closely at what's in his jaws.

He's going to regret that later.

Rane I lose for a second in the smoke — then find him near the bunker side of the property, already repositioning, already ahead of where he should be.

That's enough. They're moving.

Then I see him.

Silas. He's not fighting, just moving. Focused as he pulls away from the main fight with Harrick on his ass. A few men in black following.

He's not retreating.

I trace the line of it.

The bunker entrance.

Nova.

The dive is faster than thinking.

I scream before I hit the ground — sharp, short, so that carries — and I'm already shifting before my feet touch dirt. The landing hurts. Second shift today, maybe third, I've stopped counting. My knees take it badly and I come up breathless and naked.

Son of a bitch.

Locke is already looking at me from across the yard. He shifted mid-stride somehow. Pulling his pants up while he moves. Eyes asking me a question I'm already answering.

"Silas." I point toward the bunker. "Now."

No discussion.

They move.

Rane drops whatever he was doing to the operative in front of him and runs. Trey is already ahead of us somehow. Vaelor pulls a shirt over his head while he moves — inside out, doesn't care.

Beckett isn't with us.

Beckett is already there.

The bunker entrance is open.

Dammit.

I hear it before I can see it.

We move fast and quiet. Me first with Locke right behind. Nothing in the world is going to stop him from getting to her. The stairwell goes down —

We find Beckett on the landing.

He's not alone. An operative, bigger than him, trying to hold the lower door shut. Beckett has him by the collar. They're fighting hard against the wall and Beckett's losing ground.

Locke covers the distance and the problem stops being a problem.

Nobody pauses.

Beckett doesn't look at his hands. He looks at the door.

"They're already in," he says.

Trey kicks it open.

The voices hit us first.

Silas.

Laith.

Nova — one word — "Good."

She sounds...

I have to stop moving for half a second.

We come through the door whether they like it or not.

Too fucking bad.

Laith in the chair, still restrained, watching.

Three operatives along the walls, hands slightly up — they know what just walked in.

Harrick too close on Nova's left.

Silas closer on her right.

Nova standing between them on pure stubbornness. Shoulder wrong. Face pale. One hand at her side. She's been holding herself together through sheer refusal for longer than anyone should have to.

Alive.

That's what matters.

Locke makes a sound and it sends my blood racing. He takes one step and Rane and Trey catch him at the same time and Locke stops. His hands are shaking.

Silas doesn't look at us.

He's looking at her.

"You know what's funny," he says. Completely even. "I've been watching you since the day you walked in. And you still ended up exactly where I said you would."

I'm reading his face and I realize something I hadn't before. For Silas, this is personal. Not some Nightmare Order bullshit. This is all him.

Nova looks at him. Then at Harrick.

"It was you," she says.

Not a question.

Harrick's chin comes up. "I gave them what they needed."

"Of course you did."

She sounds bored.

I shift hiding my smirk.

"You told them," Rane says, his voice shaking. "She could have fucking died because of you and you're standing here like—" He stops. "You're proud of it."

Harrick smirks.

Rane takes a step. Vaelor catches him.

Silas moves toward Nova.

Her eyes go white.

The mark blazes. Glowing wings flicker at her shoulders — there and not there. The temperature in the room drops about ten degrees in half a second.

"If you fucking touch me..."

She doesn't finish it.

She doesn't have to.

Silas jerks back.

"What the..." He breathes.

"Enough."

One word from Laith.

Silas stops.

Laith looks at him.

"Leave her."

"She's—"

"I said leave her." Laith doesn't leave room for argument as one of the operatives undoes his restraints. "We're done here."

The silence is enormous.

Silas looks at Nova one more time as he follows his father.

I don't like the way he's looking at her.

"Now."

If Rane starts to laugh I swear to god...

Harrick follows like he just lost his favorite toy. The three operatives file out behind them. The door at the top of the stairs opens and closes. The sounds from above rush in for a moment and then it's gone.

Just us.

And Nova.

I get to her first.

"Hey," I say.

Her throat moves.

"Hey," she says back.

My hand finds her face before I decide to reach — she leans into it.

She's shaking. She's been running on adrenaline through all of it.

"Nova." My voice comes out broken. "You're okay. I promise."

Behind me Locke still hasn't moved.

Rane is silent for the first time in memory.

She nods, then stops herself.

"You can't promise that."

I feel the words sting, but she's right.

"I can for right now."

I look back at the guys, then back to her.

"Pretty sure they're going to have to kill all of us to get to you again."

I don't understand what I've said until it's too late.

She's looking at all of us. Whispering under her breath.

Counting.

One. Two. Three. Four. Five. Six.

I wrap my arms around her.

"We're here, Angel." I squeeze tighter.

"We're here."

Chapter 47
NOVA

The sunlight is a lot.

I squint until my eyes stop screaming and the Hollow comes into focus around me. Smoke still drifting. A section of fence down. Scorch marks along the storage building that weren't there this morning.

The fighting's over. I can tell by the sounds — slower, heavier. People calling to each other instead of at each other.

I start walking.

The guys are behind me. I can hear them. I try not to smile and fail horribly.

Then I see Brent.

He's sitting against the Community Hall wall with his hand pressed to his stomach. Cal's crouched in front of him talking. There's blood soaking through Brent's shirt and I change direction without deciding to.

Someone's already there with water and cloth by the time I reach them. I take it from her.

"Nova…" Cal says like he knows.

"I've got it."

He nods and steps back.

Brent looks up at me. Doesn't tell me to stop.

I crouch down and get to work. It's bad — a long cut across his side, deep — but it's not the worst I've seen. I've patched worse with less on my own body. I press the cloth down.

He doesn't make a sound.

"Nova," Trey says behind me.

"I've got it," I say again.

Someone sighs and then I hear footsteps scatter in different directions. My guys. Going to be useful somewhere else.

Good.

My guys… yeah.

Brent and I don't say anything for a minute. Just the wound and the cloth and the sounds of the Hollow pulling itself back together.

"I'm sorry," I say. "That this happened. Because of me."

"Don't." His voice is rough. "I'm the one that owes you an apology."

I shake my head. Keep cleaning.

"I saw you once," he says quietly.

My hands go still.

"You were maybe fifteen. Sleeping in an alley just outside of Shadow. I almost walked past you." He's looking somewhere past me. "We'd had an anomaly flagged for a few years. A girl. Eleven when she disappeared from the records. No mark, no file after that."

I look at my hand on the cloth. Keep it there.

I can't look at him right now.

"I was supposed to bring her in," he says. "If I found her."

I don't say anything.

"I was about to."

I look up at him.

He doesn't look away.

"And then you opened your eyes." His voice goes rougher. "Those blue eyes. Same ones that looked up at me from that basket." He shakes his head. "I'd only seen them for a few seconds that night. But you don't forget eyes like that."

Neither of us says anything.

Then he tries to sit up a little straighter.

"Ouch."

"Don't." I press down on the cloth. "Lay back, you idiot."

And suddenly we're both laughing. He moves a little too much. He winces and that makes it worse somehow and we're both trying to stop and neither of us can quite manage it.

Eventually something almost like relief crosses his face. And he settles.

"I kept looking for you after that," he says when he can. "On my own. Not for the Order. I don't know what I thought I'd do. But I didn't give up."

I go back to cleaning.

"That first time in the forest — when you came out of the trees — I was so focused on your mark I didn't even think. It wasn't until Minerva said eleven." He shakes his head. "I should have known. I should have put it together sooner."

"Brent."

He looks at me.

"It wasn't your fault." I sit back on my heels. "None of it. No reason for you to blame yourself."

He holds my gaze for a moment. "I promise. Whatever I can do to keep you safe — I will. I swear it." His voice drops. "You never deserved any of this."

I open my mouth.

Close it.

Look back at the wound.

My eyes are burning. I'm not going to cry in the middle of the street.

I'm not.

"You're a good man, Brent."

He laughs. Short and a little pained.

"I'm not." He looks at his hands. "But I'm trying to be."

I press my lips together.

"Good enough," I say.

And I keep cleaning.

A tear drops before I can stop it.

Then another.

Brent makes a sharp sound.

I watch as they fall onto the wound.

And the edges start to knit together slowly.

I'd forgotten...

"Nova?" He says quietly grabbing my wrist, squeezing once.

I let the tears come.

Chapter 48
RANE

I watch her for probably too long.

She's sitting in the dirt with Brent. The cloth in her hands and she can't stop moving.

She's crying.

She doesn't even know it.

Brent knows. He can't take his eyes off her.

I don't think he's ever seen her cry before.

The wound is gone.

I see it at the same time he does — I watch his eyes widen — and then he glances up at me and nods once.

I cross the street.

She doesn't hear me coming. I crouch down beside her and she still doesn't look up. She just keeps her hands on the cloth. Wiping even though there's nothing left to clean.

"Hey," I say.

She looks up. Eyes red.

She's been holding herself together for so long...

I don't say anything else. I just pick her up.

She doesn't fight it. That's how I know how tired she really is. Both arms come around my neck and she tucks her face against my shoulder.

I stand up with her.

Her legs wrap around me.

I hold her tighter.

Brent watches us go. Doesn't say a word.

The guys give us the street.

I don't know how they know. They just do.

I take her home.

Up the steps, through the door, and straight upstairs. She hasn't said anything. I haven't either. The house is quiet and warm and the bed is right there but I don't put her down.

"Tub," I say.

She doesn't argue.

The second bathroom is at the end of the hall. I get the water running — warm enough to do something for her muscles — and sit her on the edge of the tub while the room starts to fill with steam.

She's just looking at the wall.

I kneel in front of her and start with her boots. She lets me. Then her socks. I keep going, slow. Trying my hardest to be gentle with her until there's nothing left. She doesn't cover herself. Doesn't flinch. Just sits there while I do what needs doing.

I get her in the water.

She exhales when she's in. Long and slow. Her eyes close.

I roll my sleeves up and reach for the cup on the shelf.

She doesn't talk. I don't push. Just work through it — the days of whatever they put her in and the battle and the dirt and the blood that isn't hers. All the shit with Laith and Silas and that fucker Harrick.

I take my time. She lets me.

I reach for the shampoo and she tips her head back without being asked.

"How is it," I say, working it through her hair, "that you and I keep ending up in water together?"

The corner of her mouth moves. It's small, almost nothing.

But it's something.

I work my fingers into her scalp.

"Nova?"

"Sorry." Her voice is rough. "It just—" She stops. Tries again. "It feels amazing."

I almost say something but I stop myself.

"Good," I say instead.

I focus on rinsing the shampoo out carefully around her face. I do the same thing with that conditioner stuff she uses. I know she'd kill me if I didn't.

I take my time, wash her until she's clean and relaxed.

I can't remember the last time she looked this peaceful.

She will again. Soon.

When I'm done I get her out, wrap a towel around her, dry her off. Her eyes are clearer, she's standing steadier. She watches me the whole time.

I carry her to bed.

She burrows in immediately. Face half in the pillow. Eyes already going heavy.

I pull the blanket up over her.

"You always manage to surprise me, Beautiful," I say.

She looks up at me. "Is that a bad thing?"

"Are you kidding?" I sit on the edge of the bed. "I wouldn't have it any other way."

She smiles and settles back into the pillow.

We're quiet for a minute. The house around us, the sounds of the Hollow outside, everything slower now.

"Hey, Rane?"

"Hmm."

"Where did this bed come from?" She shifts slightly, pressing her palm flat against the mattress like she's feeling how solid it is. "I love it."

I smile.

"Locke made it," I say. "For you."

She's quiet.

Then her eyes close.

I stay until her breathing evens out.

Chapter 49
TREY

I didn't want to leave her.

I woke up with Nova curled up next to me. She looked so fragile compared to the woman glowing in that bunker yesterday.

We all need to figure out that's the same woman.

She's more than I ever dreamed.

I can tell by the time I get downstairs that none of us slept all that great. Locke's already at the table with coffee he's not drinking. At least Vaelor's at the counter doing something with eggs that smells amazing.

Rane comes down while I'm pouring coffee. Hair still half-flattened on one side.

"She okay?" Locke asks him before he's even reached the bottom stair.

"Sleeping." Rane gets his own mug. "I think she's just exhausted. She'll be better now." He pauses. "She's going to be better now."

Nobody argues with that.

I hope he's right.

I pull out a chair and sit.

"So, Silas," I say.

And suddenly they're all looking at me.

Alright, that got their attention.

"He's not going to let this go," I say. "I know him. He doesn't lose and move on. That's not how he works."

"He lost yesterday," Locke says.

"Yeah. Which is exactly why we have a problem."

Kyron turns from the window. "He walked in on his father telling Nova things he probably wasn't supposed to hear. He got publicly shut down. Then she lit up and he flinched." His jaw moves. "He's going to need to make that mean something else."

"And Harrick?" Rane asks.

"Harrick's an idiot," I say. "Always has been. But he's Silas's idiot and he goes where Silas goes, which means he'll be back too."

Locke's hands wrap tighter around the mug. "Let him come."

"We need to be smarter than that," Kyron says. "Letting him come is how we end up here again."

Locke looks at him. Doesn't argue. Which means he agrees and doesn't want to say so.

Something hits the pan. Vaelor doesn't look up from the stove.

"Then we'll be ready," Locke says.

I nod.

"Shouldn't be too hard to be smarter than Harrick," Rane mumbles into his coffee cup.

Kyron grins and shoves at him.

"Hey!"

I chuckle before I realize it. I missed this.

Beckett closes his laptop.

"She was fucking spectacular yesterday."

Locke's mouth moves. Almost a grin.

"You should have seen her with Laith." He shakes his head. There's something in his face, pride maybe, but bigger than that. Fiercer. "She walked in there alone and she just — he didn't know what hit him. I guarantee he thought he was going to manage her. And she just looked at him and started pulling the whole thing apart."

Kyron's face lights up. "I wish I had fucking seen it."

Same.

"She walked in there with her shoulder still healing," Beckett says. "And told him too bad when he said she was running out of time."

"Yeah." Locke's still grinning. "That's what I mean."

"And then Silas," Beckett says. "When she went white — the wings — the look on his face." He closes his laptop the rest of the way. "He was scared of her."

Good. He should be.

"She didn't even finish the sentence," Rane says. "Just — if you fucking touch me — and that was it. Done. The fucker standing there like he suddenly remembered he was mortal."

Kyron's laugh bursts out of him.

"And Brent," Rane adds.

Everyone's face turns serious.

Vaelor turns from the stove. "He found us after. Told us what he told her." He sets the pan down. "Her crying. The wound healing." He's quiet for a second. "All that time and he never stopped looking for her. On his own. Without anyone asking him to."

Nobody says anything to that.

"Heard Eli got hurt," Kyron says. "In the fighting."

"Zoe said bed rest for a while. He'll be okay." I wrap my hands around my mug. "Someone needs to tell Nova."

Nods around the table.

She'll want to know. She'll probably also try to do something about it. My lips twitch at that.

Rane takes the eggs Vaelor puts in front of him. Eats. I catch the crow settling on the windowsill outside. Kyron glances at it. Doesn't say anything.

"It makes me sick," Vaelor says.

He's still at the stove. Not looking at any of us.

"What they did to her." His voice is even. His hands aren't — the spoon in his grip is too tight, knuckles pale. "Like she was a thing. Like she wasn't a person."

He shakes his head.

"A variable, Laith called her. A variable," Beckett adds. I'm not sure that was helpful, but it makes my stomach twist.

Vaelor sets the spoon down hard. "She has nightmares. She reaches for food like someone's going to take it away. She spent all that time alone because of what they decided to do with her life before she was old enough to know her own name."

Rane opens his mouth.

Closes it.

Looks down at the table.

I look at my hands around the mug and think about the chair they had her in. The gown. The way she looked when Beckett carried her out. All of us taking care of her when she wouldn't wake up. Okay, Vaelor mostly. But we all helped.

That morning she saw me in front of the house.

Fuck.

The sound she made when she finally understood we were alive. When she ran into my arms.

And she still walked into that bunker yesterday.

Alone.

That's the part I can't get past.

"She keeps apologizing," Locke says quietly. He's looking at the table. "For being taken. For being the person they keep coming after. Like it was something she did."

"I know," Kyron says. He looks like he's sick suddenly.

And then it hits me.

He's thinking about how he acted in the Community Hall when we all woke up on those mattresses. When we realized she was gone.

"She said sorry to Brent. For what happened to him. In the fighting." Locke's jaw tightens. "He's the one that was injured and she's the one apologizing."

Nobody has anything to say to that either.

The crow shifts on the windowsill. Ruffles its feathers once and goes still again.

"I won't let them take her again," I say before I can stop myself.

Vaelor stops cooking and turns toward me. Determined.

"No, we won't.

Chapter 50
LOCKE

She's still asleep.

It's past noon. I checked twice. She needs to eat and there's the thing about Eli we need to tell her about. And at some point today the Hollow is going to demand her attention whether she wants to give it or not.

I sit on the edge of the bed.

She doesn't stir.

I lean over. "Hey."

Nothing.

"Nova."

She makes a sound. Something between a groan and a protest, and then she turns toward me instead of away, which I wasn't expecting, and now her face is against my arm and her hand has found my shirt.

Um...

"Five minutes," she mumbles.

I should say no. I should tell her about Eli, get her downstairs, let the others know she's up. Kind of. That's what I came up here to do.

"Five minutes," I say.

I lay down.

She fits against me like we've been doing this forever. Her head finds my shoulder without either of us adjusting. Her hand stays on my chest. I can feel her breathing slow back out, evening off, and I think she's already gone again.

I should get up.

I don't.

The room is quiet. Afternoon light coming through the curtains. I can hear something downstairs — Vaelor probably, or Rane. The sounds of the house.

Her hair smells like the conditioner she uses. It's different now. I think because she's here in a way she hasn't been.

Her skin where my hand is resting is soft. She's warm. She always runs warmer than everyone else — I noticed that early, before I understood why, before any of it made sense. Now I just know it the way I know her weight and the sound of her breathing and exactly how much space she takes up in a room.

Not much. Somehow still all of it.

I think she's asleep.

But I catch it. So quiet I almost miss it. "Thank you."

My hand stops.

I didn't know it was moving.

"For what," I say.

"Everything."

I can't say anything for a minute. Everything is too big to answer.

"Don't worry about it," I say.

She shifts. Gets up on her good arm, hand on my chest, and looks at me. Her hair is a mess. There's a pillow crease on her cheek. She looks at my face and then she looks past me, at the headboard, and I know what she's about to say before she says it.

"You made this."

I look at the ceiling.

"Locke."

"It was nothing."

"You made this for me."

"It needed to be done."

She's quiet for a second. I can feel her looking at me.

"It's everything," she says. "You know that, right?"

The back of my neck is hot. I don't know what to do with my face so I keep it pointed at the ceiling.

"Hey."

I finally look at her.

Her eyes are serious. That's worse than if she was angry.

"You always seem to know what I need," she says. "Even before I do."

I swallow.

"It's beautiful, Locke." Her voice is soft. "Thank you."

I nod. One tight jerk of my head.

I'm not going to survive this conversation.

She holds my gaze for another second. Then her face shifts and her mouth tips up on one side.

Then she giggles.

It's small at first, surprised sounding, like she didn't mean to. And then it gets away from her. She ducks her head against my shoulder and laughs and I can feel it moving through her.

I'm grinning.

I don't know when that happened.

"Come on, you brat." I'm already sitting up, reaching for her hand. "Downstairs."

She gasps. Looks at me like I've said something genuinely offensive. "Brat?"

"You heard me."

She's still laughing when I pull her up.

Chapter 51
NOVA

The bottle of pills is small enough to fit in my jacket pocket but I keep checking for it anyway. Third time since I left the house.

It's there. I know it's there.

I'm going next door... what is my problem?

The Hollow is loud — not chaos anymore, just the sounds of people putting things back together. Someone's fixing the fence section that went down. I can hear hammering from somewhere past the Community Hall. A group of shifters I half-recognize are moving debris from the east side of the main road.

I'm almost to Zoe's door when a kid tears around the corner of the adjacent house and nearly collides with my legs.

He pulls up short. Looks up at me.

"Hi Nova!"

I know his face. Darcy's boy. He was at the community meeting, staring at me from behind his mother's legs.

"Hey." I force a smile. It's not as hard as I expected. "Shouldn't you be helping with something?"

He makes a face. "Mom says I'm in the way."

"Sounds about right."

He grins and bolts back around the corner. I watch him go.

I stand there for a second longer than I need to. Just looking. I didn't realize how much I missed this place. How much it feels like home.

I shake my head as I make my way up the front steps.

I knock.

Zoe opens the door before my hand's even dropped.

She looks me over — checking for damage — and then she pulls me in. The hug is tight and I know I'm smiling before I think about it as I squeeze her a little harder.

"How is he?" I say into her shoulder.

She pulls back. Her face changes. I don't like what I see. "He's managing. It's a lot of pain."

I nod. Follow her inside.

"Where is everyone?" I ask.

"Fence. Storage building. East perimeter." She doesn't look back. "Putting things back together."

"Yeah." I check the pill bottle again without meaning to. "Mine are headed out too. Beckett's already somewhere."

Zoe stops on the landing. Turns to look at me.

"Yours..." she says.

She's not asking. Her face is perfectly serious.

Fuck.

"Well — I—" I breathe. "I just meant—"

She grins. Slow and enormous.

"Oh, shut up," I say.

She laughs. I laugh. It feels good, easy. For a second the staircase feels like any other morning and not the day after everything.

We get to the room and Zoe opens the door.

I follow her in and I stop.

My breath catches.

He's worse than I thought.

Eli is propped against the headboard with his shoulder bandaged from collarbone to mid-chest, the wrapping thick and tight. His face is pale. There's a tightness around his eyes that wasn't there the last time I saw him.

Zoe crosses to him immediately. Checks the bandaging, adjusts a pillow. He lets her.

I blink.

"I'm so sorry," I say. It comes out quiet. "Eli, I'm—"

"Hey." He looks at me. His voice is rough but his eyes are clear. "Please. You did not cause some rabid coyote shifter to do this to me. Mangy fucker did it all on his own."

I can't help it. The smile gets out before I can stop it.

"There it is," he says, satisfied.

"Stupid mangy fucker..."

He nods, smiling.

My head is still spinning as I watch them. Everything Laith has done. Everything we've all been through. What's real, what the system manufactured, and what any of it means for people like Zoe and Eli. None of us, no one in the entire Nightmare Order asked to be caught in the middle of any of it.

My stomach churns.

I take a step deeper into the room.

"There's something I need to tell you both," I say. "About — about the system, and what I found out, and—"

Eli shifts trying to sit up straighter. The sound he makes stops everything.

Zoe is already moving. Repositioning the pillow, hand at his good shoulder, saying something low and steady I can't hear. He breathes through it. His jaw is tight.

I reach into my pocket.

"Oh — here." I cross to the bed and hold out the bottle. "Vaelor got these. I don't know from where."

Zoe looks up. Her eyes widen. "Oh thank god." She takes the bottle, reads the label. "These are the good ones. Where did he find these?"

"Minerva," I say.

She laughs. Shakes one out into her palm and passes it to Eli with the water glass from the nightstand. "That woman can get anything."

"She really can," I say.

"Like some kind of magical being," Eli says. He swallows the pill. Leans back. "Honestly I think she might be terrifying."

"She is," I say. "In the best way."

"One hundred percent," Zoe agrees.

Eli looks between us. "You're both afraid of her."

"Respectfully afraid," I say.

"There's a difference," Zoe adds.

He starts to laugh and immediately regrets it — his hand going to his shoulder, his face scrunching. "Stop. Don't make me laugh. It pulls."

"Sorry," Zoe says, not sounding sorry.

"Not sorry," I confirm.

He gives us both a look and settles back against the pillow. His color is already slightly better. The tightness around his eyes easing.

Zoe tucks the blanket up around his good side. Smooths it. He catches her hand when she goes to pull away and holds it for a second without saying anything. She lets him.

I watch them.

His hand and hers. The way she stills when he holds it. The way they look at each other like nothing else matters.

The system assigned them. I know that now. The mark on their wrists isn't what mine is. It's the system's version.

It doesn't make it not real.

I can see it. Zoe's care, the blanket. The way he looks at her, reaches for her hand and neither of them needed to explain it.

That's not the system.

That's just them.

My throat goes tight.

I look down at the blanket. Look back up.

Eli's watching me now. His head tilted slightly.

"What did you need to tell us?" he asks.

I open my mouth.

Close it.

"Nothing," I say. "Nothing important."

Zoe looks at me. I can feel her looking. She knows that's not true.

She doesn't push.

"Okay," she says.

I sit down on the edge of the bed on Eli's other side and he adjusts slightly to make room.

Love isn't fated, or destiny.

Love is messy and real and so true it hurts sometimes.

That's what they have.

That's what I have too.

Chapter 52
NOVA

The sun is going down by the time I leave Zoe's.

I didn't mean to stay that long. We just kept talking — nothing important, nothing heavy, just catching up. Eli fell asleep around four. We talked over him in whispers and pretended we weren't doing it.

It was good. Things haven't been easy like that in a while.

The Hollow is quieter now than it was this morning but it's not empty. Lights are on in the windows. The smell of food from somewhere. A few people still out, moving slowly.

I'm cutting past the garden beds when I nearly walk into two women. Darcy and someone else — I know her face, not her name. They both stop.

"Nova." Darcy looks genuinely relieved to see me. "How are you feeling?"

"Better." I mean it, which is still slightly surprising. "A lot better."

The other woman — her name comes to me, Petra, she has red hair and a kid who's always climbing things — gives me the particular look of someone working up to something.

"My son," she starts. "He heard about your — um—" She gestures vaguely upward. Wings. She means the wings. "He's been asking. Constantly. I wanted to warn you."

I laugh before I can stop it.

"Tell him to find me tomorrow," I say. "I'll show him."

Petra's face breaks into a smile. "He's going to lose his mind."

"Probably." I grin.

Darcy reaches out and squeezes my arm once, brief and certain. "We're glad you're back, Nova. We really are."

I look at her.

"Yeah," I say. "Me too."

I find Trey near the Community Hall, working on a section of fence that came down in the fighting. He's got tools and wood and he's so focused he doesn't hear me until I'm right next to him.

He looks up a little startled.

"Hey, Love."

I smile before I decide to. Can't help it.

"Hey," I say looking at the fence. He's got most of it back up. "You've been out here all day?"

"On and off." He sets the hammer down. Looks at me. "You good?"

"Yeah." I actually am. "Zoe's good. Eli's managing."

He nods.

"I could use some grub," he says. "What do you say?"

"Sure." I say it without thinking about it, which is probably the most normal thing I've done in weeks.

The Community Hall smells incredible.

Better than I remember. Something warm and rich. There's a line of people around the filled tables. People talking all at once waiting for whatever is being cooked.

My stomach growls.

I want to eat it all.

I hear it and stop in the doorway.

Trey almost walks into me from behind. "What—"

Then I see it. Him.

Vaelor's at the far end of the main counter, sleeves rolled up, laughing at something Mara just said. Really laughing — head back, shoulders moving. Mara's laughing too.

My eyes move and I catch Beckett. He's toward the back, through the open kitchen door. Stirring something at the stove.

I frown. Look at Trey.

He's already reading my face. Leans down and kisses my cheek, quick and warm. "Go."

I laugh without meaning to.

Then gasp as he smacks my ass as I walk away.

He chuckles.

Mara sees me coming and smiles over the counter. "There she is. You hungry?"

"In a minute," I say. "I'll be right back."

She waves me through like she already knew.

The kitchen is warm. It smells even better in here — the soup is whatever's in that large pot Beckett's standing over, and it smells like heaven.

He's got his phone pressed between his ear and his shoulder, free hand reaching for the herb bundle on the counter.

"—I know, I know. Be safe. Love you too."

He hangs up. Drops the herbs in. Stirs.

I lean in the doorway.

"That smells amazing."

He startles. Spins around. The spoon almost goes with him.

Then he sees me and grins.

It looks good on him.

"Yeah?"

"Yeah." I walk in, move to the counter beside him. "When did you learn how to cook?"

"I mean—" He looks slightly offended. "I can cook, Nova."

"Yeah but like—" I gesture at the pot. The herbs. The whole situation. "That."

His hand goes to the back of his neck.

"I, uh." He looks at the pot. "I may have called my mother."

I stare at him.

Oh.

He's looking at the ceiling now, slightly red.

I start laughing.

"What?" He turns, laughing too despite himself, pointing the spoon at me like that helps his case. "What is— stop. Nova."

"I'm not— I'm not laughing at you—"

"You are absolutely laughing at me."

"I'm laughing with you," I say, "you're laughing too—"

"Involuntarily—"

I can't stop. He can't either.

Eventually we calm down. He stirs the pot.

"I just wanted it to be good," he says. Quieter now. "For the town." He glances at me. "For you. I thought after everything — chicken soup, you know. It's—" He shrugs. Like that's enough of an explanation, which it is.

I look at the slightly embarrassed set of his shoulders.

"I think that's exactly what the town needs," I say. "Beckett."

He looks at me.

I kiss him.

He blinks. Once.

"You're amazing," I say. "Or whatever. You get the idea."

He's still blinking when I steal a spoon from the drawer.

"What are you.."

I grin as I take a spoonful of soup right from the pot.

"Hungry, Beckett."

Now he's grinning again too.

"Hungry."

Chapter 53
KYRON

I can't get my body to work right.

This never happens. Never.

But my brain won't stop, the feelings won't stop. I'm standing outside the Community Hall like I've lost my damn mind.

Maybe I have.

Through the window, Nova's coming out of the kitchen with Beckett right behind her. They're both grinning. They look... happy.

She is. I know that.

I also know I owe her a conversation I don't want to have.

I take a step toward the door.

Stop.

The thing is — I know she didn't leave. I know what happened. I was there when Zoe told us. I understand the sequence of events.

And still. Every time I think about waking up and finding her gone —

Still.

I shake my head and start to pace again. I can't help it at this point, and fuck if I care.

It doesn't matter that how I reacted is wrong. Especially since I'm still reacting that way. Some part of my brain keeps registering that she was there and then she wasn't. The facts come after. The first thing is always the absence.

I hate it.

I take another step toward the door.

Stop.

"You deciding whether you're hungry or not?" Rane asks.

He comes around the corner and I will not look at his face. When did he become so fucking perceptive?

"Yeah," I say. "Something like that."

He nods. Comes to stand next to me. We both look through the window at Nova.

He doesn't say anything for a moment.

"So you've decided to stop being an asshole and let her explain?"

I grunt.

He laughs. Quiet and genuine. That makes it worse than if he were being cruel. But that's not Rane.

He reaches over and squeezes my shoulder once.

"I knew you had it in you," he says.

And then he starts walking toward the door.

"Don't worry," he calls, not looking back, already too far for me to stop without making it obvious. "Since you can't seem to go to her—"

No.

"—I'll send her to you!"

He disappears inside.

I'm going to kill him. I mean it this time.

If I do anything right now I'll either make a scene or catch Nova's attention.

Neither of those are good options.

Maybe I'll just go chase him through the Community Hall.

Bad idea.

Rane would never let me live that down.

Fuck!

I could run... That's it. Just turn and go.

That would be even worse.

So I stand here.

Like an idiot.

Because it's the only thing I can do.

I watch Rane cross the room. Watch him lean down and say something in Nova's ear. Watch her go still for a second and then look toward the door.

Her eyes find mine immediately.

She always does that. I don't know how she does that.

I'm not going to think about the shudder that runs through my body when she does.

I watch her say something to Rane. Watch him smile — the slow, satisfied smile of a man who has completely won — and lean down again. She kisses him briefly and then she gets up.

She walks toward the door.

I don't move.

I don't breathe.

Oh, this is bad.

I finally get a solid breath in right before she comes out. Try to hold myself together.

I don't think it worked.

She comes through the door and stops in front of me. Her eyes are too soft and it's not fair. How can I be upset with her?

Her mouth tilts up and everything melts away. She knows.

I keep forgetting how good she is at that.

"You know he's impossible, right?" she says.

"Yeah."

She waits. Doesn't make it feel like pressure.

I look at the ground. Then at her.

"When we woke up," I say. "And you were gone..."

She goes still.

"I know what happened," I say. "I know you didn't — I know the timeline. I understand what you knew and what you didn't." I stop. "That's not the point."

"Okay," she says.

"The point is that before I knew anything else — before Zoe, before any of it made sense — I felt it. Like you left." I meet her eyes. "I know that's not what it was. I'm still—" I gesture at myself. "Working on that part."

"Hey, talk to me," she says.

I look at her. The words are there — they've been there for a while, I think — but getting them out is something else entirely.

Nova doesn't say anything.

"I didn't want it. I wanted to just—" I shake my head.

The noise from inside the Community Hall feels very far away.

Her fingers wrap around mine and there's only her.

"Hey, let's walk," she says.

I exhale and look up at the Community Hall.

I meet her eyes.

"Let's go."

The Hollow is quiet at this hour. Just the sounds of people winding down — distant voices, a door closing somewhere.

She doesn't push. Just walks beside me with her hand in mine and waits.

I don't know why that makes it easier. It does.

"When I was fourteen," I say. "Whisper intelligence came for me."

She glances at me but doesn't say anything.

"They'd been tracking what I could do since I was a kid. Pattern recognition. The way I see connections other people miss." I look at the road ahead. "My parents were — they were proud. That's an understatement actually. This was everything they'd wanted. Everything they'd been building toward." I pause. "It was the highest honor my House could offer."

"But you didn't want it," she says.

"I wanted to be fourteen." It comes out too quiet. "I didn't want that yet. Ya know? I wasn't ready. I just — I wanted more time before life came at me." I shake my head. "So I said no."

She squeezes my hand.

"My parents called me a disgrace." My stomach tightens. The word still does what it always does. "Both of them. Same conversation, same word. Like they'd agreed on it beforehand." I meet her eyes for a second. "They chose the House over me."

I breathe.

"They left. Just like that. I haven't spoken to either of them since."

She squeezes tighter, like it will change anything.

The tightness loosens.

Maybe it does.

"So when I woke up," I say. "And you were just gone. No warning, no — nothing. Before I knew anything else, before I understood what happened—" I stop. "All I could think was that you chose to leave."

She stops walking.

I close my eyes as I stop walking. I know how it sounds.

When I open them again she's looking at me. I don't deserve how she's looking at me.

"I know that's not what it was," I say. "I've always known. It's just—"

"Because of your parents," she says.

"Yeah."

She brings our joined hands up to her mouth. Kisses my fingers.

Now I can't breathe for a different reason entirely.

She smiles as she pulls them away.

"No one is ever going to force me to walk away from you again, Kyron."

She steps closer.

"You're mine. I'm not going anywhere."

Chapter 54
RANE

We're absolutely not spying.

We're just — standing here. Outside. In the dark. Watching.

"Can you hear what she's saying?" Trey asks.

"No."

"Me neither."

We watch anyway.

Kyron's got his head down, which means he's actually talking,

Good, good.

That means whatever I said to him worked.

I am going to enjoy that for a very long time.

Nova's just — there. Holding his hand while he gets it out.

"I don't know what she said," Trey says, "but—"

"It's exactly what the idiot needed to hear." I cross my arms. "Whatever it was."

Trey watches them start walking. Together. Her hand still in his.

"She does that," Trey says. "Doesn't she."

"Yeah."

"Like she just — knows."

"It's not even that," I say. "It's just her being her. She sees people."

"Yeah," Trey says quietly. "She does."

We're quiet for a minute.

Then Kyron stops walking. Nova stops too. She turns to look at him and whatever happens next I can't fully make out in the dark but then his hands are on her face and —

"Damn," Trey says.

"Uhhuh," I confirm. Weakly, while my body reacts before I can stop it.

We watch for probably too long.

I'm not sorry.

Then Nova and Kyron turn and walk toward the house. Together. Not looking back.

Trey watches them go.

"So, are you gonna..." he says.

I'm already moving.

"Fuck yes!"

Chapter 55
NOVA

The door barely closes behind us before my back is against the wall.

Kyron's hands are on my jaw and his mouth is on mine and I make a sound I didn't mean to — pain shooting through my shoulder where he braced his arm.

He freezes.

Pulls back an inch.

"Fuck. Nova. I'm so —"

"Shut up, Kyron."

I drag him back down.

He laughs into my mouth — startled, broken open — and then he's kissing me like he was holding his breath the whole walk back. My hands are already moving. Down his shoulders, his sides, fisting in the hem of his shirt.

"Can't wait to get me naked?" he murmurs against my lips.

I stop. Blink at him.

"Obviously."

And tug.

He laughs again and pulls his shirt over his head. He hasn't even gotten it to the floor before my hands are at his waistband.

"Nova —" Chuckling.

"What?"

I keep my face perfectly innocent but my fingers keep moving.

His pants are open. I'm already sliding down between him and the wall, and his palms slap flat against the wood above my head.

"Fuck," he breathes.

I work his pants and boxers down. His abs shift when I look up at him through my lashes.

"Nova —"

"Hmm?"

I kiss the inside of his thigh.

His eyes close.

Closer.

"This is — *fuck* — this is not how I planned this."

"No?"

I take him in my mouth.

The sound he makes is half growl, half my name. His hand finds my hair. His fingers shake against my scalp.

His hips don't move.

I swirl my tongue. Take him deeper.

"*Nova —*"

The front door opens.

"You two love bir —"

Rane's voice.

He stops. Stares.

I don't stop, I just look up at him through my lashes and keep moving.

His mouth is open mid-word.

Kyron's hand spasms in my hair.

Rane blinks once. Twice. Then a slow grin spreads across his face and he's moving — kicking the door shut behind him, crossing the room — and he drops to his knees beside me on the rug.

"Do you have any idea," he says, low, right against my ear, "how good you look with his cock in your mouth?"

I moan around Kyron.

Kyron's head falls back.

"*Fuck — Rane.*"

"Can't help it." Rane is laughing softly. "It's true."

He kisses my neck, slow, just below my jaw. His mouth moves to my ear.

"Come on, Beautiful. Take him deeper."

I do.

Kyron's hips jerk.

He catches himself immediately — hand white-knuckled against the wall. His face does the apology before he can stop it. I almost laugh around him.

Rane is too pleased with himself. I can feel it in the way his mouth curves against my skin.

His hand slides around my stomach. Up. He pulls the fabric of my shirt down and the cold air on my skin makes me arch — and his fingers find my nipple at the same time and I make a sound I don't mean to.

His other arm comes around my waist from the opposite side. He starts to turn me — slow, gentle, his palm flat against my ribs — and Kyron adjusts with him, hand still in my hair, never breaking the rhythm I've set.

We move as one thing.

My back leaves the wall. Rane settles behind me. His chest against my spine. His mouth at the curve of my shoulder — the good one, I notice. He's probably been watching the bad one the whole time.

His hand slides down. Undoes my pants.

"You alright up there, Kyron?"

Kyron grunts.

Rane chuckles, low, and tugs my pants down just enough.

I pull back.

"Rane —"

"Hmm?"

I take a breath. Try to steady myself.

"We're in the living room."

"And?"

His hand slides between my legs.

"*Ohhh, Beautiful.*" His voice goes soft and wrecked. "Did having Kyron in your mouth turn you on a little?"

"Nope." I pop the *p*.

Rane laughs into my hair.

"Liar."

I feel him shift, looking up at Kyron.

"She's fucking soaked."

I refuse to dignify that and take Kyron deep again.

He groans. His grip tightens in my hair.

Rane pushes two fingers into me and the sound I make against Kyron is loud enough that Kyron mutters something I don't catch.

"Good girl," Rane whispers.

I shudder.

Kyron's fingers massage my scalp.

"Someone likes that," he breathes.

"*Mmhmm.*" Rane sounds delighted. His free hand is moving — I hear his own pants opening behind me, fabric catching, and then his palm is back at my hip, lining himself up. "You gonna take me, Beautiful? While Kyron takes your mouth?"

I arch back. "Mmhmm."

He slides in.

I gasp — the stretch, the heat, the way my whole body lights up — and Kyron's hand tightens in my hair and his hips finally, *finally*, move.

Just a little.

I can't think. It's overwhelming and not at the same time.

Then I feel it.

The shimmer starts at my chest first. Pale, iridescent, warm. I see it glow in the corner of my eye.

Rane's hand still cupping my breast. He doesn't comment. He just makes a low sound against the back of my neck like he can feel it.

Kyron looks down.

His eyes catch the gold.

Something cracks open in his face.

"*Nova.*"

His voice is broken.

I keep my eyes on his while Rane finds his rhythm behind me. I want him to see me. I want him to see that I'm *here*.

His thumb moves at my temple.

"*Look at you.*"

I can't speak with my mouth full. So I take him deeper instead.

His head tips back against the wall.

"*Fuck — Nova —*"

Rane's hand slides up from my hip and settles at the small of my back. Steadying. Like he's trying to protect my shoulder. He's holding most of my weight so I don't have to brace.

Kyron's breath shudders.

"Rane —" he warns.

"Good. Just means there's time for round two."

I moan before I can stop it.

"God, she wants that. But I'm not gonna —"

"I know."

Rane's free hand slides forward. Finds the place where Kyron's hand is in my hair. Covers it.

Their fingers tangle in my hair.

I feel both of them at once — Rane's pulse against my scalp through his palm, Kyron's tremor through his — and something in me goes very still and very loud at the same time.

The mark blazes.

I see it on my wrist where it's braced against Kyron's thigh. Bright enough that it lights up the skin of his leg.

He pushes in deeper and I can't think about the noise I make.

"*Nova.*" Kyron's voice is gone. "Sweetheart, I —"

I don't pull off. I just look up.

His face. God, his face. He's looking at me like if he blinks I'll be gone.

I take him as deep as I can.

I want to hear that sound again.

His hips stutter and he comes hot against my tongue. I hold his gaze the whole way through.

I swallow.

"Fuck." He whispers and exhales like he's been holding it too long.

Rane is still moving behind me. Slower now. His mouth at my temple.

I'm not going to last. The only thing keeping me upright is his arm across my stomach.

Kyron slides down the wall.

Not all the way — he catches himself, leans his back against it and lowers himself until he's sitting in front of me with his hands on my face. His thumb brushes the corner of my mouth.

"Hi," he says, hoarse.

I laugh. I can't help it.

"Hi."

Rane's hand slides down between my legs from the front and I jolt — a full-body twitch — and Kyron's hand at my jaw tightens.

"You gonna come for him?" Kyron's voice is rough and low and my hips push back into Rane on their own.

I nod against his palm.

"Tell him."

I make a sound.

"Tell him, Nova."

"*Rane —*"

"Beautiful." He breathes, his thrusts deepen. His fingers move. "Be my good girl."

Kyron's thumb brushes across my lips as I cry out.

The orgasm rolls through me as I clench hard around him. Rane curses against my shoulder and follows me, his arm crushing across my stomach, his forehead pressed hard between my shoulder blades.

I sag forward.

Kyron catches me.

He pulls me into him — careful of my shoulder — and I end up half in his lap with Rane still pressed to my back and the three of us are just breathing.

The shimmer is everywhere. My arms, my stomach, the inside of Kyron's wrist where it rests against my cheek.

Nobody says anything for a long time.

"I'm going to need more minutes," Rane says quietly.

I start laughing.

Kyron's chest moves underneath my cheek — silent and real. His hand strokes the back of my neck.

"Same," he says.

"Yeah," I agree.

Rane's forehead is still pressed between my shoulder blades. His hand finds mine on Kyron's chest. Squeezes once.

"Living room," he mumbles into my back. "I forgot about that part."

Kyron makes a sound that is almost a laugh.

"Door wasn't closed," he says.

"Yeah." Rane lifts his head finally. Looks at the door. "Yeah, knew that was gonna come back to bite me."

I smile and close my eyes against Kyron's chest.

His heartbeat is slowing.

"Hey, Kyron?" I say into his chest.

"Mm?"

"I'm here."

His hand stills at my nape for a fraction of a second.

Then it starts moving again. Slower.

"I know."

Chapter 56
VAELOR

She's so warm.

Two weeks of this as her shoulder healed. I'll never get enough.

That's the first thing my brain offers me when the light hits. Warm, and tucked against my side. Her breathing is slow against my collarbone, like she has every right to be there. She does.

One of her legs is hooked over mine. Her hair is in my mouth.

I don't move.

Everyone else is a mess around us. Kyron diagonal across the bottom of the bed. Locke dead to the world, mouth slightly open. I hope he's drooling. Beckett curled on Nova's other side with her fingers tangled in his — they fell asleep that way. Trey is somewhere on the floor.

Rane is awake.

I can tell because his weight is shifting too carefully.

A hand starts to creep under the blanket. Slow. Like he thinks I won't notice.

It moves toward Nova's hip.

I catch his wrist without opening my eyes.

"Damn, man," Rane mutters.

"She's mine. Wait your turn."

"You've had her all night."

I open my eyes.

He's grinning at me from across Nova's body. Hair everywhere. Pillow crease down one cheek. Absolutely no shame.

I smirk back.

I do not release his wrist.

Nova makes a sound — half laugh, half complaint — and burrows further into my chest.

"Stop fighting over me," she mumbles into my skin. "I'm sleeping."

"He started it."

"He always starts it."

"True." Rane is unbothered. "In my defense, you're warm and she's prettier than you."

"Debatable."

"Vaelor."

"Hmm."

"He had me last night anyway."

I don't think I've seen a grin so big on Rane's face before.

"I did."

She huffs.

I feel her smile against me.

Outside, someone shouts.

I catch it before the others do. Not a scream. Not panic. Just too loud for this early.

My body tightens immediately.

Boots on gravel. Two people, one of them with a heavier gait.

I exhale.

"Guess that's our cue to get up."

Nova groans. Loud. Aggressive.

"No."

"Sweetheart."

"*No.*"

Kyron stirs at the foot of the bed. Mumbles something into the mattress that sounds like a threat.

Locke does not move.

Beckett's eyes are open. I didn't see them open. He's looking at the door already.

He looks my way.

I nod once.

He nods back.

Then we hear Zoe's voice. Outside. Pitched slightly higher than usual, calling for Cal.

Nova goes still against my chest.

"Son of a —"

She's already pushing up on her elbow.

Then we're all moving.

Rane laughs, scrambling for pants — *whose* pants is unclear, possibly Locke's. Locke comes awake fully. Standing before I've finished swinging my legs off the bed.

"Where —"

"Outside," Beckett says, already at the door. "Brent and Max are back."

"They left two days ago."

"They should still be gone."

Locke goes still for half a second. Then he's pulling a shirt over his head. "Fuck."

Kyron is up. Rane gives Nova one last kiss on her temple — quick, like he can't help it, like he hasn't already kissed her three times this morning — and she swats at him.

"Move."

"Bossy."

"*Move.*"

I sit on the edge of the bed and pull my pants on. My hand finds the small of her back through the blanket. I rub once, slow. She presses into it.

"Take your time, sweetheart."

I bend down. Kiss her forehead. Stand up.

I head for the door.

Something is wrong. I know it the moment I step out the front door.

People are standing in groups they wouldn't normally be standing in. The neighbor's door is open and no one is in it. Two of the kids are halfway through chores and are stopped. Staring.

The supply truck is parked crooked.

It's still full.

Max is standing next to the driver's side door with his hands braced against the metal. His head is down.

That tells me more than any of the rest of it.

I'm already thinking about the unloading order without thinking. Med kits first if it's bad. Dry goods can wait. The fuel cans on the back have to come off before we move the truck.

The truck has to be moved.

He parked it pointed out.

My hands are cold.

I keep walking.

Nova is behind me. I can hear her bare feet on the boards of the porch.

She's quick.

"Vaelor —"

"I see it."

Rane gets to Max first. Drops a hand on his shoulder.

"Hey. Hey. Talk to me."

Max looks up.

His face is dry but past dry. Road dust on his cheekbones. Cracked lips. The look of a man who didn't stop to drink water because stopping meant slowing down.

"Got water?" Rane asks, already turning to wave one of the older kids over.

"They're coming," Max says.

"Hey. Water first. Brain second."

"*They're coming*, Rane."

Brent comes around the back of the truck.

His coat is covered in dust. He's not even pretending to be casual.

He looks at me first.

"How bad?" I say.

"Bad."

I'm already moving.

I'm not aware of deciding to move. Med building is two structures down. We have three full kits, six partial, the morphine count I checked last week was — I have to check it again. The generator behind the school has fuel for eight days at normal load. We do not have enough water containers if we have to move.

"How long," Locke says behind me.

"Not enough," Brent says.

"Be more specific."

"Three days. Maybe four. If we're lucky and they get held up at the river crossing, five."

"Numbers?"

He shakes his head.

"Mobilized. That's all we know."

Silence.

That's when I notice the Hollow has gone quiet around us.

"Coordinated?" Kyron asks.

"It's the Order."

I nod.

"They pulled units from Whisper."

"Pulled them how?"

"Visibly. They don't care if we see anymore."

Kyron makes a small sound.

I know that sound. He's not happy.

Join the club.

"They're coming for her," Locke says. Flat.

"Yes."

"Specifically."

"Yes."

"I'll..." Her voice from behind me.

"NO!" Six of us shout at once.

I turn to her. Her eyes are wide and I realize now she wasn't going to say she'd give herself up.

"I was just going to offer to help."

I nod. Put my hands on her shoulders, lean forward and kiss her forehead.

"Sorry, just after..."

She pulls back. "I get it."

She smiles, turns and heads toward the Community Hall. Already looking for something to do.

I'm already turning toward the med building.

"Beckett."

"Yeah?"

"Inventory. Everything. Med, food, ammo, fuel, water. I want numbers by lunch."

"On it."

"Locke."

"Get every able body who can hold a weapon into the square in an hour. I want to know what we have and what each of them can actually do. Not what they *think* they can do."

"Got it."

"Kyron."

"Already drafting it."

He hasn't moved. He's standing exactly where he was. He's focused. Has been.

"Routes," I say anyway.

"Three. North through the pass is the only one they don't have a line on yet, but it's seventeen miles of open ground. Second option is the Memory border but that's only viable if Minerva —"

"Yes."

"— okay."

"Third?"

He pauses.

"Linda."

The name sits there.

Brent's head comes up.

"Linda? You heard back?"

"No, nothing yet," Kyron says. "Vaelor?"

"Draft all three. I want to know where we stand if we have to leave quickly."

He doesn't answer, already working.

"Rane."

He's still crouched in front of Max with a water bottle.

He looks up.

"You're going to need to talk to people."

"Yeah."

"Not the speech kind. The *don't panic* kind. Pick six people who other people listen to. Get them in the Community Hall tonight at 7 pm."

"Done."

"And Rane."

"Yeah?"

"The kids."

His face changes.

It's small. It's just the corners of his eyes. But Rane has a specific face for the kids of the Hollow and that face just appeared.

"Yeah?"

"Whatever you need to make it normal for them. Whatever stories. Whatever games. I do not want them learning what *mobilized* means today."

"Got it."

I turn.

Trey is on the porch. He came out behind us at some point. He's already talking to Zoe.

Brent is watching me.

"You alright?"

It's not really a question.

"Fine."

"Vaelor —"

"I'm fine, Brent."

He keeps looking at me.

"You went pale."

"Did I?"

"Yeah."

I make myself breathe in. Out.

"Show me the maps."

"Now?"

"Now."

Chapter 57
NOVA

I wake up before the light.

Which is weird for me, but all I've been doing is resting and I'm over it. The Hollow is still quiet. That's how early it is.

Rane's arm is across my stomach. Beckett is playing with my hair in his sleep. It makes me want to stay.

It's warm. Too warm. Who knew sleeping in the same bed with six men turned it into a furnace some nights. Okay, most nights.

I ease out from under Rane's arm. My shoulder does its morning complaint and I breathe through it.

His arm tightens.

He's not awake. I catch his hand as he adjusts and bring it to my mouth. My lips brush his knuckles. It's almost nothing and I smile as he relaxes. Someone exhales somewhere behind me.

I set it back down on the bed and get up.

The floor is cold. I find my clothes by feel, get dressed in the dark. I pause, just standing there, listening to them breathe.

My guys.

I make it out the door without anyone waking up.

The morning is cool and I can smell someone already cooking in the Community Hall. My stomach growls as I stand on the porch for a second.

Two days. Maybe three now. We're running out of time.

I need to find something to do.

I know what I should do. But we're not doing that.

I'm not avoiding. I'm just being useful instead.

I see Eli. He's already up, just down the road, moving slow.

Perfect.

"You shouldn't be up yet," I say, falling into step beside him.

"I'm up." He squints at the sky. "It's morning."

"You have a hole in your shoulder."

"Had. Past tense." He glances at me sideways. "You're one to talk."

Fine. He wins that one.

"Where are you headed?"

"Cal said he might have something for me. Light work." He says the last part like it offends him. "I told him I can still lift things."

"With which arm?"

He scoffs. I smile before I realize it.

"I'll come with you," I say.

He shrugs with his good shoulder. "More the merrier."

Cal doesn't have anything.

"But there's nothing right now?" I ask.

"Not right now."

"I can lift things. Run supplies. Help with the perimeter check —"

"Nova."

"What? I can do literally anything, Cal. Tell me something and I'll do it."

He sets down what he's holding and looks at me like someone who has already had this conversation today with three other people and lost all three times.

"We made good progress yesterday. Brent's running drills after lunch. Check back with Vaelor later, he's got everything sorted."

"Of course he does." Under my breath.

Cal is grinning when I look up.

Not under enough.

Dammit.

"You heard that."

His face goes innocent. "Didn't hear anything."

I look at him. He's lying. He's absolutely lying and he knows I know and he doesn't care even a little bit.

"Fine," I say.

Eli peels off toward Zoe, squeezing my good shoulder once as he goes.

"You'll find something," he says.

I don't answer because I'm not sure that's the point.

I sigh, turning back the way I came.

Petra waves at me from her porch. I wave back and keep walking. Liam is halfway up a fence post doing something with wire that looks like it should require two people.

Kids... That looks fun.

Brent is outside the storage building, arms crossed, watching two people adjust something along the north fence line.

"Nova," he says, when I get close enough.

"What do you need?"

"Your guys should be out soon. Kyron was just —"

"I'm not asking about my guys." I tell him. "I'm ready. What do you need?"

His jaw shifts. He looks at me for a second.

"Nothing right now," he says. "We're in the lull between planning and action. Check back this afternoon."

"There's nothing? Seriously?"

"Nova."

"I can stand watch. I can —"

"Nova." Not harsh. Just final. "This afternoon."

I breathe.

"Fine."

Stupid lull.

I turn. Three steps later I glance back without deciding to. He's already looking at the fence line again.

Figures.

The Community Hall doors are open. I can see straight through to the people inside, all of them with their hands full of something. Moving. Busy.

I slow down without meaning to.

I know what I *should* do.

I keep walking.

No direction in particular because there's nothing for me to do, apparently, because everyone has got it covered, because the whole Hollow is running like a machine this morning and I am a spare part standing in the road.

I'm at the tree line before I realize it.

Didn't mean to end up here. Just did.

The ward hums further out. I stop in front of a cluster of older trees and stand there feeling extremely stupid while behind me the whole town prepares for what's coming.

Without me.

Because I'm standing in the woods.

Something lands on my shoulder.

I already know.

I brush it off. "No."

The crow lands on a branch at eye level instead. Stares at me.

"Don't." I drop onto a root. "I know what you're going to say."

It stares.

"I tried Cal. I tried Brent. Everyone in that hall already has something and I —" I stop. "I can help. That's all. I just want to help."

The crow shifts its weight.

"They're coming in two days and I can't find a single thing to do about it."

I look at the ground.

"You should go see Lena."

"I know," I say.

I freeze.

A branch snaps somewhere behind me and I'm on my feet before the thought finishes.

Minerva.

Wonderful.

She comes through the trees unhurried. Silver hair loose. She looks between me and the crow like this is a totally normal thing. Maybe it is at this point.

"You don't have anything to do," she says.

"Because everyone's already doing it."

Her mouth tilts.

"I'm sitting on a root," I say.

"Yes."

"Talking to a bird."

"Apparently."

I look at her. She looks back. She's got that thing where she can just wait indefinitely and she knows you know it and she does it anyway.

"I'm not doing anything," I say. "That's the problem."

She steps closer.

"You always have been," she says. "Whether you realized it or not."

"That's a very nice thing to say that doesn't actually help me."

"Why do you think they're coming?"

"For me." I pick at the bark on the root. "I know that part."

"Yes, but why?"

"Because I —" I stop. "I shouldn't exist."

"Yes," she says. "And?"

I look up.

"And the Hollow is full of people who are going to get hurt because of it." It comes out flat. "And I've been out here all morning getting told to come back this afternoon and I can't just... I don't know. I can't just stand here."

"You can't fix it by lifting things either."

"I know that."

"Do you?"

I don't answer.

She waits.

"The town is behind you, Nova," she says. "You're one of them. One of us."

"I know."

"Then why are you out here?"

I look at the ground. She's going to keep waiting so I might as well.

"Because they broke her because of me," I say.

"Because of you."

"Yes."

"Nova —"

The tears come before I can stop them. Too hard. Too fast. I hate it. I specifically did not want to do this today, yet here I am.

Minerva is quiet for a moment. "Cry your tears, Nova."

She turns. Takes a step. Turns back.

"They're still coming."

Chapter 58
NOVA

I can't do this.

I've been standing here for a while.

In front of Lena's door studying the wood while Beckett works fifteen feet away on something I don't recognize.

The paint is peeling on the wood. Someone should...

This is stupid. It's stupid because I already decided. I decided in the woods. I decided before the woods, probably. I've been deciding for days and somehow that doesn't make me move.

Beckett looks over again. Looks away.

He's not going to say anything. That's the thing about him — he'll just keep doing that until I figure it out myself, which I hate, because it works.

Okay.

Okay fine.

I knock before I can talk myself out of it and now I'm committed, which is — great. Love that for me. No take-backs.

Three seconds. If nobody answers in three seconds I'm leaving and that's just how it goes. One. Two.

The door opens.

Dammit.

Max looks at me like he already knew it was going to be me and already decided he didn't want it to be. Same.

"Hey," I say.

"Hey."

We stand there.

It's awkward. We both know it is.

"I don't think this is a good idea," he says.

"Yeah."

"She had a bad night and the—"

"I know."

"Nova—"

"Max." I meet his eyes. "I know. I still need to see her."

He stares at me and my stomach churns. She was my friend. Is my friend. Max knows that and...

"Problem?"

I turn and there's Beckett.

Sawdust on his sleeve, piece of wood in his hand, reading my face in about half a second. Whatever he finds there makes his mouth tip up.

My eyes go hot. Not on purpose. There's just too much sitting in my chest right now and it picked my eyes to leak out of, which — cool, great, very helpful.

He looks at Max over my shoulder.

Max makes a sound. Steps back.

"That's what I thought." Beckett looks at me. "Firefly."

He kisses my cheek. Quick. Warm. Already walking away.

I stand there.

Firefly.

My heart thuds in my chest and I swear if my face turns red...

I breathe.

"She's upstairs," Max says. "Yell if she needs anything."

I clear my throat and head upstairs.

Her door is half open. I push it.

Lena is on the bed.

Pajamas, wool socks, arms around herself. Rocking — tiny, just her weight shifting — and looking at the window like there's something out there. There isn't anything out there.

Her mouth is moving.

I stand in the doorway. Listen.

"—didn't come from Order. Linda needed — needed help for—" She stops. Starts again. "Too clean. Too clean to be—"

Linda.

Okay...

It can't be the *same* Linda, right?

I cross to the chair by the window. Slow, so I don't startle her. She doesn't look at me. The room doesn't change for her at all.

"Lena."

"—save Nova. Not like me. Nova can't be—" Her hands tighten on her own arms. "Linda's not Order."

I can't breathe.

"She's not Order. Came for Nova. Came for—" The thread breaks. "Too clean to be—"

"Lena." My voice comes out too low. "What about Linda? What did she do?"

Nothing.

She just stares, rocks a little harder.

I sit back.

My shoulder aches and I focus on it because I don't know how to think about the fact that she's been sitting here saying *Linda's not Order* like a skipping record. Linda, the only one who seemed halfway decent during processing.

"—Nova needs to know. Nova needs to—" She pauses and something shifts in her breathing. "Linda's not what she said."

Everything in me stops.

The rocking slows.

Lena turns her head.

She looks at me.

Her eyes find my face and I can see it. She's *here* and what's in her face is — relieved.

"Linda's not what she said." She says it clear. Present. Like we're having a normal conversation.

Then she's gone.

"Too clean to be—"

I move to the bed, sitting next to her. I reach over and take her hand. I don't decide to. My hand just does it.

She doesn't pull away. Keeps rocking, keeps looping, but her fingers curl around mine and hold on.

My throat closes.

"I'm sorry," I say. It comes out smaller than I want it to. "Lena. I'm really sorry."

She rocks slower.

"Nova safe," she says. Soft. Far away. "Nova safe."

I sit there and I hold her hand and I don't say anything else because there's nothing to say. She held onto this. Through all of it. Through whatever they did in there, she held onto the warning and kept trying and I didn't even—

I stay until my shoulder makes it impossible to pretend I'm not feeling it.

Then I get up. Careful. I set her hand back down on the blanket like it matters, because it does.

She doesn't look at me again.

Max is at the bottom of the stairs.

He reads my face and doesn't say anything. Good call.

I stop on the last step.

"She was trying to warn me." It comes out weird. Flat. "The whole time. That's what the loops are."

Max looks at the floor. He knew. I can tell he already knew.

Neither of us says anything.

"Okay," I say.

I walk out into the night air.

Now, I have something to do.

Chapter 59
TREY

The door hits the wall hard enough that all of us move.

My feet are under me before I've processed it's Nova in the doorway and not something worse.

She's not hurt. She's not scared.

"What the..." Rane blurts out.

She's looking for something.

"My jacket." Already past us, checking the hooks by the door. "The one I've had since the beginning. It's here right? Where is it?"

"What—"

"Inside pocket." Checks the back of the armchair. "There was a card in it."

Beckett puts down his computer.

He doesn't take his eyes off her.

"Linda's card?" he says.

Nova turns around, eyes wide.

And we all realize at exactly the same time that we've fucked up.

"How do you know that?" she says.

Beckett looks at her steadily.

Glad he's the one talking and not me.

"Because we found it. While you were gone. It fell out of your jacket." He pauses and I know it's because he's choosing his words carefully. "It was the only lead we had."

Nova stares at him.

I watch her get there.

"You called her."

"Beckett did," I say. "The first morning after we... got our shit together." I run my hand through my hair. "She answered. Gave us coordinates, timing, the entry point."

Nova doesn't move.

"She met us at the door," Kyron says. "Side entrance. Knew the patrol schedule. Knew the layout. Took us straight down to you."

"She didn't hesitate," Locke says.

"She—" Nova stops. I don't think I've ever seen that look on her face before. "She got you in."

"She got us to you," Beckett says. "Yeah."

The fire pops. Nobody moves.

"Lena said she's not Order," Nova says.

Rane sits up. "What?"

"That's what the loops are." She looks around at us. "I went to see her today. *Linda's not Order.* That's what she's been trying to say. The whole time." Her jaw tightens. "She held onto it through everything they did to her. For me."

It's hard to think about that.

"If Linda's not Order," Kyron says. Slow. "Then what?"

"I don't know." Nova shakes her head. "She couldn't — I don't know."

Vaelor's turned from the stove. Dish towel over his shoulder. "She still got us to you."

"That's not the point," Beckett says.

His voice is flat. Focused.

"Beckett," Rane says.

"It was too easy." Beckett looks up. "I've been thinking about it since the trip home. The corridor was clear. Every door open that needed to be open. Guards nowhere they should have been. The timing—" He shakes his head. "That's not one person."

"We had Linda," Rane tries.

"One woman?" Beckett looks at him. "You really think she pulled all that off alone?"

Rane opens his mouth. Closes it.

Nova's arms cross over her chest.

"Wait," she says.

Everyone looks at her.

"I met her..." She swallows. "She was there for my intake. I only met her twice. But she seemed..."

Her eyes go wide.

"You found her card."

"In your jacket," Beckett nods. "I grabbed it when we left the Academy. Didn't even think about it. The card fell out of the inside pocket."

Nova shifts, lost in thought.

"She gave me that card," she says. Quiet. "At processing. Before the Academy. Before any of this." She looks around at us. "I'd been there for days. And she was the only one who — who treated me like a person." She lets out a breath. "She said if I was stuck, if something went wrong. I could call."

Nobody says anything.

"Before the Academy," Kyron says.

"Before she knew any of us existed," Vaelor says.

"Before the cluster was even confirmed," I say.

Nova nods.

"So she wasn't watching you because of them," Rane says slowly. "She was already watching. And then they found you. And she—"

"Was there for a different reason," Beckett says.

Not sure what to think about that.

"One person still couldn't have done what she did at the facility," Beckett says. "Which means she's got something behind her. Resources. People." He looks at Nova. "Something that isn't the Order and isn't us."

"I think you're right, Beckett." She gives him a small smile.

He reaches into his pocket. Puts the card on the table between them.

She picks it up.

"Then we ask her ourselves," Beckett says.

"Yeah," she says. "We do."

Chapter 60
BECKETT

She calls from the kitchen doorway.

Doesn't ask. Doesn't look at any of us first. Just dials while Vaelor moves around her and puts the phone to her ear like she's done it a hundred times.

She hasn't.

It rings.

Vaelor turns the burner down without being asked. Rane stops mid-sentence. I look at my hands.

It keeps ringing.

Nova's nose scrunches. She's looking at the wall. Not scared. Impatient. There's a difference.

"Are you kidding me," she says.

She lowers the phone. Sets it on the counter. Vaelor puts a bowl in her other hand without a word and she takes it without looking. That's new.

"Voicemail."

"Leave one?" Trey asks.

"And say what?" She picks up a spoon. Puts it down. "No."

"So we wait," Kyron says.

"Guess so." She's already moving, restless, and then she stops pulling at the hem of her shirt. "I hate waiting."

"We know," Rane says.

"You've known me for—"

"We know," we all say at once.

Not smiling of course.

She sighs, moves back to the table. Picks up her bowl.

"Okay," she says.

Vaelor's already moving. "Sit down. All of you."

Nobody argues. That's the thing about Vaelor with a dish towel — you just don't.

Vaelor makes mashed potatoes. Said we needed comfort food.

Nova eats standing up.

She never eats like this. She's stealing from the serving dish before everyone's seated, spoon in hand, completely relaxed about it. Like food is just food.

Six months ago she'd reach for bread like someone might take it back.

Huh.

I look at my bowl.

Rane's watching her do it. I catch him watching. He catches me catching him and grins into his food and says nothing.

The conversation goes sideways when Rane notices her eating.

Not in a bad way. He's just watching her go back for seconds with this look on his face like he's proud and reverent at the same time.

"I'm glad you can eat like that," he says. Casual. Easy. "Outside of the bathroom."

The table goes quiet.

Nova's spoon stops halfway to her mouth.

Oh shit.

Rane realizes it half a second later. I watch it happen on his face — the replay, the oh no, the too late.

"Rane," Kyron says.

"I — that came out wrong, I didn't—" He looks at Nova. "Nova. I'm sorry. I didn't mean—"

She sets her spoon down. Her face has gone carefully neutral and very, very red.

"Tell us," Trey says quietly.

"It's nothing." She picks her spoon back up. "Really. It's not a big deal."

Rane opens his mouth.

"Rane." She looks at him.

He closes it.

Nobody says anything. Vaelor comes around from behind the counter and I watch him take her in — the set of them, the way they've gone up slightly — and he crosses to her without making a thing of it and puts his arms around her from behind. Doesn't say anything. Just presses his lips to her temple.

She goes still.

"Sweetheart." Low. "We care. You know that. We just want to know."

She doesn't say anything at first.

Just looks at the table.

"I woke up the first night. I was hungry." She shifts, Vaelor's arms tighten around her. "I didn't want anyone to see me eating so I took the plate to the bathroom."

The plate I made for her.

She ate it...

"Nova." My throat tightens. "Why didn't you —"

"It's fine, I promise."

Locke is fuming, but I know it's because he wishes she'd never felt like that in the first place. Same.

"It wasn't—" Nova starts.

"Hey." Vaelor's arms tighten. Just slightly. "It's okay."

She stops.

"You're okay," he says again.

She exhales. And relaxes into him.

All of us seem to relax a little too.

Rane picks up his spoon. Sets it down. Picks it up again. "For what it's worth," he says carefully, "I didn't say anything. I didn't want to... I wasn't sure... I just — closed the door."

She looks at him and her eyes go soft.

"I know," she says. "Thank you."

He nods. Looks at his bowl.

Vaelor stays where he is for another moment. Then he presses his mouth to the top of her head and goes back to the stove and nobody says anything else about it.

She picks her spoon back up.

Starts eating again.

That's what does it for me. Not the telling. Not Vaelor. Just — she picks the spoon back up and keeps eating at the same table with all of us and doesn't disappear.

It looks damn good on her.

"These are incredible," Nova says, scraping the dish.

"I know," Vaelor says.

She snorts. "You could pretend ya know."

"I could."

Rane points his spoon at her. "Third serving."

"Second."

"Third."

"Doesn't matter. They're Vaelor's mashed potatoes. And they're my new favorite."

She gets the last scoop directly from the dish. Rane looks at Trey. Trey looks at the ceiling. Locke's mouth does something.

Vaelor reaches to clear the dish.

And Rane — because he's Rane — gets a fingerful of what's left along the inside rim and wipes it across the side of Nova's neck.

The table stops.

Nova stops.

"Rane!"

"Mm." Completely serene. "Accident."

"That was not an accident."

"Too much on my finger. The physics—"

She reaches for her napkin.

Locke's hand comes down on her wrist.

Not hard. Just there.

She looks at him. Everyone looks at him. Because it's Locke.

He looks back at her. Serious, but I don't miss the smirk there.

"Sweetie." Low. Certain. "I think we should let Rane clean up his own mess."

Oh.

Nobody breathes.

Rane makes a sound.

Nova's eyes move between Locke and Rane. I watch her breathing get a little faster.

"Yeah," she says. "Okay."

Chapter 61
NOVA

Rane pushes his chair back.

That's all.

And my face goes hot.

I'm suddenly aware of everything. Them. How close they all are. Locke's hand still around my wrist.

All of them in this small room at this small table and suddenly it's very, very warm and I—

Rane stands. Smirks.

Locke leans down as Rane makes his way over.

His mouth is at my ear and his hands tighten on my wrist, not hard, just — holding me there, keeping me from doing anything stupid like standing up or running.

"Shh," He says, low. "Be a good girl for Rane."

Oh no.

Good girl.

I know instantly. The shower. Me... Rane... The things I said, the things Rane said, the sounds I made that I thought — It all comes flooding back and heat pools low.

I glance at Kyron. He looks like he wants to devour me.

I take a breath, but it doesn't help.

My face is on fire. My whole body is on fire. I can't look at any of them. I'm staring at the table and my ears are ringing and Rane is next to me now, crouching to my eye level with that smile. The one that means he's going to make this so much worse and enjoy every second of it.

"Don't worry, beautiful." His voice drops. "I'll be gentle."

I open my mouth to say what, I don't know. But he doesn't hesitate, he leans in.

His mouth finds the side of my neck, warm and slow, and my eyes close before I decide to close them. His hand comes up to the other side, holding me there, and he keeps going — unhurried, deliberate — and somewhere at the table someone says *fuck* under their breath and I feel it more than I hear it.

A hand lands on my thigh under the table.

I don't know who's.

My breathing is doing something I can't control. My fingers curl around the edge of my chair. Rane's mouth is still at my neck and Locke is still at my ear and there are six of them and I am aware of every single one.

"Guys."

Rane hums against my skin.

"You can't — we can't—"

"Why the hell not?" Kyron says like he's offended.

I open my mouth.

Rane beats me to it.

"Because then she'd have to admit it," He says slowly. Pulling back to look at me. "That she wants it." He looks down at my lips, then back up. "Wants us." He breathes. "All of us."

The room doesn't move.

My face is on fire. "That's not — that's not what this is—"

"Isn't it?" Rane tilts his head. Kisses my neck again. Slow. Like he's got all the time in the world.

"I just—" My thoughts scatter. "It's not that simple—"

"It's okay to admit it, Nova." Trey. Quiet. Not pushing. Just steady, the way he always is. "We already know."

A moan slips out before I can stop it as Rane does something with his tongue.

"I think she just did," Vaelor says.

"Vaelor." My voice comes out embarrassingly unsteady.

"Mm."

Rane pulls back again. I drag in a breath. Two.

"You make it really hard to think when you do that."

"That's kinda the point." His eyes find mine. Soft under the smirk. "Isn't it, Nova."

Not a question.

I look around the table.

All of them looking back at me.

Waiting for me to catch up to something they've all known for a long time.

My throat tightens.

"Yeah," I say. "I do."

I look at my hands.

"All of you."

I breathe.

"More than anything."

The room goes quiet.

I stare at my hands. My face is still hot. My heart is going too fast.

I look up.

Kyron's jaw is tight and his eyes are dark and he's not even pretending anymore. Vaelor's mouth has curved into something soft.

I turn my head, look at Rane.

He's grinning like he won something, which he did, which I hate.

Beckett's just quiet. I can't read the look on his face.

He's been still this whole time. Watching.

Then he moves. Shoves Rane out of the way.

"Hey—" Rane starts.

But Beckett doesn't pause, doesn't answer. He gets one hand under my knees and one at my back and then I'm up, over his shoulder, the chair scraping back behind me, and I shriek because I wasn't ready, nobody warned me, this is not—

"Beckett!"

He's already walking toward the stairs.

"You better hurry up," he calls back over his shoulder. To all of them. Like it's obvious. Like this was always where the night was going.

It was always where the night was going.

Behind me I hear a chair scrape. Then another. Then what sounds like Rane and Trey hitting the doorway at the same time and someone swearing.

Kyron yelling at them like they're idiots.

Vaelor telling everyone to calm down.

He's not calm.

"Beckett." I'm laughing. I can't help it. "Put me down."

"No."

"I'm serious—"

"I know."

He starts up the stairs.

We make it to the bedroom and he throws me on the bed.

I bounce and giggle and my brain is everywhere at once — Rane's mouth, Locke's hand on my wrist, *more than anything* still ringing in my ears — and I don't even register my shoulder until it's already done.

Locke walks in.

With purpose. Like he already knows exactly how this is going to go.

He looks at me on the bed and smirks.

The others come in behind him. All of them. The room gets very full very fast.

"Get her clothes off." Locke's voice. Easy. Certain. "Now."

Beckett moves.

Locke holds up a hand.

"Except for the panties." His eyes make their way down my body. "White ones today, right?" He tilts his head. "I like those."

I stare at him.

"Bet you do," Trey says from somewhere behind him.

"They're your favorites too, Trey."

"They are." Zero shame.

I look between them. "Since when do you guys pay that much attention to my underwear?"

Beckett stops.

Looks at me.

"Since always," he says. Completely serious.

Oh.

Oh.

I open my mouth. Close it.

They're all watching me figure it out and nobody is helping and I think my face might actually be on fire.

"Oh," I say out loud.

"Yeah," Rane says. Grinning. "*Oh.*"

Suddenly, there are hands everywhere.

Someone finds the hem of my shirt. Someone else gets my jeans. I lift my arms without being asked. The shirt moves over my head and before I know it I'm lying there in just the white cotton while five men look at me like I'm the only thing in the room.

I wait for the feeling.

The one where it's too much. Too exposed. Too seen.

It doesn't come.

"Huh," I say out loud.

"Huh?" Rane raises an eyebrow.

"Nothing. I just—" I look down at myself. Look back up at all of them. "I thought this was going to feel weird."

"Does it?"

"No." I blink. "That's the weird part."

Trey laughs. Short, surprised.

Vaelor's hand finds my jaw. Tips it up. He looks at me for a second like he's looking for something. He must find it because his face relaxes and his thumb brushes my cheek before he pulls back.

"Good," he says. Simply. Like that's all that needed to be said.

Rane opens his mouth.

Locke walks back in.

Everyone stops.

He's in the doorway. We all notice what he's holding at the same time I do.

I see Kyron's smirk.

Dammit.

Locke's eyes find mine across the room.

"I want—" He stops. Rubs the back of his neck like he's nervous. He tries again. "I know we don't know what happened in there, not really." Still just looking at me. "But if this is okay—"

I look at the rope.

Look at him.

He's standing in the doorway looking like that, and I don't know how I can deny him.

"Yeah," I say. "It's okay."

He nods.

"Tell me if it's too much and they're gone. Okay?"

"Okay."

Oh no...

I see it — the moment the switch flips in Locke. Something in his face goes from asking to certain and he crosses to the bed and the room reorganizes around him without a word.

"Hands up," he says. To me, not them.

I put my hands up.

Beckett takes my wrists. Gentle. Positions them above my head against the headboard and holds them there while Locke works the rope. It's soft. I don't know what I expected but not this — not soft, not slow, not the way Locke's hands move like he's thought about exactly how this goes and he's in no hurry at all.

I test it once when he's done. Just to feel it.

He watches me do it. Watches as my wrists catch.

He smirks.

He likes this. He likes this way more than I understood.

My thighs clench at the thought.

Trey shifts position beside me and pulls his shirt over his head and I don't know what thinking is anymore.

It doesn't matter how many times... Because right now with my wrists tied and my body on fire, I just — stop. On his stomach. The definition there. The way it moves when he breathes.

"Nova."

"Mm?"

"You're staring."

"I'm aware."

Locke's hand finds my jaw.

Turns my face back toward him.

"Eyes here," he says. Calm. Like redirecting my attention is as natural as breathing.

I look at Locke.

He nods. Satisfied.

Rane's mouth finds my collarbone, working his way up my neck.

I tilt, giving him access and the sound he makes shoots right through me.

"That's it, Beautiful," He whispers in my ear.

Vaelor's hand moves along my side, slow, like he's been waiting to learn exactly this and now that he can he's not going to rush it. His thumb brushes the bottom of my breast and my back arches.

Trey's mouth finds mine and I make a sound against his lips that I feel everywhere. Because Beckett is low on my stomach, kissing his way down.

My body feels on fire. I stop trying to track anything.

Just feel it.

Just like I know someone isn't here.

"Where's—"

Locke's hand stills. Someone shifts.

I lift my head and—

Oh.

Kyron pulled a chair into the corner of the room.

He's sitting in it. Fully naked and completely relaxed. One arm draped over the back, the other stroking himself, slow and deliberate.

He's not even slightly embarrassed about any of it.

His eyes never leave mine.

"Damn," Rane says.

Kyron raises an eyebrow. Daring someone to say something.

Nobody does.

"Carry on," he says.

Vaelor turns back to me. His mouth finds my shoulder. His hand moves and I stop thinking about Kyron for approximately four seconds before I look back over because I can feel his eyes and knowing he's watching from that chair is doing something I didn't expect it to do to me.

He notices me looking.

His mouth curves. Slow.

Locke's hand finds my jaw.

Turns my face back.

"Eyes," he says.

I look at him as he kneels between my legs.

Locke moves closer.

Beckett pulls back. Murmurs something low.

Locke doesn't look up from me. "Just like I thought." His thumb presses against the white cotton. "She's ready."

I make a sound I wasn't planning on making.

"I told you these were my favorite." His thumb moves. Slow. Deliberate. "You were wearing them the night we were first together."

The room slows down around us.

"I remember that," Kyron says.

I turn my head toward him. He's watching from the chair with that look. The one that always means trouble.

"You liked watching then too," I say.

He smirks. Doesn't deny it.

Locke presses a little harder and my attention snaps back to him.

"But Sweetie." His voice drops. "I like them so much because you get so wet." His thumb drags slowly across the fabric. "And they show me exactly how wet you are."

He slides them to the side.

"And there's nothing you can do about it right now."

He pushes one finger in.

I cry out. My hips lift off the bed without my permission.

Trey kisses me. Swallows the sound.

Locke adds another finger and my whole body arches into it, his fingers curling, finding the right angle immediately like he already knows exactly where, because he does, he's memorized this, and my hands pull against the rope above me.

My hips move. I can't stop them.

"That's it," Rane says low. "Just like that, Beautiful."

Beckett's mouth finds my nipple.

Vaelor's hands move to my legs, pulling them up, opening me further. I hear Locke make a sound that's almost not human as he pulls his fingers out and drags his pants down.

He presses himself against me.

I groan. "I forgot how—"

He pushes in.

I cut myself off with a moan that bounces off every wall in the room.

"Vaelor." Locke's voice. Controlled. Barely.

Vaelor pulls my legs higher. Just like that. Changing the angle and I feel every inch of it and my fingers curl into fists above the rope.

Locke moves. Slow at first. Deep. His hands on my hips keeping me exactly where he wants me.

Then Rane moves, pulling away. When he comes back his clothes are gone. His cock hard, as he makes his way back onto the bed.

These men are going to kill me.

He presses himself to my lips. "Come on, beautiful." His voice is rough. "I want to feel your mouth around me."

I open for him.

He pushes in slow and the sound he makes when my lips close around him goes straight through me.

"Fuck," Trey says under his breath. He's watching. Too intently. His pants are coming off and his hand wraps around himself and he's watching my mouth and—

Rane's eyes dart between me and Trey's hand on his cock.

Something in his expression shifts.

Rane moans and I lose whatever thought I had because there's too much happening at once and all I can do is feel.

All of it. All of them.

Locke's rhythm changes.

I feel it immediately — his control slipping, his pace going harder, deeper, less deliberate and more desperate and I moan around Rane because I can't help it. The vibration of it makes Rane's breath catch above me.

"God," he breathes. "Do that again."

I do.

His hips push forward and his grip in my hair tightens and I feel it pulling low in my stomach. Tension coiling tighter. Locke feels it, his hands grip my hips harder.

"That's it," Trey says from somewhere to my left. Low. Filthy. "Let them feel you."

I moan again before I can stop it.

Locke's angle shifts. Just slightly. Just enough. And Beckett chooses that exact moment to run his hand slowly down my body — past my hip, lower, lower — his fingers finding my back entrance and pressing gently while his mouth pulls hard at my nipple at the same time and—

Everything goes white.

I come so hard my whole body lifts off the bed. The rope catches my wrists. Rane's hand holds my head. Locke's hands anchor my hips and he keeps moving through it, drawing it out, every thrust making my toes curl and my thighs shake and sounds come out of me that I've never made before.

Locke's rhythm stutters. His hands crush my hips. A sound tears out of him that I feel in my chest — and he shudders and stills and I feel every second of it.

Rane's hand fists in my hair.

"Nova—"

He pushes a little too deep. I gag around him and his whole body shudders and he comes, hard into my mouth as he groans.

In the corner Kyron makes a sound like something broke loose.

I open my eyes.

All of them are glowing.

Every set of eyes in the room lit up and bright before they start to fade, one by one, like embers going soft.

Except Trey's.

He's still stroking himself. His eyes cycling gold then dimming then gold again, right on the edge and unable to tip over. His jaw is tight. His whole body is tense with the effort of holding back something he can't quite let go.

When he meets my eyes, my breath catches.

He's looking at me like he doesn't deserve...

I pull at the rope and Rane is already there, getting my hands free.

I move, swing my leg over his hips and sink down slow. He makes a sound so broken it goes straight through me before I've even started to move.

His hands find my waist. Shaking.

"Nova—"

"I know." I start to move.

His eyes flood gold immediately. Holding this time. Staying.

I lean down and kiss him.

Slow. Just that. His mouth finding mine like he's been waiting for exactly this and didn't know how to ask.

For me.

I break the kiss, moving up his jaw.

Close enough that he'll hear me.

"You were never broken, Trey," I say quiet. Just for him. Moving slow against him, rolling my hips, feeling him start to unravel beneath me. "You were just always meant to be mine."

His arms wrap around me and pull me against his chest as his hips move into me. Faster, harder and I can't do anything but take it.

The orgasm builds again so fast I can't breathe. It rolls through me as his whole body shakes and he comes inside me.

He breathes deep and I watch the glow in his eyes slowly fade.

He doesn't let go of me.

I don't move.

Vaelor pulls a blanket up from somewhere. He doesn't say anything. Just tucks it around me like that's his job, which maybe it is. Maybe it's always been.

I wiggle free just a little and end up between Vaelor and Trey without anyone deciding it.

Trey's arm stays around me from one side. He presses his mouth to my hair. He doesn't say anything. He doesn't need to.

Vaelor on my other side. His hand finds mine under the blanket.

"You got the short end," I say. My voice comes out rough.

"Did I?" He sounds almost amused.

"You barely—"

"I held you through all of it." His thumb moves across my knuckles. "I felt everything you felt." A pause. "I got the best part."

I turn my head and look at him.

He presses his lips to mine and pulls me closer.

Trey makes a sound in protest.

I laugh and snuggle in between them.

Somewhere Rane says something about voyeurs. Kyron throws a pillow.

Men...

My men.

Chapter 62
NOVA

I wake up and can't move.

Trey's arm is around my waist. Vaelor still has my hand — I don't think he let go at all. There's weight across my legs that is definitely Rane and when I try to shift Locke's hand tightens on my ankle from somewhere at the foot of the bed like he's been waiting for me to try that.

I stare at the ceiling.

Every single one of them is touching me somehow. My whole body is just — still. Relaxed.

I don't know when that happened. I can't find the moment. It just isn't anymore.

I didn't know how nice this could be.

"Ugh," I say to no one. "Coffee. I need—"

Vaelor kisses my cheek. "On it."

He gets up, drags his pants on and heads downstairs.

I stare after him.

"Already addicted, huh beautiful?" Rane. Smug. Not even slightly asleep.

I glare at him.

"Just like she's addicted to all of us," Kyron says.

I gasp, not even a little bit offended.

"I am not—"

"Oh you are," Trey says.

And then he tickles me.

"That's it—" I'm laughing before I finish the sentence, pulling myself upright, climbing over whoever's in the way. Hands grab at me from every direction. Rane actually whimpers and I pause looking at him.

"Seriously?"

He grins.

Such a brat.

Trey is still grinning, but Locke catches my wrist for half a second. I lean down and press my lips to his.

"See you downstairs."

He nods and I find my clothes, barely.

I find clothes. Pull them on fast.

"You don't need to—" Beckett starts.

I raise an eyebrow at him.

He turns red.

I've never seen Beckett turn red before in my life.

"You're adorable."

I grin and head downstairs.

Pretty sure he's redder now.

Vaelor hands me coffee before I hit the bottom stair.

I take it with both hands and don't say anything because some things are beyond words and this is one of them.

The kitchen is warm. Vaelor opened a window. I can hear the Hollow starting up outside — voices, movement, the ordinary sounds of a place that's still standing.

I hop up on the counter.

Vaelor looks at me. Looks at the counter.

"What are you..."

"This is my spot now," I tell him.

"It's a counter."

"My counter spot."

He grins as he moves between my legs. I try to stay serious but this man grinning does something to me. I'm grinning back by the time his hands rest on my thighs.

"Your counter spot," he murmurs kissing me.

Then he winks, and turns back to whatever he's making.

I drink my coffee. It's hard to actually drink with this smile I can't get off my face.

The rest of my guys filter down in pieces.

My guys... I'll get over that one day.

Rane immediately goes for the food. It's absolutely not done yet.

"Fuck!"

"Burn yourself?"

"Shhh," he says, already pouting.

Trey stops long enough to kiss my cheek before making his way to the coffee.

Kyron jumps down the last few stairs way too awake.

I hate him.

I grumble and take a few sips of my coffee.

Beckett comes down last.

He looks at me on the counter. His ears are still slightly pink.

Adorable, I mouth. He shakes his head trying not to smile.

"So... Last night," Rane starts, mouth already full.

"Don't," Locke says.

"What? I was just—"

"Rane."

"It was good!" He gestures with his fork. "I'm allowed to say it was good."

"It was good," Trey agrees quietly into his coffee.

Vaelor sets a plate next to me on the counter.

"Eat," he says.

"Thank you." I pick up the plate.

Kyron leans back in his chair. That smirk on his face.

"You've come a long way," he says. Casual. Unbearable. "From the girl who could barely be in the same room as me."

"I could be in the same room as you."

"You went red every time I looked at you."

"I did not—"

"You did."

"It was bad lighting."

"Kyron," Beckett says, without looking up from his mug. "Did you see how far you came last night?"

Everyone stares at Beckett.

I choke on my coffee.

Rane drops his fork.

Kyron processes it two full seconds after everyone else and then a piece of toast comes from nowhere and hits Beckett square in the face.

Beckett doesn't flinch. Picks up his mug.

Rane is pointing. He can't form words. He's just — pointing at Beckett and making sounds.

Trey has his face in his hands. His shoulders are shaking.

"Beckett," I manage. "You can't just—"

"Too far?"

"No," Rane wheezes. "No that was exactly the right distance."

Kyron throws another piece of toast.

Good thing he's out of toast now.

After a while the kitchen quiets down and it feels like home. All of it.

Rane's stolen the last of my toast. Trey gives me a soft smile as he grabs more coffee.

Vaelor's washing dishes and somehow talked Beckett into drying.

I reach over and steal a piece of fruit from Rane's plate.

He moves it closer without looking up.

But I catch the smile on his face.

Yeah, home.

"I'm going to try Linda again today," I say.

Locke grunts like it's nothing.

"It's strange, isn't it?" Beckett says. "All of that and then just — gone."

"She's not just gone," Kyron says. "People don't vanish like that without a reason."

Nobody argues.

"After coffee," I say.

"That's your second coffee," Rane says.

"Might have a third." I shrug and smile.

He shakes his head again.

"You're going to be bouncing off the walls."

Vaelor laughs as he dries his hands and starts to brew another pot.

I can hear the sounds from outside, someone talking low. See the neighbor on her porch across the street. It's normal, peaceful.

This really is my counter spot from now on... I hope Vaelor knows that.

I'm about to say something when the sound comes.

Hoofbeats.

Fast.

Too fast.

Everything stops.

I'm off the counter before I decide to move.

Chapter 63
NOVA

I'm the first out of the door and I do not give a shit.

Behind me chairs scrape. Trey's coffee hits the counter.

Outside the Hollow is already reacting. Doors opening. People on porches with their hands shading their eyes. Someone down the road calling a name. The normal morning sounds from thirty seconds ago just — gone.

I get to the porch and stop.

Movement in the tree line. Crashing. Wrong.

The hoofbeats are louder now and more uneven and I can hear breathing that carries and that's how I know it's bad, that's how I know before I see him because something that big doesn't breathe like that unless—

Marcus bursts from the trees.

One antler.

That's what I see first. One antler where there should be two, the break ragged and dark, and he's moving but barely staying upright. His legs going wrong under him, blood on his flank catching the morning light.

"Marcus—" Rane's voice. Not loud. Just broken.

He's already running.

Marcus makes it to the road.

Tries to keep going.

His legs buckle.

The shift when it comes is violent and incomplete and wrong, bones cracking too fast, and he hits the road in human form hard enough that I feel it in my chest from the porch.

I'm moving before I decide to.

Rane reaches him first, dropping to his knees in the dirt, hands already on Marcus's shoulders.

"Hey. Hey, hey, hey—"

Brent comes from somewhere down the road at a run. He gets there fast, dropping beside Marcus, hands moving with the specific efficiency of someone who's done this before. Checking his neck. His side. The blood.

The Hollow is gathering. I can feel it. Doors opening wider. People stepping off porches. A woman pulling her kid back by the collar. Someone asking what happened, what happened, what—

Marcus's eyes open.

He finds Rane first.

Then he finds me.

"They're coming."

His breathing turns ragged.

His eyes close.

Rane's hands tighten on his shoulders. "Marcus. Marcus—"

"He's breathing," Brent says. Not soft. Just fact. "He's breathing."

No one's talking. They don't have to.

"Where has he been?" I hear myself say it. "All this time — we thought he just — where has he been?"

Brent doesn't look up from Marcus.

"Out there," he says nodding to the treeline. "Every day. Trying to catch them between him and the other shifters before they got to the town." He takes a breath. "Trying to warn us if they did."

The road is quiet.

"Silas," Locke says. Low.

Brent nods once.

"He was there," he says. "When Silas came. He tried then too."

I look at the broken antler on the road.

He's been out there alone this whole time. Fighting a war none of us could see. And Silas got through anyway. Now whatever's coming broke his antler and he still ran here because he needed to warn us.

To give us a fighting chance.

I won't let that go to waste.

"How long?" I say, flat. "How long do we have?"

Brent looks up at me.

"Not long," he says.

I look at my guys.

At the Hollow spreading out behind them.

At my home.

"Alright," I say. Loud enough for the road to hear it. "Let's go."

Chapter 64
KYRON

Nova said *let's go.* The Hollow listened.

The Hollow moves fast. Brent's already barking orders before he gets up off the ground. Cal appears from the storage building at a run. Someone's hauling Marcus toward shelter — I don't track who, I'm already checking the street, the tree line, calculating which way they'll come if they're already that close.

"I can go up," she says.

She means her phoenix.

Absolutely not.

"No, I'll go," I say immediately.

Rane looks at both of us. "A flaming bird or a giant owl." He clears his throat. "You really think that's subtle?"

Locke frowns. Vaelor makes a sound that sounds suspiciously like *you're both idiots.* I don't have an answer because he's right and I hate that he's right.

The street is controlled chaos. People know what to do here — Brent made sure of that. A woman pulls her kids off the road. Cal's already gathering the women and children and the ones who can't fight. Doors slamming up and down the main street.

Marcus said *they're coming*. Not *I think*. Not *I heard something*. Present tense. Certain. Which means he saw them close enough to know.

The crow hits her in the face.

Out of nowhere, wings everywhere, screaming, talons catching her hair and Nova ducks and shoves it away and it comes right back.

"What the—"

It dives again. She throws her arm up. It screams at her, circles, comes at her a third time and she shoves it hard and it veers off—

And comes for me.

It's screaming in my ear and I grab for it and miss and it pulls back and goes straight for my face and I catch it finally, both hands around its body, and it's still screaming—

Looking.

Not at me. Not at Nova.

At the tree line.

"Okay."

I let it go.

It lands on the fence post. Feathers puffed. Eyes on the trees.

"Uh, guys," Rane says. "Isn't that what it did right before..."

I hear it before I see anything. Branches. Too many branches. Moving wrong.

"They're already here."

Chapter 65
LOCKE

The first panther walks out of the trees.

Not charging. Walking.

I see it immediately — the size, the way it carries itself, Shadow House from the set of its shoulders — and then the second one steps out beside it. Then a third.

A raven lands in the branch above them. Just sits there.

They stop at the tree line.

Just stand there.

Behind me the Hollow erupts. A woman screams a name. Doors slam. Brent's voice cuts through — orders, fast, clear. Minerva somewhere to my right, standing with her people.

I respect that.

I don't look back. Don't look away from the treeline.

More shifters emerge. Panthers mostly. Two black wolves flanking. A viper low in the grass that I almost miss — almost.

Cal's with Jonah at the bunker entrance. I catch it in my peripheral. Moving people through. Good.

Nova takes a step forward.

I put my hand on her arm. She looks at me. The air between us is warmer than it should be.

"Not yet," I say.

"I know."

None of them have moved. Panthers. Ravens. Hawks in the trees watching everything. Shadow doesn't hide what it is. It just makes you look away.

Fuck that.

Twelve visible.

No way that's all of them.

Twelve don't stand at a tree line and wait unless waiting is the point.

"Behind us," Beckett says.

Already turning.

South road. More. Black wolves and bears this time, spread across the width of the road, same slow deliberate pace. No urgency. No aggression.

This isn't right.

I run the math. North tree line. South road. East and west—

"They're surrounding us," Kyron says.

Not attacking. Surrounding.

I look north again. Back south. The pieces land in order and the last one hits hardest.

They let Marcus through.

The whole run. The broken antler. All of it. They let him come because they wanted us looking north while they closed everything else.

These aren't the ones that matter.

These are the ones they want us to see.

Nova's hand finds my arm.

I look at her hand, her face.

She's everything.

I won't fail her again.

My eyes move back to the treeline.

The panthers still haven't moved.

They're waiting.

Chapter 66
NOVA

The panthers haven't moved.

That's what gets me. A dozen of them at the tree line, wolves across the south road, ravens in every branch above us, and none of them are doing anything. Just standing there. Watching. Like they have all the time in the world and they want us to feel it.

They're right. That's the sick part. They do.

Brent's still moving people toward the bunker. I can hear him behind me — low commands, controlled — and the sound of the Hollow trying to stay quiet while it falls apart. A child crying, cut off fast. Footsteps on gravel.

It's like we're all trying to hide while completely surrounded.

It's not going well.

My wrist is burning.

I don't know why. I can't think about it right now.

Silas walks out of the tree line like he planned the whole thing in advance.

Bet he did.

Which is somehow the most infuriating part.

His hands are behind his back. Looking directly at me as he takes his sweet ass time crossing the open ground between the trees and where we're standing because he wants us to watch him do it. He wants the Hollow behind us to see who has authority here.

Harrick is one step behind him, because of course he is, because Harrick has never once in his life let Silas walk into a room without being the second person through the door.

He stops maybe fifteen feet out.

Harrick nearly runs into him.

"There was a time when all of you would be considered abominations..."

He's been talking for two minutes and I stopped hearing the words around the thirty-second mark because something else is happening.

Something is wrong with the air.

Like the pressure dropped before a storm, except the sky is clear and whatever's coming isn't weather.

I look at Locke.

His jaw is locked. The tendons in his neck are standing out. His hands are flat at his sides and very, very still.

Too still, even for him.

He's holding himself back from something.

I look at Rane, beside me, and find the same thing. He's staring at the tree line with his shoulders up and his hands half-open. He's not even blinking.

Then Silas says something and I catch it this time.

"You will not shift." Said like a command. Like he has any fucking authority here. "Whatever you believe is happening here, it will not help you. Organic shifting is not permitted in front of anyone without a second mark. Not without authorization."

He smirks. "Which you do not have."

Nobody answers him.

That's when I realize.

They're not answering him because they can't.

It's already happening.

I feel Beckett first.

He's behind me, slightly left, and there's heat coming off him that I've never felt before. I turn.

He's trembling.

His face is careful. His eyes are on me.

The smoke comes first.

I gasp.

Just like I saw during testing.

A curl of it from the corner of his mouth, like he breathed something out and it didn't go away. Then more, from the spaces between his fingers. His exhale is wrong. Too dense. Too dark.

"Beckett—"

He shakes his head. Once. Sharp.

I know.

The smoke pours out of him.

It comes from everywhere at once, from his skin and his mouth and the spaces where his shirt meets his wrists, and it doesn't dissipate. It moves. It curls against the ground like it's looking for something and everything in me says *run* and my feet don't move because this is Beckett.

My Beckett.

The bones go. I hear it and he almost folds into himself. The smoke closes around him and what comes out of it is wrong and right and ancient all at once, a wolf made of living smoke, bigger than any wolf should be, its outline not quite solid, its eyes glowing gold.

Familiar. Completely, terrifyingly familiar.

Someone in the crowd behind me makes a sound like a prayer or a curse. I can't tell which.

Silas has stopped walking.

Then gold fractures.

That's how Vaelor happens — light splitting through him like he swallowed something that got too big to hold. The sound he makes isn't human and it isn't animal, it's somewhere underneath both. He goes up. That's the thing I wasn't ready for. He goes *up,* the bear form rising and rising and not stopping where it should, wings tearing out of his back that catch the morning light and throw it everywhere, and the Hollow residents who hadn't already moved backward take three steps at once.

Not because he's terrifying.

Because he's impossible.

And *mine.*

The others go fast.

Locke doesn't build. He arrives — panther, black and low and absolutely controlled, and even shifted his eyes track immediately to where I'm standing and don't leave. He doesn't pace. He's positioned. There's a difference and I feel it.

Rane's antlers catch the light. The stag he becomes is massive and still and ancient in a way that makes the air around him feel older, like it was always meant to be.

Trey goes centaur — and it's strange because I've seen it before, from above, when everything was chaos and fire, and seeing it now on the ground is completely different. He reaches for something at his side. Ready before he's fully himself.

Kyron rises. The snow owl ascends above the road and the ravens in the trees scatter, all of them, every single one, in the same instant — and when the air empties of ravens it fills with the shadow of something enormous and white, and the sky is different. The sky belongs to him.

All of them, these beautiful, mythical creatures... mine.

I don't choose it.

It just happens.

The mark warms. Then my back. I know what's coming and I don't fight it — just brace, and let it happen.

The wings come out slowly. Gold and red, then white bleeding through, and the air pressure around me changes before I've fully processed that they're there. I don't try to stop it.

Silas has not moved a single inch.

There's a vein working in his jaw. His hands are still behind his back and I would bet everything I own that they're fists back there.

Harrick looks like he's trying to figure out if he's allowed to be afraid yet.

Silas finds his voice first.

"I said." Each word sharp. "You will not shift."

The bear's wings settle.

The panther sits.

Nobody listens.

Silas takes three steps forward and his composure is cracking at every seam. "You do not have authorization. What you are doing is illegal and a violation of—"

"Look at your army," I say.

He stops.

I nod toward the tree line. Toward the south road. Toward the ravens in every branch that scattered the second Kyron rose.

"Your shifters. Come from every house within Nightmare Order." I look back at him. "They're already shifted. They walked in here that way. Did you authorize that?"

His jaw moves.

"Because you don't actually work for the Nightmare Order, do you Silas?"

I try to hold back the smile, I really do.

I fail, miserably.

"Of course I..."

"But do you? Self protection is allowed within the Order. Even during military intervention."

He didn't. I can see it. How he got this entire army to follow him I have no idea— but I do know he doesn't work for the Order. Not yet.

"That's not—"

"The same?" I ask. "Or are the rules different when it's your army?"

Harrick puts a hand on Silas's arm. "Silas—"

Silas shakes him off. He's looking at my guys. At the shadow wolf and the winged bear and the panther and the stag and the centaur and my giant fucking owl. His eyes are moving too fast, trying to figure out how to get the upper hand.

There isn't one.

Silas looks at Beckett in his wolf form and his lip curls.

That's what gets me. Not fear. Not shock. Genuine, visceral disgust — like he walked into something rotten and can't extinguish it fast enough.

"This is what you've become," he says. Quiet. Almost to himself. Then louder, sweeping his gaze across all of them. "This is what you call a bond. This corruption. This—"

"Organic shifting," I say. "That's the word you're looking for."

His eyes cut to me.

"It's illegal."

"It's real." I tilt my head. "Which I think is actually the problem."

"It is an aberration." His voice is controlled again, which is worse than when it wasn't. "It is exactly what the Order exists to prevent. Unregulated transformation, unauthorized power, clusters operating outside sanctioned boundaries—"

"Says the guy who showed up with an army he doesn't actually command."

Harrick growls. Silas ignores it.

"The system exists for a reason," he says. "Order. Stability. The protection of—"

The words are out before I decide to say them. "If you believe that," I say, "shift."

He stops.

"You have a Shadow mark. You live for the Order. Daddy groomed you for it, right?" I hold his gaze. "So shift. Show me what the system produces. Show me what all of this is actually worth."

The silence goes long.

His hands are still behind his back. The air around him is still. Completely, perfectly, horribly still.

Nothing happens.

I wait. He knows I'm waiting. The Hollow knows I'm waiting. Every shifted operative surrounding the Hollow knows I'm waiting, which is maybe the worst part for him.

Nothing.

His face turns red, I can't tell if it's in anger or embarrassment.

It's not that he won't shift.

"You can't," I say.

His jaw moves.

One of the Shadow panthers growls.

A second follows. Then the third.

They're pissed.

I don't blame them.

Silas turns in place as his army blames him.

Harrick takes a step back. I notice because Harrick has never taken a step back from anything in his life, and now he's doing it without meaning to, his body answering something his brain is still catching up to.

Silas doesn't move.

The horror on his face isn't about power. It's not even about me. He gave everything to this. And it left him standing here with nothing.

And exposing it to everyone.

Harrick takes a breath and steps forward, eyes filled with hate.

"You're going to regret that."

Chapter 67
TREY

Harrick steps forward and I already know how this ends.

Not because I'm smart. Because I know Harrick.

"You think this means something?" His voice carries across the road. He's looking at us and his face isn't afraid.

He's not afraid.

He's angry.

And anger makes you stupid.

"You think because you can do this, that makes you right?"

Nobody answers.

"You're defective." He says it like it's just a fact. "All of you. A cluster that shouldn't exist, shifts that shouldn't be possible, built around something without a mark—"

"She has a mark, maybe your intel is out of date," Brent yells from behind us.

I watch Nova's mouth tip up.

"She is an anomaly." Harrick's jaw is set. "The system exists because things like this—" He gestures at all of us. "—are what happens when you don't contain corruption early enough. When you tell people that broken marks are just different."

He looks at me.

Right at me.

"You of all people should understand that."

Except they do. The whole of the Hollow does, just not in the way that he expects.

I feel them, all of them.

They form a line on either side of our cluster.

Backing us.

Backing Nova.

And everything it means to be broken in a system that doesn't tolerate it.

I hear Beckett growl.

My wrist burns, even shifted. The mark that isn't deformed anymore — he doesn't know that. He's still seeing what I used to be. Dream and Memory fighting each other on my skin, proof I didn't fit anywhere. That I was broken.

I almost say something.

I don't.

The smoke shifts wrong. To my left. Low.

I've felt it twice before — outside the facility, on the road when the Hollow first fell — and I know it before I see it. The air changes around Beckett like weather. You don't see it. You feel it.

My eyes snap left.

He's already gone.

Not gone. Moving. Threading through the space between bodies like he was never solid to begin with. No sound. No warning.

He's behind Harrick before Harrick finishes the sentence.

Fuck, yes.

I look at Harrick.

Harrick who believed every word he just said. Harrick who is Silas's whole world, has been since before any of us arrived at the Academy. The guy who made cruelty feel like clarity because Silas needed someone to agree with him loudly and Harrick was more than willing.

He threw burning trash through her window and called it order.

Beckett looks at me. I nod, no hesitation.

It's fast. That's what I wasn't ready for even knowing it was coming. One second Harrick is talking. Then the smoke closes in from behind and there's a sound I'm not going to think about and then he's not talking anymore.

The silence is total.

Beckett steps back. The smoke dissolves.

He's looking at Nova.

I watch her nod and he turns to smoke, positioning himself right beside her, leaning in.

I look back at Harrick.

Silas crosses the distance in three steps and goes down on his knees in the road.

His hands find Harrick's shoulders first. Like he's trying to understand. Like if he's fast enough it stops being true.

Then he just stops.

His hands are shaking.

I've spent two years watching Silas be untouchable. Composed. The boy groomed for authority who grew into it so completely you couldn't find where he ended and the system began.

There's none of that left.

He's in the road with blood on his hands and grief on his face. Plain and ugly and real.

Harrick mattered to him.

He gave everything to the system.

Look what it gave him back.

He squeezes Harrick's shoulders, and looks up.

At Nova.

"I am going to fucking kill you," he says too calm, "and everything you care about."

He can fucking try...

Nova doesn't move.

Silas gets to his feet. Slowly. Eyes still on her. Whatever was ideology in them is gone.

It's just hate now. Personal.

We all move closer to her.

He's going to have to go through all of us first.

Every operative in the road is frozen. Watching him stand up with blood on his knees and nothing left of whatever authority he arrived with. Watching to see what happens next.

What happens next is going to be bad.

I know it. The cluster knows it. The Hollow behind us knows it and...

"You will do no such thing."

From behind Silas. Flat. Absolute.

Everything stops.

Laith walks out of the tree line and I think we all stop breathing.

He takes it all in without expression.

His eyes land on Nova.

Then us.

And for just a moment something shifts in his expression.

Approval?

No. Impossible.

It's gone before I can be sure and his eyes flick to Harrick on the ground. His son on his knees.

And Silas — still shaking, still with blood on his hands, still the most dangerous thing in this road sixty seconds ago —

Turns toward his father.

And looks afraid.

Chapter 68
NOVA

Nobody moves.

I don't either.

Laith is standing at the tree line and I don't know how long he's been there. Long enough to see all of it, probably.

He looks at Harrick on the ground. His son on his knees.

Then past Silas.

At Trey.

Just for a second.

Then he finds me.

"Stand down."

Doesn't raise his voice. Doesn't need to.

They obey. It moves through the army like water — operatives stepping back, some of them shifting back to human, the whole thing dissolving in under a minute. Whatever authority Silas arrived with, it was always borrowed.

Silas is still on his knees.

He looks up at his father and for just a second his face does something I wasn't expecting.

Hope.

Until he sees Laith's expression.

"She's an abomination." His voice is cracking. "You can see what they are. The system — everything we built—"

"Is not your concern right now."

"It's all of it. It's everything, Harrick is dead and you're just standing there like—"

"Silas." The way Laith says it closes a door. "Enough."

Silas stares at him.

Laith looks at the two operatives still close. "Get him out."

They move.

Silas doesn't go quietly. His hands grip the road. He twists away, still talking — corruption, abomination, thirty years of ideology coming apart at the seams — and under all of it there's something that sounds less like conviction and more like a question his father won't answer and he can't stop asking.

Laith watches him go and doesn't say a word.

It's not the army. It's his own father who makes the call, and watches as Silas is dragged out of the way.

He doesn't even bother to tell him why.

The trees take him.

I feel like it should be satisfying.

It's not.

The road goes quiet. The Hollow is still holding its breath behind me. The guys shift around me, still on guard.

Laith looks at me.

"You knew," I say.

"Yes."

"The whole time."

"You could say that."

Things are clicking into place too fast. The Hollow. Minerva. The people who kept finding her — scared and lost and somehow making it here, to this specific place, in the middle of nowhere. The infrastructure. The way this place existed at all.

Oh.

Oh no.

"You guided them," I say. "You're the reason these people all ended up here."

He stands there looking at me like he's waiting for something.

Of course he does.

"It wasn't an accident," I say. "None of it was."

"I knew who Minerva was," he says. "What she'd do if the right people kept arriving." He takes a breath. "At least that was my hope. So I made sure they did."

Behind me Minerva makes a sound like she's disappointed.

"I built this for you," Laith says. "I set Minerva, the Hollow, all of it in motion so you would have somewhere to go."

Somewhere to go.

I can't breathe.

Fifteen years of nowhere. Alleys and exits and making myself small enough that the system looked through me. And the whole time there was a door. Someone making sure it stayed open.

Not for kindness.

Not for me.

For the experiment.

"You set my whole life in motion," I say.

"I did."

"And then you watched."

"Yes."

It's the same tone as the bunker. Fact. He did what he did and he's not going to apologize it just because I'm the one who paid for it.

I almost respect it.

Almost.

The whispers start.

Minerva moves through the crowd without looking at anyone and stops a few feet away. She's looking at Laith with an expression I've never seen on her face before. Not anger. Something underneath anger that's been sitting there a lot longer.

"You sent them to me," she says.

"I knew what you'd do with your access, your knowledge of the archives. And I knew what they needed."

"You used me."

"I trusted you." Something shifts in his face — not quite a flinch. "There's a difference. I wasn't certain you'd take them in. I hoped."

Minerva's mouth presses thin.

She doesn't say anything else.

She doesn't step back either.

I look at her. All the time she spent building, believing it was her rebellion. Believing she'd stopped closing the door because she chose to.

Laith just destroyed almost thirty years of her life in one sentence.

And she's still standing.

We both are.

I look back at Laith.

He doesn't get forgiveness. That's not what this is.

"You're staying," I say.

He doesn't argue.

"You don't go anywhere until I figure out what to do with you."

Vaelor growls.

I look at him, then to Minerva.

She's already watching me.

She nods, barely.

I meet Laith's eyes.

"Until *we* figure out what to do with you."

Cal and Brent are there before I even think about it. They step up beside him and that's that. Laith goes. He's not fighting it. I didn't think he would.

I turn and watch them go.

I look around, I can't help it.

Because the Hollow is still here. All of us— the forest shifters, Brent, Lena with Max's arm around her, Zoe somewhere in the back with Eli— watching me.

My men.

My home.

Laith put the Hollow into motion.
But he didn't make it what it is.

Chapter 69
NOVA

I'm shaking.

Not visibly, I don't think.

A fucking experiment.

That's all I ever was.

Minerva's hand finds my elbow.

"Community Hall. Thirty minutes."

She's gone before I finish processing it. The Hollow starts moving with her — people dispersing, conversations starting up, the town remembering how to be a town. Lena and Max are already halfway down the road. Mara behind them. Zoe in the crowd pulling Eli away, glancing back at me once.

And then it's just us.

They've all shifted back... noticeably.

I try to focus on their faces. I swear I do.

They're all moving at once. Closer. Around me.

Touching me, all talking at once.

It's overwhelming and chaotic and I love it.

I love them.

"You were—"

"—that was incredible, Nova—"

"She made him confirm it," Kyron says, to Locke, right over my head — and Locke's hand is at my jaw and Rane's arms are coming around me from behind and Vaelor is right there and they are all —

Naked.

Every single one of them.

So naked.

My brain goes sideways.

I'm still trying not to look. I look. I try to stop looking. My eyes just — they keep going, moving down, before I can get them under control — Locke's chest, Kyron's — yeah — Vaelor, who is, I knew this, but damn — Rane's arms around me, which means Rane is directly —

I get back to six faces.

They all saw me do it.

My face goes hot.

"Hi," I say.

Rane makes a sound against my hair that is pure delight.

"Don't," I say.

"I'm not doing anything."

"You're about to."

"She did the full rotation," Kyron says to Locke. Conversational. Like reporting weather. "All the way around."

"I was looking at the — I wasn't—" I stop. "It was a general survey of the—"

"She stopped twice," Trey says.

"I didn't—" I look at him. He looks back at me, completely straight-faced, which is worse than if he'd smiled. "I didn't stop."

"The road is very interesting," Beckett says.

I stare at him. Beckett. Two words, perfectly flat, and somehow that's the thing that makes my face feel like it's going to actually combust.

Rane is shaking with it. I can feel it — he's laughing into my hair and trying not to and failing, his arms tightening around me, and —

"Pants," I manage. "Someone needs to—"

Locke's thumb moves against my jaw.

I forget what I was saying.

He's looking at me the way he gets sometimes — like he wants to pad my entire body with pillows while devouring me — I don't hate it.

He leans closer and he says, quiet, "You were terrifying."

"You said that already—"

"I mean it more than when I said it." His hand moves to the side of my neck. "You stood against him. For the Hollow. For us."

I open my mouth.

Vaelor gets there first — his hand coming to the back of my head, warm and certain, fingers gentle in my hair, and his voice too steady. "I always knew you had it in you, sweetheart."

"I—" My chest is doing something. "Thank you, I—"

"She's flustered," Rane announces.

"I'm not—"

"You are. You're blushing." He sounds like he's just received a gift. "Kyron, she's blushing."

"I can see that," Kyron says. His hand finds my arm, thumb pressing in — too firm, like he needs to know I'm really here— and his voice is even but his grip isn't. "Just how I like you."

Bastard.

"I just—" I try to get my brain working. "Bad lighting. That's all."

"Pretty sure it's how we all like her," Trey says. Low. Something in it that isn't quite joking anymore.

"That's— I mean, guys—"

"Nova," Beckett says quiet. He hasn't touched me yet. He's right there, close enough that I can feel the warmth off him, and he still hasn't touched me, and somehow that is the loudest thing in the road. "We almost lost you."

We all stop moving.

It never occurred to me... I didn't think...

But to them, it was.

Everywhere they're touching me tightens.

And that's when I realize, they're shaking too.

All of them.

I can feel it now — the tight grips, the hovering, the way nobody is more than six inches away from me. Beckett's hands curled at his sides because he doesn't trust what they'd do. Kyron's fingers pressing in.

Holy shit, I think. *We're alive. All of us. Together.*

"Hey," I say. "I'm here."

Locke exhales, his body relaxing.

"Yeah," he says. "You are."

Thirty minutes, I think. Minerva gave us thirty minutes and the Hollow has dispersed and the road is empty and they are all right here and still shaking and so am I and —

"Thirty minutes," Rane says against my hair. Like he read it off my face. "That's enough time."

"For what?" I say.

They all look at me.

Oh.

I see it a second before it happens. Beckett grins and then I'm over his shoulder.

"Beckett!" I yell as he moves.

"Tree line," Beckett calls back.

"We're supposed to be at—" I start.

"In thirty minutes," Kyron says, loud as his footsteps get closer.

"Someone could see—"

Beckett puts me on my feet, still grinning.

"Nova." Locke, stepping in behind me, hand at the small of my back. "Look at me." He smirks. Waits.

I turn to face him. All of them.

My eyes drop.

Dammit.

When they meet Locke's again, he's smirking.

"Do you actually care if they see?"

Nope. I do not.

Rane's had enough. "Thirty minutes," he says again, pulling, grinning, completely unabashed and completely naked and moving me back until I hit Beckett's chest — and I laugh, actually laugh, out loud, in the middle of everything, because we're alive and I'm shaking and Rane is ridiculous and Beckett's hand is on my waist now and Locke is looking at me like—

"I'm trying to maintain some dignity here," I say.

"No you're not," Rane says.

He's not wrong.

Chapter 70
NOVA

There is come running down my thighs.

This is not okay.

Who thought this was a good idea?

It's me. I did.

It was.

I pull a leaf out of my hair and walk.

The guys are behind me, apparently completely fine, which is — good for them, genuinely, I'm happy for them. Some of us have logistics. Some of us are doing the math on how far the Community Hall is and whether anyone is going to notice and the answer to both of those questions is bad.

"Guys! Someone give me my pants. I am *not* walking into the Community Hall like this."

Rane snickers and pants hit the back of my head. "Thanks," I mutter, dragging them on.

Sliding them up wet thighs is not recommended.

Brent is waiting twenty feet from the entrance.

Of course he is.

He sees us coming and something moves across his face that he's fighting very hard to keep under control. He loses. His shoulders start going. He looks at the sky. Looks back at us. Loses again.

Then he reaches behind him and pulls out a stack of pants.

The guys descend on them without missing a beat, like this is completely normal, like Brent standing outside the Community Hall with spare pants was always the plan.

"You timed that," I say.

"Thirty minutes," Brent says. Still not fully recovered. "Give or take."

"We were—" I stop. "We were almost on time."

He looks at me.

He looks at the leaf still in my hand.

"Everyone's waiting," he says.

I stick my tongue out at him.

He's still chuckling when we walk through the door.

The Community Hall is packed.

Every seat, every wall. Kids asleep on shoulders. The injured tucked in wherever they fit — Eli's arm in a sling, Lena against Max's side, Marcus in a chair near the front looking like he'd rather be literally anywhere else.

Even the forest shifters are here.

And the crow.

They go quiet when I walk in.

Nope.

I walk faster.

Minerva is at the front. She looks at me when I come through the door and I go to the nearest empty seat before she can direct me to it.

She doesn't waste time.

"We know what happened," she says. Not to me. To the room. "We saw it. What we decide now is what comes next." She smooths her pants. "The Hollow has always governed itself. That doesn't change tonight."

Nobody speaks.

"Laith Crux is contained. He stays that way until we decide otherwise." Her eyes move across the room. "That decision — like every decision about this Hollow — belongs to the people in this room."

Then she looks at me.

No.

I hear a chair screech and turn around.

Lena tries to stand.

Max steadies her but she only gets halfway up before she starts.

"Nova not here." Thin, her voice still catching. "She wasn't — Nova not—"

She sits back down. Max pulls her in close.

Brent stands up.

He doesn't look around first. Just stands.

"I spent a long time enforcing what I was told," he says. "Told myself it wasn't my job to ask questions." He stops. Starts again. "I'm done with that."

He looks at me.

"I think it's time for a change. And I think Nova should decide what comes next." He gives me a sad smile. "Not just Laith. All of it."

He sits back down.

Zoe's hand goes up. "I'm in."

Then Cal's hand follows. Then the forest shifters, one by one. The woman who gave me bread on my second day. The man whose kid I pulled out of the rain. People whose names I know and some I still don't.

My guys.

Every hand in the room.

I turn back to the front.

I watch Minerva's hand go up.

My throat closes.

I stand up before I can stop myself.

If I think about it I won't stand up at all.

I don't want to turn and face them all, but I do.

"I didn't plan on this," I say. "Any of it." My hand moves to my wrist. "I didn't know what coming here would mean. I didn't know it would mean anything, honestly."

Someone near the back makes a sound.

"But it became — you became —" My voice cracks and I try to breathe through it. "You're the first real home I've ever had."

The silence somehow makes it more real.

"Laith says the Hollow was set in motion because of me." I say, trying and failing to stop the tears. "But it exists because of all of you. Because Minerva opened a door and kept opening it. Because every person in this room chose to stay." My throat is doing something. I talk through it. "That's not his. That's yours."

Minerva's hand lands on my shoulder, and I find her eyes. "It's ours."

I nod and look back at the room.

"So this isn't my decision," I say. "It's ours. Together."

The doors slam open.

Linda runs in.

Linda. Yeah, that one.

She's out of breath, coat half off, hair everywhere.

"I'm sorry I'm late — I came as fast as I could, Silas left with the whole army and Laith went after him and I didn't know if you were still—" She stops.

She takes in the packed hall, every face turned toward her.

"...Nova, we need to talk."

Chapter 71
NOVA

Linda.

I don't think I can forget her face. She was the only person at intake who talked to me like I was a person. She gave me her card — I still don't know why — but I kept it where it wouldn't fall out. And that card is the reason I'm standing here instead of still in that chair.

Or worse.

Minerva clears the room with one look. Zoe squeezes my arm on her way past. Then it's just us — me, my guys, Minerva, Brent, Linda.

The guys move in around me without discussing it. Not between me and Linda. Just — there.

She's not the same woman I remember from intake. She looks tired, a little frazzled, her eyes brighter now.

She's looking at me like I have answers.

I do not.

"I'm not Nightmare Order," she says. "I never was."

Lena said that. Over and over, looping, holding onto it through every-thing they did to her. *Linda's not Order.* I believed it. I just didn't know what it meant.

"Then what are you?" I say.

She takes a breath.

"I'm from the Fourth," she says. "I've been embedded inside Nightmare for twenty-five years. Looking for you."

Rane moves closer.

"For me?"

"For you." Her voice is steady. "We knew you existed. We knew the system would eventually surface an anomaly without a mark — it was only a matter of when and where. I needed to be there when it happened."

I shift where I stand.

"So not really me. Just someone without a mark?"

Linda leans forward slightly.

"You know how rare it is, Nova. You lived it."

"I did. So why?"

"Because you're an anchor," she says. "It's an old word — older than everything you've ever known." Her eyes stay on mine. "You don't hold things together by force. You're the reason they hold together at all. The bonds. The people around you."

I stare at her.

"The healing," Rane says quietly. From somewhere behind me.

"Yes," Linda says. "And the shifts coming back. Your bonds stabilizing, possibly from a distance. The marks changing." She looks around at my guys and back to me. "Things that shouldn't be possible started happening the moment you found each other. That's not coincidence. That's you."

That's you.

I don't know what to do with that.

"Why didn't you take me?" The words come out before I've finished deciding to say them. "At intake. If you'd been looking for twenty-five years. Why did you give me a card and walk away."

Something in her face shifts. Not guilt exactly. Closer to grief.

"I couldn't," she says. "Not then. Extracting you before the path was clear would have burned everything — twenty-five years of cover, both our lives, any chance of this." Her voice is careful. "I had to wait. To be sure. Especially since you were assigned to a cluster. If that was real..." She stops, looks at them. "I had to give you a chance at that. At your bonds."

I get it. I'm just not sure if it makes it better or worse.

"There are people in the Fourth's territory," Linda says, quieter now. "Who have been waiting." She gives me a small smile. "I want you to come back with me. You and your bonds."

The Hollow is on the other side of that wall.

First real home I've ever had. Twenty minutes ago I said that out loud to a room full of raised hands.

Linda is offering me another one.

I don't answer. I can't answer.

How can I give that up?

But more than that, how can I give up the chance at finding my parents? Not Celeste and Hunter, the ones Laith assigned. My *real* parents.

My chest aches and I don't know how to deal with it right now.

"The facility..." Beckett says from near the window.

Linda looks at him.

"That wasn't you alone."

Of course he needs to know. For some reasons that eases the ache just a little.

"No," Linda says. "It wasn't."

Beckett nods once.

The room goes quiet.

"I'll need to leave, soon."

We don't have much time.

Chapter 72
NOVA

Minerva clears the room.

One look. Linda goes, Brent goes, Minerva herself goes, and the door closes behind them.

Just us.

My guys settle without discussing it — Rane close, knee against mine, Trey on my other side.

It's hard to focus. There's been so much.

Vaelor at the counter trying to keep his hands busy. Locke in the chair across from me. Kyron against the wall. Beckett near the window, not quite looking at me.

I look at my hands.

What if they're here?

Not Celeste and Hunter. My real parents.

The ones I don't have names for, faces for, anything for except the fact that I exist and someone made that happen. What if they're somewhere in

Nightmare Order right now? What if I'm closer than I've ever been and I'm about to walk away from it.

I look up.

I don't want to.

"So what do we do?"

Nobody jumps in.

That's not like them.

Locke is watching me.

"If we stay," I say, "we're still inside it. Still a part of it." I shrug. "Laith is here now, but for how long? And that means the experiment continues."

I take a breath because I know.

"If we stay, then we did all of this for nothing."

Locke's mouth tilts up.

"And if we go," Trey says. "We choose it."

"We remove ourselves completely," Kyron says. "That's the difference."

I nod.

"So what's the problem?" Locke says.

I look at my hands.

What if they're here.

"What if I'm leaving something behind," I say. "Not the Hollow. Something else. What if there are answers here — about where I actually came from — that aren't anywhere else? And I walk away from them."

Nothing.

Nobody says anything.

I look down at my hands again.

They're just looking at me and I know. I know what the answer is.

"I love you."

It comes out so quiet.

"I love you."

I try again and finally look at them.

They're all smiling. Every single one of them.

"We wondered when you were going to figure it out, Beautiful," Rane says, grinning.

"Shut up," I say.

He grins wider.

"I'm serious, Rane."

"I know you are."

"I will end you."

"You love me."

I open my mouth. Close it. Look at the ceiling.

Trey makes a sound beside me that he's trying very hard to keep inside his chest.

"Trey…"

"I didn't say anything."

"Your face said something."

Locke is looking at me from across the table. Smirking.

"I hate all of you," I say.

"No you don't," Rane says.

"Profoundly. Deeply. With my whole—"

"Nova." Trey says quietly.

I stop.

He's looking at me. His face serious.

"I love you too," he says.

My breath catches.

Rane's hand finds mine. His thumb moves.

Vaelor turns from the counter. "You already know I love you, Sweetheart."

I nod, blinking back tears.

"I made you a bed," Locke says, flat.

The laugh bubbles out of me before I can stop it.

I shake my head, the smile stuck on my face.

Kyron comes up, drops onto one knee in front of me.

"I was gone for you the moment I saw you walking down that path, Nova," he says, and I watch him breathe deep. "Even when I thought... Maybe more. There's no one else."

I lean forward and press my mouth to his. His hand cups my jaw, and I don't want to pull back but I do anyway.

He stops me. I stare into those blue eyes.

"He needs to know. From you," he whispers and stands.

Beckett still hasn't moved from the window.

I get up and walk over. His arms come around me as he pulls me down onto his lap.

"You know I'm yours, right?"

"I know."

He leans forward, kisses my nose.

"Even when you're covered in sawdust."

The way he looks at me makes my throat close.

"I knew," I say. My voice cracks right down the middle of it. "I've known. I just—" I stop. "I've loved all of you since before I had words for it. Since before I understood what was happening to me." I press the back of my hand to my mouth. "I know."

Then they're all there.

Rane pulls me up, his arms come around me and I go. Locke's hand at the back of my neck. Trey's forehead against my temple. Vaelor's palm between my shoulders, warm and steady. Kyron's hand over mine.

Beckett puts his hand on my ass.

"This is mine now," he murmurs.

This time I hold back the giggle.

I take a breath and close my eyes.

There might be people in Nightmare Order who have my face.

But there are six people in this room who chose me anyway.

I breathe out.

"We go," I say. Into Rane's shoulder. Quiet.

Locke's hand tightens at my neck.

I pull back. Look at all of them.

Wipe my face with the back of my hand.

"We should go tell Linda," I say.

Rane's grin comes back. Enormous and immediate.

"Yeah," he says.

"We should."

Chapter 73
TREY

We come out of the Community Hall together.

All of us, together. And I don't think I've ever felt like I belong to something more. I watch Nova, I can't help it.

For the first time, I see it.

She's lighter.

We're not free yet, not really. But she feels it.

It's exactly how I feel.

She loves me.

I know I'm hers, and she's mine.

And not Laith, not the system... Nothing is going to take that away.

She leans over and kisses Locke's cheek.

He's totally blushing. Though I'll never say that.

I do not have a death wish.

The Hollow is still moving — people putting things back together after the chaos of the morning. Kids already running like nothing happened.

Minerva is waiting with Brent and Linda.

She looks at Nova's face and doesn't ask.

"You decided," she says.

Nova nods.

That's it. No ceremony. Minerva's already turning to Brent before the nod finishes. "Get everyone back inside." Then she looks at Linda. "You too."

Then she looks at me.

Not Locke. Not Kyron. Me.

"Would you bring him up?" she says. "He should be there."

"Yeah," I say. "I'm on it."

Locke falls into step with me. We head around back to the bunker entrance. He stops at the top of the stairs. Nods.

I go down alone.

Laith is sitting in the chair, restrained. He looks up when I come in.

"They sent you?" he says.

"Looks that way."

I pull the other chair out and sit.

"We've only got a few minutes, but I just need you to know that whatever fucked up reason you have in your head for all of this?" My hand clenches. "Nothing makes it okay."

He scoffs like what I think doesn't matter.

It probably doesn't to him.

"You were isolated," he says. "I couldn't have picked a better friend for Silas if I'd tried." He smiles but it doesn't reach his eyes. "Your mark was deformed, no bond, not flagged by the system for a cluster... It should have worked."

I look at him.

"You were going to be curious about them. Maybe even friendly. Enough that you would have had information that no one else did," he says. "Why do you think you ended up in Mark Theory with her?"

I sit back, let out a breath.

"Answers. I needed answers and you are exactly who you are, Trey. It should have worked."

His arms pull against the restraints.

"You were supposed to watch them, not become one of them."

The laugh comes out before I can stop it.

"You really thought I would do that?" I say. "You never knew me at all, Laith."

He looks at me for a long moment.

"Maybe I didn't."

I stand up, because this is over. "They're waiting."

He stands without argument as soon as I undo his restraints. I let him go up the stairs first because I'm not turning my back on him.

I'm not an idiot.

Locke is at the top. He grabs Laith's arm and we make our way back.

The Community Hall is packed again. Same faces, but everything feels different somehow. Brent is by the door. He takes over, grabbing Laith and hauling him to the front of the room.

I find Nova in the crowd. She finds me at the same time.

We make our way over. My hand finds hers, squeezing once.

Minerva stands.

She looks at the room the way she always does — like she's seeing every single person in it.

"The Hollow has made its decision."

Minerva's eyes land on her.

"What happens to Laith Crux belongs to Nova."

I watch Laith's face fall.

Good.

Chapter 74
NOVA

The Community Hall is packed again.

Same walls, same faces, but it feels different now. Everyone is looking at me and I know what they think they're here for. Laith is at the front with Brent standing beside him. Linda off to the side. Minerva in her chair, watching me walk up like she already knows something is about to go sideways.

Probably is.

I get up there.

I look at Laith.

Then I turn away from him.

"Before I get to that," I say.

The room goes quiet.

"My guys and I made a decision," I breathe. "We're leaving the Hollow."

The whispers start immediately. I look for Lena without meaning to and find her in the middle of the crowd. Her face just falls. One of the moms near the back presses her hand to her mouth. Eli's arm moves around Zoe. I turn back and Brent is looking at the floor.

I open my mouth.

"I know this place has become my—"

I stop because I need a second.

My guys will follow me anywhere. I know that.

I look around the room. At everyone I've come to know — the forest shifters, the kids. They're all...

I shake my head.

I look at Linda.

"I can't," I say. "I can't go."

She looks surprised. "What do you mean you can't go?"

"I won't go without them."

"You can bring your bonds—"

"No." I look around the room again. "Everyone. Everyone who lives in the Hollow."

Dead silence.

Linda looks at me. Then she looks around the room — the kids, Lena, the forest shifters three deep at the back.

She looks back at me.

"Done," she says.

I can't stop the smile that comes.

I turn back to the room.

"You don't have to come," I say. "You can stay. You can go somewhere else. Whatever you choose." I stop. "But this is the only way I know how to be free. All of us. Outside a system that spent our whole lives telling us we were the problem." I find Lena's eyes. "We're not the problem."

"Hell yes!" Someone yells from the back and I laugh. Everyone is talking at once and I can't make it out and I know I have to—

I turn to Laith.

Brent is beside him. He gives me a soft smile.

He has no idea.

"Let him go," I say.

Brent goes still.

Laith looks at me. "You're letting me go? Just like that?"

"Yeah, because me and all of my fellow misfits are leaving." My hand moves to my mark. "And you get to live with the mess you made."

His mouth opens.

Closes.

Brent reaches over and pulls him up out of the chair.

Cal takes over and escorts him from the town.

When I turn back, everyone is already moving.

People gathering kids, bags, whatever they can carry. Forest shifters scattering to the perimeter. Brent helping someone with something heavy. Linda at the front with Kyron, pointing ahead.

Minerva is already packed, which shouldn't surprise me. But I don't have time to think about that.

Lena is with Max, moving.

My guys and I move to the road.

The crow is flying overhead. It banks, coming down low, right in front of us — almost like a goodbye.

I watch it go.

Locke's hand finds the back of my neck as we walk.

At the edge of the tree line I stop.

"Just give me a minute," I say quietly. "I'll catch up."

The guys nod and keep moving.

I turn around and look at the Hollow.

Empty now.

The blue door at the end of the road, closed. The Community Hall, quiet. The fence Brent fixed. Zoe's house next door. The road where everything happened, still and ordinary in the morning light.

Nobody left inside.

Nobody waiting.

Just a town I didn't know I needed.

I take a breath and try to imprint it into my memory.

I don't want to forget it.

"You coming, Firefly?"

Beckett catches my hand.

I smile and squeeze once.

"Yeah," I say. "Let's go."

THE END.

Chapter 75
BONUS

One more thing...

You didn't think I was going to leave that gap between Chapters 69 and 70 unexplained, did you?

Because apparently some of you are nosy.

If you'd like to see exactly what happened between those chapters, I've got a bonus scene waiting for you.

Join my reader list and I'll send it straight to your inbox.

https://geni.us/MisfitBonus

You're welcome.

— CeeCee

THANK YOU

Well.

We did it.

Three books.

One very stubborn phoenix.

Six men who desperately needed therapy.

A crow with questionable boundaries.

And enough emotional damage to keep everyone busy for years.

Thank you for taking this journey with me.

Thank you for loving Nova.

Thank you for loving the guys.

Thank you for giving this strange little story a place in your heart.

I'm grateful you came with us.

Take care of yourselves.

And remember:

Some stories end.

Some stories just stop where you're allowed to see them.

Later, bitches.

Tick tock...

— CeeCee

;)

About The Author

CeeCee Crow writes dark, slow-burn romance for readers who like their heroines guarded, their heroes obsessed, and their bonds impossible to walk away from. Her books live in the tension — the half-glance, the held breath, the moment someone realizes they're already in too deep.

She's drawn to feral women, quiet devotion, and the kind of love that doesn't ask permission. If a character is morally gray, emotionally unavailable, or one bad day away from burning it all down, she's probably writing about him.

She lives in Wisconsin and writes the books she wishes someone had handed her years ago.

CeeCeeCrow.com

ALSO BY CEECEE CROW

Nightmare Misfits Series

Destiny

Chosen

Order

Clockwork Rebels Series

Coming soon

www.ingramcontent.com/pod-product-compliance
Lightning Source LLC
Chambersburg PA
CBHW050130170726
47995CB00001BA/6